At Night, White Bracken

Gareth Wood

Stairwell Books //

Published by Stairwell Books
9 Carleton St
Greenwich
CT 06830 USA

161 Lowther Street
York, YO31 7LZ

www.stairwellbooks.co.uk
@stairwellbooks

Cover art Susie Williamson

ISBN: 978-1-913432-98-0

For Claire, Foley and Duc. Thank you for the perfect balance of love, space and lunacy.

For Birmingham. The place that made me. The bluest of cities, the reddest of nights.

For all the monsters I adore.

'You can see the weakness of a man right through his iris.'
RZA, '4th Chamber'.

.

The fire is dying back now.

Only occasional flames lick from the shattered windows of The Red House.

The palls of dark smoke, only recently like enormous murmurations, have splintered and faded. Soon, all of the rage and violence seen here will be invisible.

Even the corpses will be nothing more than charred furniture.

Regardless, I am not even facing the stone cottage, I am facing the woodland. That permitter of unblinking eyes. I am waiting for the Undertundrans to light the jagged bark and bracken.

I am waiting for the white stag, for the creature christened Bone Stairwell by Hickey. I have learned that when he appears, it heralds the arrival of the others, of the ethereal masses. When they arrive, that grinning parade, I will ask them to show me everything, to show me their world beneath the world, their city under dirt.

Hickey wanted that more than anything. He was content to kill, maim and maul to get even a glimpse of the inhuman universe and, well, he did. He was able to stare into that void. I wonder whether the image is now printed on his eternal eye, fixed there forever, the last frame on the cinema of the soul.

I couldn't care. He was everything I thought he was from the start. Every ounce of him, flesh, bone, marrow. If only Cooper had realised earlier on, if only he hadn't been hypnotised by his own anger, his own humanity.

Dusk is turning to night now. It shouldn't be long until Bone Stairwell appears between the ashes and oaks, its face stoic, hardened, on its throat a garland of human faces.

Until then, whether I want to or not, all I can do is look back.

I believe I know how this began, the very moment the door opened, the second the shadows began to face the figures who cast them. I can trace it, the way it unfolded. That blueprint is all I have now, all I will have until the Undertundra opens its maw to me.

I pull my coat tight as the temperature drops. I'm weak, I've barely eaten. It's hard to keep my eyes open, but I must do the best I can.

1.

Figment of a beginning

THE PUB STANK OF BAD guts and Cooper's face was a void at the end of a glass.

I watched him guzzle the second half of his lager with a brutal thirst. He burped into his large, red fist, threw the gas in the air and nodded at me to get another round.

I did so, silently, my headless pint sat on the rickety table, barely touched. Like Cooper, like that pub, it was one more startling and anachronistic figment of a beginning, a figment of a time now splintered and gone.

I leaned on the bar and waited for old Sylvia to come and crank out two more glasses of piss water. The same dead faces haunted the stools either side of me. Their fingers rusted by fags and gnawed filters, grotesque as they thumbed crumpled newspapers.

It was either the racing form or the latest public outrages splattered across the pages in gaudy, enormous headlines. It was rapes and taxes, foreigners and monsters. Tabloids screamed about anyone worse off than their idiot readers. They wanted to rage on about those who had it coming, the slurs boiling at the back of their throats. They used their perfect coded languages, their sinister inferences. They suggested the horrors to the slobbering mobs and that was enough to whet their appetites, to rile them into dynamite furies.

It was the same thing, the churn, the endless nagging rot which kept us livid on the estate. Despite

knowing better, I could feel it coming through me like bugs in the blood.

Sylvia had bare legs marbled with varicose veins. She limped over and smiled painfully. Her teeth were like cricket stumps, more gap than bone. I didn't have to say a word. There were only three working taps at The Gladiator. Mild was for geriatric dossers, cider was for the ladies, lager for the rest. I was in the rest, making up the numbers.

I didn't wait for the change. Let her have it. *Pay it forward, you poor sod.*

I sat down hard and the stool nearly gave way.

'Easy, pal,' Cooper cackled, 'spill my beer and the next one's on you.'

The next one.

Then the next one.

Always the next one.

It was Wednesday night and that meant nothing to us. Thursday was empty, we were both out of work.

I had a few quid salted away, saved from the last job, the place I met Cooper. It wasn't much, but it was enough to cover my rent to him and to keep him oiled at The Gladiator.

Cooper never looked more like a fallen General than when he was six pints deep and had his broad bulk pressed against a wall in the bar. Like some landlord of souls on the estate, Cooper eyed his starved flock with a mixture of love and loathing. He knew them all, the regulars in there, the usual skeletons, waifs, loons and other assorted residents who lived at Balsall Heights and they, oh they knew him, even if they didn't want to.

When I'd met Cooper at Easton Automotive, he was just another shape on the assembly line. Head down, fat fingers and thumbs dunked in grease, he did what I did, pressed two parts of a drum brake together and sent it down the line for the next fast fix. The presses boomed, the gears yelled, the cogs cranked and bashed.

It was too loud for chat on the line, but we started to talk during break. I was living in a house-share then, over in Deer Wood. A house full of professionals. I kidded myself I was something of an academic, leaving unread copies of *Notes from the Underground*, or *The Road to Wigan*

Pier in the shared kitchen in the hope they wouldn't think I was just some beardy tumour who worked odd hours and stole their butter in the night.

When Cooper offered me a room at his house, I jumped at it. Fuck those cappuccino dandies, I thought. Fuck them with their olives and fashionable décor, their natural wines and casual parties. Fuck pretending I was an academic when I was just as happy to suck the wet end of a spliff and watch the cosmetic holograms of reality TV at 2am before skulking beneath my dirty sheets and crying myself to sleep.

Fuck them. Fuck me too.

If I'd known where it would lead, I'd have started turning up the legs of my jeans and talking about free-trade chocolate and local elections.

'Cheer up, Danny boy,' Cooper leered and winked over his latest pint, already half gone, 'you've got a face like a rat's arse tonight. What's bothering you?'

'Nothing,' I said, 'just bored probably, that's all. Could do with the agency coming up with some work, any work.'

Cooper waved the notion away, 'They'll be in touch, mate, don't fret. Men like us weren't made for the dole. We're proper, we're up for whatever,' he tilted his head to one of the jaded middle-agers at the bar, 'leave them to suck the government tit. Clowns like that were born into it, born to die at fifty-five, no more teeth in their heads than Sylvia.'

Something was brewing, not just with me, but with Cooper. I could feel it, like impending rain. It had weight, it gripped the sides of our conversation. It had talons. It was ugly and I should have done something to get away from it.

'Gym in the morning?' Cooper wasn't really asking. He was an organiser, a foreman.

I nodded. I could already smell the musk and arse of Body Swell. As rundown as it gets, but it was always good to sweat out the fears and panics.

The way Cooper's eyes narrowed over the next few beers, he was running something through his mind.

Occasionally, like a crescent moon glimpsed beyond fog, his lips curled into a thin, private smile. He was always clean shaven, his head and face. I never asked him how old he was, but always guessed around forty-two. It just never came up.

He didn't ask me either but, for the record, I'm the same age Christ died – the first time – thirty-three. I had recently read an article in a public toilet which claimed thirty-three was the most desirable age for humans. It didn't feel that way. It felt like anchors in the gut, like needles in the neck. I didn't feel free or ideal. I felt like mud at the centre of a crusted puddle. I felt malleable and insignificant. Cooper was the boot which broke the dirty water.

'Hey,' he leaned in and lowered his voice, 'you ever really…have you ever really given someone a hiding. You know, a real kicking?' His face was rosy with amusement. It shone brightly as he let the words fall effortlessly from his wide mouth.

I told him I hadn't. 'Last time I had any kind of fight was probably ten years ago. Even that was just a scuffle outside a chippy in town. Some bloke walked past and slapped the cone out my hand. I'd had a few, so went for him.'

'Left him on the pavement?'

'Nah,' I laughed as I recalled the idiocy of the confrontation. 'It was just windmills, Coop. Pair of us were plastered. Couldn't hit a tractor with a bat. Waste of time.'

'How'd it end?'

'Like they always do. Well-meaning posers careful not to get their white shirts dirty jumped in-between and threw us in different directions.'

'That's a shame.' Cooper leaned back and plaited his fingers until they clunked, a terrible habit, 'I'd like to have heard how you bloodied him, you know. You're good with words, Dan. I hoped you might be able to tell me something…to tell me something meaty, to give me some bone-on-bone, you know?'

I nodded. 'I'll write a diary if it ever happens again.'

'It will,' Cooper's eyes were neon tetra. 'The way the world is now, violence is just something like the flu. Everyone'll get it. Some worse than others.'

◊

WE LEFT THE GLADIATOR AT closing time.

Sylvia waved us away. Best wishes from a poor, old ghoul.

I'd left my tepid lager for so long that I had to down three pints in a row. Cooper hated waste and worshipped parity. He was a pub socialist, a true believer in the equality of intoxication. It didn't hit him the same way it hit me though.

I weaved across the pavement, he walked in a straight line. Cooper moved in a confident, unalterable way. His skinhead high, his eyes took in every detail of Balsall Heights. The streetlights bathed him in golden yellow. A gilded Lord, he seemed as large as the tower blocks and as dangerous as the underpasses which linked them.

Yet there was always something likeable about Cooper, despite his prevalence for prejudice and blanket hatreds. He came with a discordant panache. He didn't seem to exist in the same reality as me. Mine was one of worry and self-exposition. He always seemed content to let the rest of the world exist beyond his orbit, only entering it when the mood took him, crashing against its surface with blistering heat.

We stopped at Eastern Days to get some grub.

I always read the menu before ordering, even though I had the same thing every time.

'Egg fried rice and chips,' I slurred to the humourless owner.

She carried a look of total revulsion, and I appreciated it. I would be disgusted looking at me too. Some pissed-up loser in his hood, lank hair across the face, untrimmed beard like dirty laundry on the chin.

Cooper didn't blink when their eyes met. It was a test for him, I knew that. It was a barometer of control. He liked these instances and, as he would always do, he didn't order anything until she changed the tone of her voice. As it lightened, as it tilted towards a friendlier, welcoming tone, Cooper placed his order for sweet and sour chicken and boiled rice, 'The crispy balls, right,' he added, 'not that soppy chicken and peppers. Hate that.'

We slumped onto one of the frayed leather sofas and I closed an eye and began to read the flyers. A circus two months ago. A missing cat, its name – *Pixel* – written in a child's crayon. Mental Health awareness clinics. Odd-job men with their own vans. An advert for a local wrestling federation, with their event featuring *Baron Thump, Lockjaw* and *Miss Vamp.*

'Hey, Dan.' Cooper nudged my arm as the door opened and a shabbily dressed older thug wandered in. He had a few blue-smudge tats on his neck and face. Dreadful work, completely incomprehensible lettering which was likely the name of a dead parent or some nick in which he'd spent a few months on remand. The man snorted loudly and dropped two heavy elbows onto the laminated counter.

'Oi, oi,' he bellowed into the unseen kitchen, separated by strings of chipped, wooden beads.

The owner returned, her face as stony and numb as I expected.

'About fuckin time,' he sniffed. 'Get me a curry, yeah. *British curry sauce,* right? None of that fuckin *Chinese shite,*' and he turned to us and raised his wild eyebrows, as if he expected agreement.

I turned to Cooper instinctively and saw that he offered nothing of the kind. His face was blank, unmoved.

The man turned back to the counter and chucked a handful of coins down hard. Some of them rolled over the side and fell onto the tiles beyond. Their clinking racket sounded like foundries in the night.

Our food arrived first. I stood up and grabbed the carrier bag. Cooper opened the door and shouted his usual *thanks, doll* to the owner. She didn't reply.

We walked down the steps and, as we rounded the corner, Cooper grabbed my shoulder, 'Wait up a second, Danny. I want to see this bloke.'

I felt the tone of Cooper's words. They were measured, but he seethed behind them. I'd heard Cooper use racist slurs a thousand times. He didn't seem to see it as the same thing at all. His was delivered in what he saw as a natural, inoffensive way. He saw them as friendly, pally, salt-of-the-earth terminologies. They were descriptions in a lexicon born of this estate and every other city centre periphery zone he had existed in before.

I saw it as the same offence, the same remark, the same intonation and prejudice, but when I had mentioned that to Cooper in the past, he'd just waved it away as bollocks, as overreaction and the go-to bastion for the average white, of *political correctness gone mad.*

I didn't think for a second Cooper gave a fuck about the woman being insulted by that bastard in the takeaway, he just wanted to focus whatever violence was being amplified in his mind on a convenient target.

I took a few steps down the street and Cooper whistled me back. '*Wait,*' he growled firmly. I leaned against a garden wall. The overgrown grass was lousy with children's toys left out from play. Dog turds were scattered between the three-wheeled plastic bikes and wild-haired dolls of naked babies with their rolling eyes in the roofs of their skulls. It was better to look at them and hear the inherent and permanent background fuzz of ten-thousand televisions than it was to watch was about to take place.

Cooper unzipped his coat and moved his head in slow rotations. He was an intimidating, bullish figure. A pulverizing invention of muscle and meat.

I remember even now how I began to tremble as I waited in those long, heavy seconds. I had never liked violence, even the idea of it. The brutality, the gnashing of teeth, the fierce, bursting eyes of those frozen for a moment in the melee. It disgusted me. It was something I never thought I would feel.

Eventually I heard the creak and slam of the takeaway door and the textbook racist tumbled out into the sheets of neon cast from the flickering signage above him. A staggering shadow, fluttering, weightless.

He turned towards us and began to walk our way but then, with some implicit feral instinct, he stopped suddenly and stepped backwards. He scanned the silhouettes ahead of him carefully and eventually reached the monstrous sight of Cooper staring bloodlessly from the mouth of an alleyway.

Meticulously, with all the failed pretence of a bad dancer, the man backed away towards the corner and then, his takeaway slopping at his thigh, ran in the opposite direction.

Cooper emerged from the dark fastening his coat. He was agitated. He shrugged at me, 'That's a shame,' he said blankly, 'he could've done with a lesson in politeness.'

'Best off not getting involved,' I said, keen to get away from that bristling street, keen to get back to our place and eat.

'Maybe,' Cooper joined my side, matched my pace, 'but people *need* that release, Dan. It's natural, something we're owed.'

'Gym in the morning though,' I offered meekly, aware of the higher pitch of my own voice.

'Yeah,' Cooper agreed sadly, 'but weights ain't nothing compared to flesh and bone.'

◊

IT WAS JUST AFTER MIDNIGHT when the documentary aired.

The half-eaten takeaways lay like indistinct artefacts on the carpet by our feet. We leaned back on the long sofa and passed a joint between us.

Cooper had opened a bottle of vodka but, whenever I exchanged the dope for the liquor, I took a phoney sip, stifling the spout of the bottle with my tongue. The cheap lager churned in my guts, only marginally suffocated by the takeaway.

Cooper had the remote and cycled through channels endlessly. Snippets of shows, films and adverts zoomed in and quickly vanished. They moved ahead of me like aspects of dreams barely remembered, the faces and products went by too quickly to be anything other than alien.

It was some sort of inherent, browser instinct which caused Cooper to stop on Channel 4. It only took a moment, a few frames for us to realise what the documentary was about.

Vigilante groups catching online predators.

I don't even remember what it was called. Something like 'Netting the Beasts', or 'Undercover Heroes: Nonces Must Die'. Some throwaway trash title for the late-night zombie crowd. It didn't matter what it was called because, for Cooper, it was simply the fuse. It lit the Semtex at the base of his hatred and gave him everything he needed.

I was pretty baked, so just watched with my usual disinterest as hard-to-hear microphones picked up the nasal conversations of pixilated pedo-hunters crammed into the seats of their vehicle, hung there in stark, multi-story carparks.

Screenshots of horrendous exchanges with potential offenders were flashed across the TV, with every foul and wretched description imaginable somehow immediately available or inferred.

The show only wanted extremes. The *hunters* needed us to know that this adult male wanted to get hold of this toddler and defile her in every brutal way possible. The hunters insisted on it. They gaslit these seedy rubes day after day. Just from the few minutes we saw, they demonstrated how they hung out in chatrooms, how they pretended to be teen or pre-teen victims waiting for the monsters to slap their gristle against the screen. Then they could hunt them down.

The show only featured one confrontation. We had missed the rest. What I saw was the usual shaky-cam pursuit through a crowded bus-station. A man, his face also pixilated, leaned against the railings of a bus station somewhere down south. A smog-spewing vape protruded from his hidden head. The two men, their voices gruff and hateful, grabbed the man's arms and, it seemed to me, made sure they addressed him and his crimes loud enough for everyone nearby to hear as they wrestled him back through the triggered throngs, towards their car.

As they waited for the police to arrive, their informal court of justice kicked into gear. They slammed their mobiles into the man's face, slavering as they showed him their digital snares, their cosplay performances as a pre-teen girl. These two men, both middle-aged, had spent weeks messaging from the viewpoint of a child. They weren't terrified by their actions, or seemingly even horrified by the predator's.

The display was one of sport, of blood-sport. 'You're fucking done for, dirty cunt!'

I reached out and took the joint from Cooper's motionless hand. I could see then as the light from the screen bathed him in flickering blues, something had ignited in Cooper. Some malignant idea, some new obsession.

As the TV show splintered to credits and sombre electronic music, a wider, toothy smile lit up Cooper's face.

I didn't know then just how far this would take us, nor how barbed the path would be. When I look back to that moment, high on estate hash and half-drunk off flat Carling, I now see an equinox, a moment of blinding ferocity which crashed across everything that happened afterwards, leaving it scorched and bloodied.

The notion of the void had always intrigued me. As we sat there, past midnight, past existence, I should have realised we weren't just staring into the void, we had our toes over its edge, teasing the eternal beasts below.

2.

A testament to dead intentions

BY THE TIME I MADE it downstairs the next morning, Cooper was up and glued to the computer.

Hunched there like Buddha's mad brother, Cooper slurped at a huge bowl of cheap cereal and scrolled through video after video on YouTube.

I didn't need to see them to know what they were, but glanced at the top of his screen as I walked past to the kitchen.

Spaz nonce confronted in carpark.

'Look at the terror on this bastard's grill!' Cooper was excited. 'These groups, mate, they get these buggers banged to rights. *Banged to rights.*'

I made a coffee and held it with shuddering hungover hands. 'Don't believe what you see on there,' I shrugged and sat down on the sofa, 'could all be actors for all you know.'

'For all I know?' Cooper spun around on the chair, dark luggage beneath his eyes. 'I know what's real and what isn't, Danny boy. These nonces are the real thing. This one here, state of him, squirming around on the pavement, begging to be let go.'

'So what are they gonna do, eh? Why do they need to brace him like that when they can just send his details to the coppers?'

'Cops.' Cooper turned back to the screen and slurped at his stodgy Weetabix. 'Cops ain't worth shit, you know that. Lazy bastards would rather be down on the canal busting gypsies for stripping copper wiring than doing the work to get these fuckers. Nah, groups of real characters, folks who want to see things done, that's who's best doing this, blokes like us.'

I didn't answer. We got on, but I never wanted to see us as similar. The situation we were in was a coiled snake. We didn't come together because of shared interests, we collided because of mauled fates.

The scratchy audio of another dozen ambushes played out as I tried to cough out last night's wreckage at the window. The lace curtain acted like a mosquito net between me and the rest of the estate. Only I didn't know which of us were the bugs.

It was school time. A parade of fag-mouthed parents dragged their mewling toddlers across the field towards St Delphi's Primary. A cabaret of screams and barking adults, it played out like a violent conga. Some of the parents were as hungover as me. Some more so. Their language was harsh, brutal. Some of the kids were pacified with breakfasts of crisps and chocolate bars. Others were fed swift backhanders, their cheeks blooming with fingerprints.

They made their way through the shadows cast from the four main high-rise flats; from *Benton House* to *Weston House*. Like sheer ice floes, they dominated the skyline of Balsall Heights with their imposing incarceration, with their bladed edges and inherent sense of dread. Like all estates in the centre of the country, the tower blocks were the focal point, their pallid terraces surrounding their windows like kneeling mourners.

Our front garden was overgrown. The pathetic wire fence had buckled in a thousand places and the gate was missing. A hollowed-out lawnmower sat in the centre of the grass. A testament to dead intentions. The rusted husk seemed perfectly at home here in Balsall Heights. Like a jacked car with its wheels nicked, it was just one more sedentary wreck with nowhere to go.

◊

COOPER SWUNG HIS KITBAG MERRILY.

I walked behind, belching loudly with each step.

Not only did I have no idea how Cooper could drink so much and seem to exhibit no after-effects, I couldn't believe he was able to work out so hard when we hit the gym. I would have put it down to the steroids which flowed liberally from the hands of dealers like Mack or Turkish Lee, but he was terrified of needles. He didn't even have any ink, which would've seemed inevitable for someone like him. It was just his constitution. His impossible, nuclear system.

We walked through the arcade. Only two shops still had all their windows – *Fryer Tuck's Fish & Chips* and *Select & Save*. The others, even the charity shops, had at least one boarded up.

At night the goblins came. Circling on mountain bikes and BMXs, faces obscured by scarves and hoods. They tortured the owners and patrons with their ever-present violence, their undying desire to impose their dread on anyone who frequented the shops.

I was usually okay. I was with Cooper. I was a face on the estate now. I ate from its shops, I drank at its pub, I walked its streets and pissed in its sewers. Rats move in groups, so did we.

Cooper and I walked down to the canal and edged through the thorns onto the path. It was the quickest way to the gym. I took the opportunity to puke into the fly-tipped hedgerow.

'Best get that out before we hit the metal, Danny boy.' Cooper paused and watched with interest as I wretched. 'I reckon it's those nonces,' he grinned, 'turning your stomach. Makes sense, I feel the same.'

I wiped my mouth and said it was the lager at The Gladiator. 'It's off, Coop. They've never cleaned the pipes there. Not once.'

'Bollocks, it's fine. Mind over matter, sunshine. Think yourself stronger.'

We carried on down the canal path. Rows of stalled cranes peered over us, their cabins derelict homes for pigeons and sparrows. The development of the neighbouring industrial zone had ceased months earlier. I didn't really give it a second thought, but Cooper was intrigued by it. He and the other regulars at The Gladiator speculated for weeks about the reason. The Council were crooks, the company was some Hong Kong rip-off firm out to bleed the country and fill their pockets. One grizzled lush in a permanent raincoat even suggested they had found fossils beneath one of the bombed-out forges. Not fossils as we knew it though, but alien fossils, occult bones stashed beneath a few workshops and lockups.

14

I just took my sips and shut my mouth. It was best to listen to the muzac without humming along.

As we crossed the bridge towards the old Maddox Dog Food Factory, the last of the night's working girls were ending their shift on the desolate corners. Mostly smack-haggard waifs with track-mark tattoos, they hugged themselves and licked their chapped lips.

Cooper smirked as one of them asked him whether he was up for quick shuffle round back. 'My lovely,' he bellowed, 'If I didn't need my energy for the gym, I might just take you up on it.'

'Another time, lover?' She tried to smile, but ten hours of unwashed gristle can really dull a person's humour.

'Why not.'

They were a crumbling quartet of boot-trodden workers. I looked down at the pavement as we passed them. They were staggeringly pitiful, no matter how often I saw them on the way to the gym.

I never ventured this way late at night, so I just had to imagine the feral thuds and yelps which echoed through the abandoned building where they took their johns. Even then, even during the workaday morning, a car slowly eased to the kerb and one of the prostitutes came dutifully to the passenger side and slid behind onto the leather. She teetered as she walked, her legs like porcelain wickets. The car moved away and turned down one of the flooded paths which encircled the building.

I heaved again, but there was nothing left inside.

3.

Hickey

MEN LIKE COOPER WERE AGELESS at the gym.

They were symbiotic with the metal, the equipment and, when gathered in circles of bulbous meat, each other.

I was an outsider at Body Swell. No way around it. Trim, lean enough, but lacking in width, weights and bars just didn't respond to me in the same way they did to Cooper and the others there. I couldn't lift the same weights many of them could, but even when I pushed myself, I didn't get the shapes they got. I didn't get the elevated highways of veins which seemed desperate to escape the skin.

Free weights, benches, squat-racks, bars and bags, there was nothing else there.

This wasn't a high-end fitness centre with hydraulic presses and treadmills. Body Swell was as raw as it got. Shaved mammoths screamed under bending steel, or bled gallons of sweat from their thudding heads as they hit rep after rep after rep of agonising lifts.

It was one of the only places where Cooper left me to my own devices.

Ever since I'd taken the room at his place, we were usually together. Shopping, drinking, eating, even the jobs we worked. Not at the gym though.

He barged upstream with the ogres and I stayed in the shallows, shaping my meagre muscles like a child left in a prison creche.

16

I was happy to doze on the lateral pulldown. I whirled the bar as Cooper went to work with all the energy and fury of a freed bull. He tugged and lifted, squatted and wrenched. Sweat became opals on his neck, his flushed face.

There was a blankness to his eyes when he exercised there. It was as if he was somehow able to turn his mind off during the warm-up, to leave it outside of the gym and pick it back up from a locker on the way out. He moved effortlessly from one perfect exercise to the next, in unison with the other beasts.

It was the same with the others.

There in ragged vests, in bollock-high shorts, the leathery doormen and night-shift killers tore themselves apart. Communications were gruffly coded. They spoke through grunts and roars, through rolled shoulders and pulsing forearms. There were tectonic blasts as they slammed the weights down to the ground, as they holstered the enormous bars and screamed about their violent successes, or sucked at plastic water flasks, half the water spilling down their raging necks and chests.

I lifted a little, squatted a little. I humoured Cooper by bench-pressing as he spotted me. He liked to slide more weight on, each plate making me struggle more than the last.

'Don't worry, Danny Boy!' he bellowed, meeting the eyes of the other silverbacks in the gym, 'Not like I'm gonna let this fall on your neck, is it?' Then, of course, he'd pretend he was about to drop the bar as I laboured desperately to the tenth press.

The same routine, the barbed circuit of the days before it all happened.

When I think back to that day at the gym, I realise it was really then that things truly developed, when they began to take shape. A smoke-ring just before it inevitably splinters into greying chaos, into oblivion.

Hickey was suddenly there, near to us.

I had always been uncomfortable around Hickey, right from the moment Cooper had introduced us a few months earlier.

He was a frightening man.

I suppose that's why I disliked him, because he terrified me. Hickey wore a cowl of intimidation. He was a permanently dark presence, a sinister shape. Shadows seemed to glide around him like sneering vapours. He stood out in the gym because, despite him being smaller than Cooper and the other bulldozers, he carried a type of vulgar menace in his limbs, in his face. His muscles seemed to have outgrown his skin years before, with the meat refashioned to accommodate them. He didn't bulge and swell, he just wore ugly, brutal strength. It bled from his pores. His frizzy, greying hair tied back, his thick, long beard like a gaping maw, his silver eyes fast and mean. Hickey's mouth was always shaped into a malicious smile. When I say always, I mean *always*. When he spoke, when he drank, when he slept...Hickey smiled constantly. For me, it may have been the most disconcerting aspect of him. That smile.

I can see it now, as I later saw it through tears, through blood, through flames.

Cooper liked Hickey. He valued him highly. As soon as I looked out through the veil of greasy sweat – a mixture of mine and Cooper's – and saw Hickey, I knew it was too late to exit before he joined us.

'Ah!' Cooper pushed out a fist and Hickey punched it, his eyes fixed on mine. 'If it isn't the phantom. Where you been, Hick?'

'Around and about,' he replied, rolling his shoulders and clicking the joints of his thick fingers, 'just out in the dark, howling at the traffic.'

Hickey's body was tramlined with mangled tattoos. Images of butchered faces, of incoherent symbols smudged to nothingness at the time they were inked. The colours of much of his tattoo work had faded, which gave him the impression of having an inhuman skin; a mixture of scales and graffitied granite.

'What about you two true believers?' Hickey nudged me off the bench and proceeded to easily press the weight Cooper had foisted on me. He showed no strain whatsoever, he exuded no effort.

'Keeping our eyes peeled for work.' Cooper removed his vest and used it to wipe his face and neck. 'Hitting The Gladiator to look at the damned. Passing the time, you know.'

'Aye,' Hickey slid from the bench and began to add more weight than either me or Cooper had lifted, 'I know about passing the time.' He sat back down. 'Only true benefit of time in the big house...it teaches you about time. About true time.'

We watched as Hickey threw out a set of twelve and sat up again, barely a change in his pallor or breathing. 'What type of work you looking for?'

'Whatever we can get,' I answered. 'Well, whatever the agencies can sling our way.'

'That's cute,' Hickey winked at me, 'boy like you could sell his body out the back of the canals whenever he wanted to. You could be a retired whore by thirty-five.'

'Wouldn't want to jeopardise my modelling career,' I replied, aware my humour and quick wit were perhaps the only factors which kept Cooper and Hickey believing I inhabited even the furthest reach of their own, peculiar stratospheres.

'Hear that?!' Cooper slapped my shoulder. 'Our Dan's got a bite on him.'

Hickey didn't respond. We stood and watched him finish the sets. A strange observation of required worship.

When Hickey broke for a stretch, Cooper leaned in conspiratorially, his words only audible to our weird trio. 'Dan and I have been thinking about taking a punt catching nonces on the internet.'

I began to protest, but the words died in the sewer of my neck. There was no point saying anything then. I remained quiet.

'That right?' Hickey's eyes widened. 'Public service?'

'Had the thought last night,' Cooper continued, 'caught the tail-end of some doc on the telly about these groups who go around catching the bastards at it.'

'Groomers getting groomed,' I interjected. Neither man acknowledged me.

'Way I see it,' Cooper placed a hand on Hickey's naked shoulder, 'it'd be a good way to let off some steam whilst also doing something productive.'

'The perfect crime.' Hickey grinned broadly. 'Need a third?'

Cooper was immediately elated. 'Yes, brother!'

'Let me know when you're making a move. Got some new boots I want to break in.'

4.

Katie Pop

IT MIGHT'VE BEEN A WEEK later when I came back to the house to find Hickey sat next to Cooper at the computer.

I'd told Cooper I was heading out for a run. He hated jogging, so never wanted to join me. I didn't really go out for exercise. I just found a quiet bus-stop at the edge of the estate and cried myself stupid.

I didn't know exactly why I sobbed that day. It just came upon me, like a spring storm.

It could've been the idea of my Mom at the hospice, the notion I would need to go and see her again soon. Just a flicker of that picture, of her and the other jaundiced demi-dead waiting for their hearts to putter out. That could have done it. Even then, it may have just been the fact that I felt anchored to that estate, just like the estate on which I'd grown up. The way a person feels trapped, caught in some unspeakable gravity. Even the bus-stop I sat at to cry was on the periphery of the estate, on a hill, looking down into that bowl of spoiled food. It was as if I couldn't leave, couldn't get any further away. When I had, in the past, when I'd tried to move into some other alley of society, I'd felt alien, filthy, an imposter.

Yet, I wonder now whether it was an acknowledgement of something sinister to come, of what did come. I have grown to understand that there's so much more to what happens than what I know, than what we know. I don't mean the kind of predetermination so many bogus cash-hungry religions use to work the dumb, I mean something else, something completely intangible.

I thought about the dream I would always have as a child, the kind you remember when you wake up, the kind which you never really forget.

It wasn't a dream of action, a mechanical dream of super-powered abilities, or one of quicksand feet and tumbling teeth. It was a revealing dream, one which simply showed me something essential, but terrifying.

In the dream, I was there as normal, in the places I knew. Oak trees shook with warm autumn winds, the dashing tits and sparrows joined the magpies on geriatric branches and sang intermittently. Beyond, always visible from a bedroom window, the city raged with emissions and neon, its rattling jaws never silent, never still.

I saw myself, my child self, watching from the window, my meagre elbows on the sill, my empty, bug-eyed face at the glass. As I sat there, my mind empty, something showed itself to me.

Above the city I knew, I glimpsed – through clearing cloud – another city above it. Then, above that, another city, then more and more, fading in concentric impressions. Echo cities, the image of each weaker than the last. I was stricken with panic, with absolute horror. I looked down from the window, the sounds beyond the glass suddenly slurred and maudlin. There, as the ground itself cleared like the clouds I had only ever witnessed above me, I saw more cities beneath me. Like spiral steps, they corkscrewed into oblivion.

Only now, after everything that's happened, only now can I understand why the dream was so frightening, so devastating.

I was given a chance to understand my pathetic place in an unending universe, the sheer indifference of the cosmos to me. I have grown to believe the dream scared me so much because, above all else, it inferred there was more to the world I thought I knew than I could ever believe.

Forces of sinister magic. Shuddering, ghastly malevolence. Vulgar, inhuman puppeteers.

It was a warning. Stigmata on the horizon.

I had been thinking of the dream that day, as I cried in the bus-stop.

It had seemed ludicrous then.

21

'About time you made it back' Cooper nodded at the computer screen, Hickey didn't even acknowledge me, 'fucking jogging. That's probably why you can't put any real meat on, Danny boy.'

'Maybe,' I threw my hoodie over the back of the frayed sofa, 'or maybe I've got cancer.'

'Jesus, Dan,' Cooper shook his head slowly, without looking back at me, 'you educated types love a bit of drama. Speaking of which, come and take a look at this.'

I meandered over to where the neon of the screen bathed the hunched duo, making their faces monochrome. They were on a chat site, *FishTank*. Bubbles of dialogue rose upwards, almost too quickly to read. I asked what was happening.

'We made a profile,' Hickey answered tonelessly, 'we're baiting ourselves a pervert.'

'Jesus.' I ran a hand through my hair, sniffed my fingers with disgust at its greasiness. 'You're serious?' I asked, but knew they were.

'Course we're serious, Danny boy,' Cooper turned to me, amused eyebrows raised, 'we knocked up profiles on all of 'em. FishTank, MeetMe, Natter, the whole shebang.'

I leaned in and read their online name. *Katie*.

'That's right,' Copper seemed proud, like he'd cracked an unfathomable code, 'Katie. We're fourteen, into R&B and looking to meet older blokes.'

I couldn't help but laugh, *looking to meet older blokes*. I told them they sounded ridiculous. 'Honestly, that must be the most basic fishing profile I've ever heard.'

'Oh yeah,' Hickey turned to me, his lips downturned, annoyed. 'You want to have a go, see if you can do something better?'

I told him I didn't want anything to do with it. 'Your business, boys. Keep me out of it.'

Before I turned away, I noticed they had copied some photos from image searches. A glossy, smiling teen, the sea at her back, a captured sun making her already blonde hair neon as it rose into a cloudless sky behind her. It was an advert face, something torn from a billboard in the city. Nobody in their right mind could believe she was the person they were talking to, that this was real. Nobody.

As I made a coffee and receded into the sofa to flick through the tripe of afternoon television, I kept an ear on them, more from disbelief than curiosity. I mocked them silently, running the idiocy of their fumbling mousetrap over in my mind.

I could hear their excitement when they caught an occasional comment, Cooper's quick desperation to think of something *teen* to say. 'Who's a good R&B artist? One that sounds real?'

'Doesn't matter,' Hickey yawned, 'make up a name. They're fishing for a piece of arse, not recommendations for their playlists.'

It went on like that for a couple of hours. They mumbled suggestions to each other, opened a second window on the browser and began to search for music acts that fitted, for comments that fitted, for clothing, for films, for anything that legitimised them.

I started watching some BBC2 fluff documentary about the renovation of a church spire. Soporific stuff, the kind that dulls your thoughts, that rounds them, takes away the edges. My mind felt sanded, wiped. My eyes grew heavier with each second as the greying TV flakes chatted and awed, pointed, hummed and faded.

As I was about to fall asleep completely, a shout from Cooper jolted me horribly.

'Got you!'

I turned to look over at them and Hickey was already eyeing me. Unblinking, somehow ravenous, he seemed keen to involve me, 'Awake now, eh? Didn't think we'd get a bite, did you, Daniel. Well, come and have a look at this greasy bastard.'

Cooper was typing, his breathing heavy.

I stood between them and read the exchange. It was a snippet from a longer conversation. They had obviously aroused the interest of their inaugural target a while earlier. Maybe their searches had yielded enough content to seem legitimate.

I only needed to see the final few messages.

[Katie Pop: Dunno, reckon I'd be nervous. Ain't done anything like that before.]
[Big Barry: I'd be gentle and all that. Honest. You'll love it LOL]
[Katie Pop: Yeah?]
[Big Barry: Defo babe. Best thing ever]

[Katie Pop: What would we do first then LOLS]
[Big Barry: Whatever you want beautiful LOLS]
[Katie Pop: ROLF I'm blushing!]
[Big Barry: Come on girl! Let me know when and where and I'll be there!]

They had found one. A slavering rube. Clear as day. At least as far as the chat was concerned. I asked them to show me his profile.

'Into it now, are you?' Hickey flashed a thin smile at me.

I told him I still wasn't, but couldn't believe someone would actually fall for the shit they were putting out, even if secretly I was a little impressed by how measured Cooper was as he impersonated *Katie Pop*.

Leaving Big Barry with a necklace of garish emojis, Cooper clicked into Katie's friends list and found his profile. I expected Big Barry's profile photo to be fake too, to be some kind of perfect avatar, his dream self, the image he wished to occupy.

No, from the photograph, there was no way it could be anything other than real.

A large, shaved head, domelike. Two raisin eyes sat beneath the looming brow. A flat, once broken nose jutted out over a smile of occasional teeth. A thin, hairless throat, the drooping neck of a football shirt. An absence of muscle and shape, skin like the cast on a broken arm. An alabaster thing, an alien thing. The picture was ugly, the man seemed pitiful, grotesque.

I told Hickey and Cooper he looked slow-witted, sickly, dumb.

'He ain't dumb,' Cooper sipped at a mug of cold tea, 'he's on here fishing for *kids*, Danny boy. He might be sick in the head, but he ain't dumb.'

'He's pretty stupid to have fallen for this.' I waved the screen away, a feeling of seediness enveloping me, even though all I'd seen was those few messages. 'You can report him to the moderators on the site,' I suggested, 'get his profile locked, get his info to the cops.'

I watched as Cooper and Hickey exchanged a fast look.

'We're not going to do that,' Hickey said calmly, 'we're planning to push ahead, Daniel. We're going to arrange a meeting.'

'Why?' I was appalled, disgusted they would even bother. 'To be like those clowns on TV, on YouTube? They just do that shit for clicks.

They could hand over the info to the police whenever they want to. They only brace them in public to get a reaction, to feel good.' I told them we didn't need that kind of thing.

'*We* is it now?' Hickey spun around on his chair to face me. Even sat there, looking up at me, he was larger, stronger, more powerful with each passing second. 'Well *we* didn't think you wanted anything to do with this.'

'I'm just saying, you're better off out of that stuff. It's a waste of time. Just report this goon and move on.'

'Nah.' Cooper stood up, stretched out the hours of being slouched at the computer. 'We want to catch this fucker in the act. It's all well and good us just passing his name and chat profiles over to the cops, Danny, but that only nails him for some online shenanigans. We want to prove he was going to follow through, that he was going to turn up and mess with our Katie.'

'Our Katie,' Hickey echoed, as if they were talking about their adopted daughter.

'See,' Cooper placed a hand on my shoulder, 'like I was saying to you the other night, Danny, we're stale, we're just hanging around, waiting for something to happen and I *need* this. I have something building in me, you know? I need to get it out and now I've found something useful, some way I can do it all.'

'Or get a job,' I suggested, 'we both need that more than anything else.'

'Don't worry about work,' Hickey sniffed. 'You two can come down the yard and get a few days' pay from me whenever you want.'

The yard. The fucking yard. It was like some mythical crossroads, some place where all trades seemed to intermingle, legal and illegal alike. The yard. I'd heard Hickey mention it a hundred times, but me and Cooper had never taken him up on it, never wanted to.

'See, Danny,' Cooper smiled broadly, 'we can get some work down the yard. It'll all work itself out, just you wait and see. In the meantime…' Cooper leaned over and pulled something out of a carrier bag. It was a new mobile phone, a cheap one. He bent it out of the plastic and turned it on. 'A burner,' he announced proudly, 'we're gonna give this Barry bastard the number, get hold of him outside of FishTank, arrange to meet.'

I remember backing away, just a few inches. It was some facile attempt to leave that atmosphere, the gravity they were creating. I insisted I didn't want to be a part of it, yet there was a fraction of me that did. That cretin, that Big Barry, sat there, somewhere, leering at his computer screen, his phone screen, pants around his ankles, rotten. That's the image I had then, the idea that demanded I see it. It felt like it was being transmitted to me by Hickey, even by Cooper. They were lacing up my boots, breathing air on behalf of my lungs. They were infecting me, spore by spore.

Cooper didn't wait long to give Big Barry the number. Having done so, he and Hickey waited around the phone, like they were sat over a Ouija board. They waited for the black magic, for the summoning to appear. It only took a few seconds. *Ping. Ping. Ping.* The messages began.

Elated, his eyes fiercely bright, Hickey congratulated Cooper and made the inevitable suggestion. 'Few down The Gladiator? We'll take the phone and message this bastard from there.'

5.

A dream of different places

I drank the flat lager as quickly as I could.

Pint after pint, I wanted to be drunk. Hopelessness had hit me hard that day. It wasn't just Hickey and Cooper, the new crusaders, it was everything. I wanted to be numb, to be blank. I wanted to be deleted and redrawn. That was impossible so, in place of being able to shut down and restart, I just opted for blindness.

Hickey and Cooper were high on their catch. They laughed as they messaged Big Barry. Inevitably, he wanted to send Katie a picture of his prick. He wanted a picture of her too, of her *of her pert little tits.* Everything in his messages was big or little. He was Big Barry. She was little Katie. She had a little body, a little mouth.

The more I drank, the more of Big Barry's messages I heard or saw, the more I fostered hatred for him, the easier it was for him to become a target of loathing for me too. I'm ashamed now, ashamed to believe I could have felt that way, that quickly, but I did.

I watched Cooper. It was easy. Suddenly, every frustration, every fear, every worry, every unresolved roaring rage could be funnelled into a single target. A series of texts, a badly taken photograph of a repugnant man. That was the enemy. Big Barry and the others like him could become the reason for everything wrong. Just as he was grooming the ethereal Katie Pop, so I was being groomed by Hickey, perhaps even by Cooper.

And so we all were being manipulated by them, by the white bracken.

By the time we staggered out of The Gladiator after last orders, zigzagging our way between the other fleeing rats, I was yelling my disgust for Big Barry too. I was talking about kicking him to bits, about dragging him into some anonymous stairwell and punching him until my fists no longer existed.

Slobbering drunk, I couldn't have seen Hickey watching me, knowing it was all coming together the way he wanted it to. Yet he was there, omnipresent in the night. Like a Hunter's Moon, Hickey lit the way.

As we stormed along the street, our voices booming, our words incomprehensible, I felt Hickey's hand on my shoulder. It may have seemed a small gesture, but it wasn't. He had gripped my reins; he was steering me forwards. There, indestructible in our inebriation, it was a sign of three, the formation of a triangle. Hickey didn't speak as he did it, he just allowed our eyes to meet, my singsong stupidity to quieten beneath his unblinking eyes. Cooper, patrolling his estate, chest out, sleeves rolled over bulbous biceps, merely recognised the gesture with one of his own. He pulled me away, held me in a headlock, ruffled my lank hair, laughed until he was hoarse, the joke unknown to any of us, the punchline one we would never forget.

Back at the house, one more saccharine takeaway poured onto scratched plates, we slurped and slobbered, we sucked lager cans dry and then crushed them in our atomic fists. Hickey seemed content to let mine and Cooper's voices rule. Our house, our volume. He sat back, much of his food left on the plate as Cooper talked about Big Barry, about what he was going to do to him.

'We'll give him up to the cops eventually,' he slurred, 'after we've given him a shoeing, you know. Just a few kicks, punches, wrestle him a bit. We're owed that much,' he belched, his voice deepened with supressed gas, 'we're owed a workout on the bastard. We'll get the cameras and -'

'No.' Hickey leaned forward from the shadows, the crooked shade on the standard lamp lit his face like a nightclub crooner. 'No cameras, none of that shit.'

Cooper hiccupped, seemed bloated with confusion. 'I-I thought we...I thought we were gonna sort a YouTube channel out, y'know? Like the others on there?'

'No YouTube channel, no profiles, no public.' Hickey plaited his fingers, clunked them, unfolded them. 'Don't forget why we're into this now,' he grinned, his plan manifest, at least in his own mind. 'It's about catching these creeps, it's about working out some fury on them, terrifying the cunts.'

'Getting them nicked,' I added, like some feeble punctuation, 'after we're done.'

'After we're done,' Hickey echoed, his grin widened, 'sure, we'll let the police have them. No cameras though. No photos. This isn't posturing, boys. This is a tribute to those who watch from night.'

'A tribute!' Cooper lifted his can, saluted a comment he didn't understand and downed the remaining beer.

I didn't understand the comment either. Not then. *Those who watch from the night*. A tribute. It was all there, in those early hours. Yet, I was beer blind, misery blind, fury blind. I was locked into the cycle, churning in those maligned moments.

I left Cooper and Hickey to carry on without me. I knew we would have to be back at the gym the next morning, that the life of Katie Pop would continue afterwards. I was wasted, rubber legged. I stumbled up the stairs, the roars of the bears beneath me.

I staggered into my room, my clothing scattered across the bed, the floor. Panting heavily, labouring to even remove my shoes, I stared out of the yellow window, through the torn net curtains. The streetlight right outside the glass bathed everything in that stagnant gold. Three AM, maybe even later, yet still the lost youths circled the small green area over the road on their bikes, their faces anonymous beneath hoods, scarves. Near silent, they obeyed their strange routine, the same routine I had adhered to as a kid. I often referred to them as goblins, maybe due to some recall of a Fall song I'd heard years earlier. It had always been easy or amusing to me to think of humans in that way, as goblins, ogres, werewolves, ghosts. It felt like the perfect assessment of us, like the most apt exaggeration.

As I lay down on my side, still mostly clothed, the few lads on their bikes who circled the litter-strewn green became a strange carousel. In those dozing moments, one eye shut to avoid doubling their numbers, I began to see them as the pulse of the estate, as its silent heart, as the muscle beating beneath the bone, the fat, the gristle and blood. They were the heart, they were the womb. They were the next in line to climb into my shape, into Cooper's shape, even into Hickey's. When we faded into the long grass, when we rotted at the stovetop, they would emerge as us, as the next versions of us.

I thought then that they would follow in our paths, either between or over the landmines.

Eventually, in the weeks to come, I would realise that their path could never be like ours, that their future belonged here and ours, ours belonged amongst the multiple cities of my childhood nightmare.

♨

I HAD A CALL FROM the hospice the next morning.

Mom was asking for me.

Humiliated by the tone of the nurse, disgusted by myself, I admitted that I hadn't visited for almost two weeks. I apologised, claimed I had been working shifts, that I'd been ill and didn't want to risk giving Mom a cold. I conjured every fast and convenient lie I could, snarling them out, growling them from a dry throat.

I promised I'd be there later that morning, that I'd *call work and tell them I couldn't make it in today.*

The nurse hung-up without replying. She knew I didn't really exist.

When I made it downstairs, my hands like frightened birds, Cooper was already up, stretching out the hangover. He couldn't have had more than five hours sleep, but he looked fresh, strong.

'Jesus, Danny boy, you look crippled from the booze.'

I told him I was sick with it, done with it. 'I can't carry on like this, Coop. Fuck's sake. We must've sunk a boatload.'

'Fair go of it, that much is for sure.'

I asked what time he and Hickey called it a night.

'No idea,' he yawned, 'we got into a bottle of scotch. It was starting to get light when Hickey split. He walked straight through the lads on the green. Shoulda seen them move. He's got a way about him, hasn't he, our Hickey?'

I agreed. There was a way about him. 'Yeah, like a shark or a wolf.'

'That's about right,' Cooper agreed, and passed me a coffee, 'get this down you, gym in an hour.'

'Can't, mate, have something on.'

Cooper thought I was just trying to get out of exercise. 'Now, come on, Danny boy,' he shook me by the neck, 'you'll feel a world better when you sweat it out. Think yourself stronger. You know how it goes.'

'No.' I explained I couldn't, that I had a family thing. I hadn't told him about my Mom. He had never asked about my family, I'd never asked about his.

'Can't get out of those,' he agreed after a few more jibes about me dodging the gym. 'Hickey'll think you bottled it.'

'Fuck what Hickey thinks,' I snapped, my head like a thunderstorm, 'I can't worry about my reputation in hell today.'

'Okay, my lovely,' Cooper wriggled his fingers at me, 'guess you'll have to get over your monthlies in your own time.'

I ignored him and set about shaking off my hangover. The hospice would be horrible enough.

The bus ride was brutal.

I had never felt so nauseous in my life.

I swallowed puke on every corner, leaning against the glass as the bus rocked and stuttered. The hangover drummed at my skull from the interior, the cackle and yammer of the other passengers from the exterior. My thoughts were drummed into some neutral trench, cowering there, hoping the monsters would pass them by eventually.

A stagnant district, one cursed with the *new town* stink. Adderley was a former estate, not unlike Balsall Heights was now, but one swept clean by some new home initiatives, its sickly tower blocks felled by emotionless bulldozers, rows of nondescript beige homes erected in their place. Amongst the terraced nowhere, the hospice sat on the same row of buildings as a school for the Deaf and a building for local council meetings.

Caked in yellow décor and undying flowers, it was a nothing place too, something you could easily walk past, without even seeing it. You could never tell it was a place where the ill gathered to die.

I waited outside for a few minutes, framed by ringlets of purple and red flowers. I took deep breaths and tried desperately to feel well again. It was hopeless. I had a thrumming pulse, aches in every organ, a headache that drilled outwards, eager for sunlight. My bones felt like they were rebelling against me, my guts too.

It was just the booze. I was a matter of feet away from people counting their final hours. I swallowed my discomfort and slid through the door.

Daniel Solomon, here for Violet Solomon, I whispered at the desk, aware of the reek of my own breath; the liquor and onions, the concentric rot of spent screams.

The nurse on duty nodded me in the direction of my mother's room. I knew where it was. I wasn't sure why I had to show myself at the desk beforehand. Some opportunity for humiliation, a reminder that I hadn't visited enough.

I made my way down the bleached hallway, stifling belches, swallowing the vomit which threatened to pour outwards at any moment.

Some of the doors lay ajar, offering glimpses into the ersatz tombs. Like the very graves the occupants were moving towards, many of the rooms were littered with flowers, some fashioned into garlands, bouquets; others simply stood in vases, their solemn observation offset by the neon colours of their petals. Competing television channels blared from most bedrooms, merging in the hallway in some kind of anonymous dispute. Music of comfort also seeped out. They must have been tunes important to the patients, songs which elicited gilded memories, moments of value from their past. Most of the music was slow, maudlin. Unsubtle romance, loves lost, wedding dance tap-along melancholia.

I eased my way into Mom's room and found her sleeping.

I sat next to her bed. She was smaller with every visit. Little more than a doll of her former self. I couldn't stand the way disease shrank the infected person, the way it went about whittling them to some kind of sickly caricature. It was a cruel device, a savage starvation of features and verve.

Mom had always been a loud woman, yet now she was quiet. Even her dreams failed to bustle, to bellow. They too must have been silent. Her eyes moved faintly beneath the folded, yellowing lids. I wondered what she thought of then, in that ether, that void. I found myself thinking of my childhood nightmare again; concentric cities, bursting outwards, growing malignantly from one another, falling downwards in concrete birth muck, arrowing upwards from the spines of those cities below. I tried to put it out of my mind.

Unable to look too closely at Mom's withered frame, I instead looked past her, into the carefully maintained garden beyond the glass. There, some hunched over their metallic walkers, others being wheeled around by yawning relatives, the occupants who could leave their cells were basking in the splintered sunshine. An essence of orchards, of Tuscany lemon groves, I was impressed and thankful for what the hospice was able to do for its residents. Even if just for a moment, just as those few rays of sunlight caught their sunken cheeks, they were likely transported to another place, perhaps to another city, one beyond this one, at the periphery of their consciousness.

I wondered then whether I would ever know that feeling. Now, to look back on that thought, it seems so silly, so pathetic.

Caught up in looking outwards, I hadn't noticed that Mom had woken up.

I felt her hand gently rest on mine. A tired butterfly on a wind-shaken leaf.

'I didn't hear you come in, Danny,' her voice was so faint, less than a whisper.

'I haven't been here long, Mom.' I straightened up, tried to find a smile for her in the cabinet of painted faces. 'I wasn't sure you were going to wake up whilst I was visiting.'

'I would have hated to have missed you.' Mom sat up awkwardly. I propped cushions behind her, passed her the water she motioned for.

'I haven't been here enough,' I said then, to air the fact, to ensure she understood that I knew it. 'I've been tied up with work. Hard to get out during the day and, by evening, I figure you might be too tired, you know.'

'I don't sleep so much at night,' Mom replied, 'I find it the loneliest then.'

'Aren't the staff on?'

'It isn't that type of loneliness. It can't be fixed by someone passing the time with me, by small talk.'

'Yeah, work has been...' I tried to move on, to move away from her loneliness, her sickness.

'What are you doing now?' she thinned her bloodshot eyes, trying to recall my earlier lies. 'Are you still...are you still with the bank?'

'Yes,' I nodded, swallowing dryly as I did so. 'They're pleased with how it's all going, you know. They think I have uh, that I have some real prospects there.'

'That's good, Danny.' Mom gripped my hand a little tighter. 'Are you still writing your poems.'

'No,' I snapped, the first truth I had spoken since arriving. 'I don't have time for that now.'

'That's a pity, I liked them a lot. You're so talented with words, Danny. They come naturally to you.'

'Words come naturally to everyone,' I withdrew my hand, worried it was saturated with cold sweat, 'I'm no different from the rest. I'm nothing.'

'That's not true. You know it.'

'This isn't about me, Mom. I'm...I'm here for you.'

'For me,' she smiled, 'there's not that much of me left to be here for. I want to think about *you,* Danny. You're all I have left to think about now.'

I told her it wasn't true, that she seemed better, that there was every chance things would pick up. Mom ignored me, saw through that rubbish, that idiocy.

'I had a dream last night,' she replied, 'a dream of different places, of woodland places.'

'Woodlands? We've never spent any time in places like that, outside of parks.'

'I have. You will.'

I didn't answer. Instead, her voice as temperate as windless water, my mother related her dream to me.

An impossible forest, an ethereal place of knitted branches and leaves that shone like tearful eyes. At night, white bracken. The trees leaned into one another, from the glooms between them, a billion weightless figures, some barely vapours, others mean, leering, monstrous. A place of both dread and merriment. A city of glooms, tower blocks replaced by unyielding oaks, as silver as starlight. Ash trees that giggled at the skeletal birds that haunted them, thorns that danced from their grimacing flowers. At the centre of it all, kingly, maybe even godly, a huge white stag.

Half as tall as the trees from which it glowered, the stag wore complex antlers. Woven bone, the horns spiralled upwards from its shimmering skull. They were entwined with berries and moss, as if the stag had burrowed its way out of the very earth beneath it. Something in the stag's expression, something sold by its eyes informed my mother that it was there for her; to deliver a message. Yet, it was unable to speak, to communicate in a way she would be able to fathom. Instead, surrounded by the hushed banshees of the dream wood, the stag could only snort, could only dig its hooves into the wet earth and leave deep furrows in the black.

Mom drifted off to sleep here, her voice fading like the last chimes of an echo.

I felt her grip on my hand loosen, saw her thin face turn away into the softness of her pillow.

The dream sounded incredible. I put it down to the morphine, to the enormous doses of painkillers they shot into her daily. In my entire life, Mom had never really spoken this way, in such a magical way, in a voice of images and pictures, in a voice of poetry.

I suppose it was easier for me to think of it as being a result of the drugs, of some kind of side-effect. It didn't feel like that though, like an accident. I should have seen it as a message then, rather than discount it as something fleeting, as a cancer dream. I would come to know the white stag, to see it myself, outside of dreams. I wonder now, as I recount this, when I next see our white stag walking through the concentric cities of my own nightmares, if I'll know then, for sure, that my time has come.

I left her room quietly, gently pulling the blankets up to her neck before I went.

I didn't return to Cooper's place that night. Without really meaning to, I found myself in the city centre, on Barrow Street, the place of dreadful, neon bars, strip clubs and cheap hotels. I didn't know why I went there, at least not consciously. I gravitated to the gaudy ruin of it, the thundering shouts and heart-attack light shows, the grimacing squads of perfumed boozers out for violence.

I walked amongst them, pub to pub, blue-lit bar to blue-lit bar. The haggard faces, the gin-crushed imbeciles, the bicep boys and handbag dancers. They didn't see me at all. I could have sat before them, could have licked the rims of their glasses and they would have just looked past me, into the bristling void beyond, unaware of me. That was fine, it was what I wanted, that momentary nothingness.

I drank in each place, glass after glass. Eventually done in, suddenly stagger-drunk, I shuffled down to the canal basin and found a bench. The lights from the moored barges doubled on the black water. Behind them, the horizon of tower blocks and high-rise offices, the sporadic lights from their windows also multiplied in the water, as did the outlines of the buildings themselves. I saw it once again, a city beneath the city.

I lay back on the bench, not caring for a second if carrion birds tore me to shreds during the night. I looked upwards at the spoiled sky, to where only a few stars were visible. I dreaded it, but I wanted to see another city there too. Instead, drunk, I just saw the stars double, the throbbing moon flex and thin, flex and thin. Eventually, hiccups subsiding, I fell into a stupor and slept.

I made it back to Cooper's the next morning. My hangover was a power-drill in my bones.

When I stepped through the door and shivered into the living room, I was met by Cooper and Hickey, their faces wild with excitement.

'Clean yourself up, Danny boy,' Cooper beamed, 'we're meeting Big Barry at the Bus Station!'

Hickey nodded his approval, a grin slashed across his jaw.

6.

Big Barry

COOPER TOLD ME ALL ABOUT it as we waited in the bustle of the bus station.

Big Barry was keen, couldn't stop messaging the previous day. 'Honestly, Danny boy, fucker might've sent a hundred messages in an hour. Sick stuff, mind you, all about his tackle, where he was gonna put it. Hickey here figured we may as well drop anchor, invite the bastard over. We fed him a line, told him the family was away for a few days, our Katie's first chance to have the place to herself for a bit. He was dribbling when he heard this, drove him absolutely nuts. Course, he jumped right at it, didn't he? *What time should I come? Where should we meet? I'll bring beer, vodka, pills.* The works.'

I listened as best I could, my headache worsening with every word. I watched the travellers come and go, boarding their coaches. I wished I was one of them, any of them.

A hive of noise, the taut faces of hurry and panic, those who had arrived late, those rushing for their connections, their holidays, their escape. The serenity of older travellers, their arrival achieved early, ample time. The steam from their tea flasks hid their mellow faces like veils. The chaos made me feel drunk again. The carousel blurred, but Cooper shook me awake.

'Eyes peeled, Danny boy,' he gripped my shoulder, shook it, 'that weird fucker'll be here any minute and we want to brace him the second we see him.'

I nodded, swallowed some bile. I stood and walked over to a vending machine that faced the first row of departure bays. We were triangulated again; me there, Cooper opposite, then Hickey amongst the bays themselves. He looked so wolfen there, so predatory. Hickey's thick black hair and even thicker beard hid much of his lean face. His eyes were silver beneath the electric bulbs, his thin mouth turned up slightly at the right side. A butchered smile. His mouth seemed capable of saying anything, showing anything, tearing into anything.

Perhaps Hickey noticed me looking at him and he turned his eyes to me suddenly. Even through that rushing crowd, we saw each other. Neither of us looked away. Me due to the slow-wittedness of my hangover state, Hickey maybe due to his inherent curiosity of me. That's how it felt, that he was catlike, toying with me. I could feel his enormous claws at each side of the building, holding me there.

Cooper told me that Big Barry was coming in from up North, somewhere near Blackpool. Cooper guessed the coach was from Glasgow, heading all the way to the capitol. It made sense. We watched the bays for anything coming from that way, our eyes keen, perhaps even hungry.

Oddly, when I think back, my objections to the coercion Cooper and Hickey were already knee-deep in had begun to fade. I don't know whether it was because of seeing my mother at the hospice the previous day, or perhaps it was just the black mood of a hangover, but humanity had already started to feel more distant, more unimportant.

Human beings were beginning to fade, their features blurring, their voices increasingly alien, disparate.

Cooper spotted him first.

At least I think he did. Hickey had suddenly vanished into the blur of fast, sexless heads.

Cooper tried to whistle to me, his forefingers fish-hooking his lips. All I heard was a loud splutter, a hissing, spitting snarl. I turned to where Cooper was positioned and saw he was frantically nodding over to bay B.

I looked but could only see a yawning queue of bag-heavy travellers exiting the tall, dirty coach. I snatched the picture of Big Barry from my thoughts and, owing to his prefix, naturally looked for a fat or towering figure. I searched above the heads of the smaller men and women who waddled in from the cold and saw no one matching the image I had of Big Barry.

I looked back at Cooper and shrugged. I even mouthed *Can't see him* as slowly as I could.

Cooper nodded again and began to march over to the splintering queue.

I began to walk over too and that's when I noticed *Big*.

As I should have expected, as we all should have, the Barry who had arrived at the bus station was far from big. Maybe 5'6", maybe even smaller, the figure which carried the unmistakeably slack-jawed, flat-nosed, low-browed face we had seen online was tiny, weedy.

He sniffed and wiped the dampness from his nose with the back of his free hand. In his other hand, he held a carrier bag. A four-pack of lager embraced a half bottle of vodka. Crammed in alongside them, visible through the cheap plastic, a few packets of crisps acted as a buffer as the bag banged against the leg of Big Barry's scuffed and knee-torn jeans. He wore a leather jacket several sizes too large. Maybe some kind of hand-me-down, the coat drowned him. Its sleeves were rolled back several times, exposing thin, bone-white wrists and tiny, doll-like hands. Most notable of all, Big Barry wore a lost, dumb expression. It was the kind of daydream somnolence I had seen on a thousand cartoon idiots. A feckless, dull admission of stupidity, of inanity.

Cooper moved like a bull through the throngs. His shoulders nudged families out of his path, porters, drivers. I could see his wide eyes, the intensity with which he barged his way towards Big Barry.

I walked as slowly as I could, dragged the worn soles of my trainers. My stomach knotted and burned. I was immediately scared. I had no idea what would happen, what they would do, what *we* would do. Yet, in that bewildering moment, I also felt excitement. The frisson of anticipation pocked the flesh at the back of my neck, the hairs on my forearms stood like splintered wood.

As Cooper came within arm's reach of Big Barry, Hickey appeared behind our target, his teeth brilliantly white, his grin manic.

Before Cooper or I could grab Big Barry, Hickey reached around the small man's throat with his left arm and lifted him from the floor in a sickening choke. I saw Big Barry's eyes widen with terror, his mouth contort as if he was about to scream.

Big Barry didn't have chance to make a fuss. Hickey silenced him with his arm and, although I couldn't hear what he said, he thrust his face against Big Barry's right cheek and growled some threat into his ear.

Big Barry did not resist.

Cooper reached them and gripped Big Barry's free arm. Together, Hickey and Cooper marched the tiny man towards me.

'Come on, let's go,' Cooper snarled, his teeth pressed together, his jaw taut and distended.

I asked where, but Cooper and Hickey ignored me completely. I followed them through the thinning crowd, towards the station's exit.

I don't know to this day whether they knew where they were going beforehand, but it all worked perfectly, without even the slightest sense anyone would stop us, would try to interfere in what could have looked like anything from a kidnapping to an arrest.

We moved through the taxi rank, the tired drivers intoxicated by their crumpled newspapers and radio stations. They didn't even look up.

Rounding the corner of a closed Irish bar, we found ourselves at the back of the old wholesale markets. It wasn't market day, so the stalls were skeletal, empty of even a single item. They were frighteningly bare and seemed to go on for an infinite distance. Apart from a few scurrying rats, scrounging for the previous day's litter, there was nobody around.

Hickey pushed Big Barry into one of stalls, finally hurling him off his feet, onto the shelf itself. Masked by the awning, Cooper and Hickey crowded the terrified man, me between them, like a vapour trail.

'Alright cunt!' Cooper backhanded Barry hard across the face. 'Tell us what you're doing here, eh!' Cooper hit him again, another open palm. Barry reared up from the impact, shocked, blood already evident between his lips, from his nostrils.

'I'm…I'm *just visiting,*' he pleaded, his voice so pathetic, so frantic, 'what you want with me? What is this?'

'You're here to see Katie, aren't you?' Copper lifted Barry off his feet by his jacket, scrunching the leather in his fists, making the material squeal. 'Here to see a *fuckin kid?*'

Barry begged, claimed he didn't know anything about a girl called Katie, that he wouldn't do anything like that, meet up with a child. 'I ain't…I ain't no sicko!'

Hickey, who had been silent, coolly pulled the mobile phone he and Cooper had been using from his pocket and dialled Barry's phone. A few heavy seconds passed and then, loudly, it began to ring. In the shuddering violence of the moment, it was oddly hilarious to hear the lame, middle-of-the-road Bon Jovi song Barry had as a ringtone blare loudly in the naked marketplace.

'Well, *fucking* well.' Cooper punched Barry hard in the guts. I didn't think it was possible, but the punched seemed to shrink Barry. He folded up, breathless.

'Fact is,' Cooper continued, 'we've got you banged to rights, you filthy little nonce. We've got your messages, your call logs, we've got you asking for pictures of *Katie's little body,* we've got you begging to send pictures of your prick over. You're done for.'

'Please, *please,*' Barry continued to beg, to plead. He clasped his small, thin fingers together in some kind of prayer. 'I…I've got mental health issues…been going through a hard time…lost my job and…'

Cooper kicked his legs out from under him and, with Barry down on the ground, planted another kick in his stomach.

I don't know why, I hadn't even said a word, but seeing Barry there, down on the ground, feeble, broken, I had a terrible compulsion to kick him too. I didn't fight it. As he clutched his stomach with one hand, tried to protect his face with the other, I stepped in and kicked him hard in the chest. He made a vile, retching sound in response.

Hickey hadn't laid a hand on him yet.

Cooper eventually lifted Barry up and threw him back on the shelf. The blood ran from his face in thick, bright channels. His eyes rolled in his head.

'We've got everything we need to take you to the coppers, you understand?'

Barry nodded slowly, his face swelling, his features disappearing under bruises.

'Maybe we will, maybe we won't,' Cooper spat at Barry, 'but you *better* keep away from kids, you hear me?'

Again, Barry nodded, his eyes gaining some of their focus, 'I...I will...*I will.*'

At that, Cooper released Barry and watched as he fell back into the glooms of the stall, battered, crushed.

I turned away, my mouth dry, disgusted by the exhilaration I had felt during those grotesque moments. I thought we were done. I was wrong.

'Hold on,' Hickey's voice was cold, deep, his breathing loud, laboured with something almost like arousal. 'You two need to keep an eye out. I want to leave Barry with a reminder.'

'What?' Cooper instinctively grabbed Hickey's arm, went to pull him away. 'Let's get the fuck outta here before anyone shows up.'

Hickey shrugged Cooper off like wet newspaper, his strength reinforced, his power undeniable. 'You've done what you wanted to do,' he smiled, 'but I have a responsibility too.'

A responsibility, that's how he said it. I know now to whom he had a responsibility, why he had to leave his tribute.

Hickey spun Barry round, bent him over the shelf. Barry protested, fought back. Hickey silenced Barry with a hard chop to the back of his neck.

With Barry limp, Hickey tugged up his jacket and t-shirt.

I remember Barry's bare back, the scarring from the skin-grafts around his kidneys, from old burns. I felt dreadful then, sick with myself, appalled by my actions, by my involvement.

I was terrified when I saw Hickey pull the Stanley knife from his back pocket.

Calmly, with Barry barely conscious, his earlier screams replaced by a low, toneless groan, Hickey carved the symbol into Barry's naked back. Smaller than a dinner plate, but large enough for Cooper and me to see it, it was the first time I saw what would eventually mean so much more to me as the weeks went on.

42

Hickey worked quickly, little more than a minute and he was done. He snapped the blade from the Stanley and pocketed the knife. Turning to us, content with his artistry, Hickey smiled warmly. 'Something so he won't forget.'

I looked back once more before we hurried away.

His arms splayed out, his body shaking with shock, Big Barry's back had become a flag, a beacon. The image didn't mean a thing then, yet I immediately remembered it, recognised it somehow. Later, before we wasted ourselves in bizarre celebration, I scribbled it down on the back of a beermat. I still have it.

The outline of an eye. A pupil at its bottom right corner, a second pupil at the upper left. An eye which looked in two directions. An eye which beheld two worlds.

7.

Shanice

I DON'T KNOW IF I truly thought it would stop there, but I would have been a fool to believe that.

It took a few days after Big Barry, but the evolution of Katie Pop continued, her outline quickly filled with a human incarnation.

I had been distracted in the days since the incident with Big Barry. I had been there, in the house with Cooper and, increasingly, Hickey, but I had also been back there, in the empty markets, replaying everything from the kick I planted in his chest, to the strange and gory insignia Hickey carved into his burn-scarred back.

I was at war with my feelings, my thoughts.

At one moment, I was sick with the exhilaration I felt when I kicked him, at others I was indifferent to it, appalled by Barry himself and, more so by the hour, the human species. In fact, there were moments I wished I had smashed Barry's face to pieces. Whilst my mother was lay in a hospice, drug-somnolent with her morphine dreams of a white stag, filth like Big Barry were trying to net underage victims, travelling the length of the isles, giddy with molestation kicks.

I hadn't even noticed the shifting dynamic, or rather the developing dynamic.

Hickey had become omnipresent since the confrontation at the bus station. He often slept at the house, occupying the sofa, looking out at me from beneath sheets of black hair. More than that, Hickey had assumed the role of foreman, of organiser. I saw Cooper yielding to him, listening carefully as Hickey directed the continuance of Katie Pop, pointing to the sections of sullied water into which Cooper was to cast the glistening lure.

My role didn't change then. I remained on the third-place podium, looking up at the stronger swimmers, wondering how I hadn't drowned.

Perhaps it was that fog which prevented me from seeing the direction in which the situation would move.

One morning, on the usual walk to the gym, Katie Pop was given a real face, a real body.

Cooper and Hickey walked ahead along the canal towpath, deep in gruff conversation. I lingered behind, as disinterested in ninety-minutes of *clang and bang* as ever. Smackheads and dossers lined the towpath like forgotten Halloween decorations, left out to deflate. They didn't trouble us, of course. Even those lost in the whirl of dope psychosis could see that bothering the likes of Hickey and Cooper would see them pulped in their rags.

Between the canal-side zombies, flowers attempted to grow through the litter. Mostly flowers which gripped the puzzling knots of weeds, but flowers all the same. Occasionally, forcing their way from the violent thorns, dog roses shone in defiance.

I was lost in the idea of the flowers when we peeled away from the towpath, as usual, up towards the abandoned factories, the red-light zone.

Out in the middle distance, the early-morning prostitutes shivered in the shadows of the gutted workshops. Waif-like, mere bone and perfume, the usual girls smoked and watched the road and pavement for johns. Their legs reminded me of a butcher's window. The pallid, livid meat hung there, devoid of life, blue at its edges.

Seeing them ahead of me, as a collective, I hadn't noticed that Cooper and Hickey had slowed down and were staring at a figure who stood away from the gaggle of miniskirt stiffs.

She leaned against the corner of one of the dead units, the blown-out windows above her.

I thought she was a child at first. Her figure, the slender tick of a face which sat between two curtains of lank, blonde hair. It was only as I caught up to Cooper and Hickey that I could see her features more clearly, the deep black rings around her eyes, the downturn of her thin mouth.

Cooper and Hickey said nothing as we approached. I made some throwaway comment about *new meat for the fire,* but they didn't answer. I suppose I knew what they were thinking, even then.

When we grew nearer, having to walk past them first, the usual girls said hello, tried their best to be saucy, even demure. A hard act when you've been on shift all night and are beginning to wither with the shakes for a fix. Cooper, ordinarily keen to joke with them, said nothing. Hickey seemed to hate them and never said a word. The most he would offer was a chilling, unblinking stare in their direction.

Cooper stopped ahead of the young prostitute. He towered over her. Hickey hung back, flanking me. If some godly eraser could have rubbed away the track marks on her thighs and forearms, smoothed the sunken features of her tiny face, she could have been thirteen or fourteen years old.

Cooper introduced himself. His voice was gentle, almost soothing. A tone I hadn't heard before. 'What're you doing out her, on this lark?'

The girl shrugged, looked over at the older girls, the flesh veterans. 'Ain't the only one out here,' she smirked, 'you ask them?'

'I'm not interested in them.' Cooper slid the rucksack from his shoulder. 'What's your name, love?'

'What's it matter?'

'I want to know, that's what it matters.'

'Shanice,' the girl flicked the hair from her check, a few strands stuck there, 'you?'

'Call me Cooper, everyone does.'

'You and your mates want some action? It's a tenner a piece, if you do. No twos up, I don't like that.'

'What?!' Cooper seemed flabbergasted. 'We ain't punters.' He even blushed when he spoke.

'Coppers then, whatever.'

'Not pigs either,' Cooper fished around in his kitbag and pulled out his wallet, 'just locals, that's all. Lads from the estate.'

'So what?' Shanice's eyes glinted a little as she spoke. 'Plenty of lads, plenty of estates.'

'So *this*,' Cooper handed Shanice a folded twenty, 'get yourself something to eat, something warm. Stay off the streets, especially *these* streets.' He shot a glance at the other hookers. They glowered hatefully in Shanice's direction. One even asked where her twenty was.

'Mind your fucking business,' Hickey snapped at her. 'Dead fish can't swim upstream,' he added, as they turned away, paling, somehow aware of Hickey's edge.

'Thanks,' Shanice seemed genuinely grateful, 'I didn't want to go off with any of the blokes what drove by in the night.'

'You shouldn't,' Cooper picked his bag up, hoisted a strap over his huge shoulder, 'nothing in this way of life but more misery. Listen, you ever come down the café on the square, Blue Micks?'

Shanice nodded, 'Yeah, he does tea and toast for one-fifty. Bargain.'

'Alright. I pop down there for a cooked brekkie on a Wednesday, after the gym, about eleven. I see you there, I'll shout you that tea and toast, eh?'

'Alright, cool.' Shanice smiled and Cooper shot one back. He turned away from her, passed us, and continued onto the gym. We followed.

I looked back at Shanice and saw she was already walking away from the strip. I guessed the twenty would be shot in her arm by lunchtime. I think Cooper knew that too.

That wasn't important though. What mattered was that our slavering Geppetto had wished life into his Pinocchio.

♦

I FIRST FOUND SHANICE AT the house a week later.

I had probably expected it. When I look back from here, the heat of the fire dying away, I knew Cooper and Hickey would make the approach from that very first moment they saw her.

It made perfect sense. Perfectly appalling sense.

I had been working at Hickey's yard.

A sprawling concrete nowhere of sheds, storage units, various machinery, the yard seemed to be a hub for numerous businesses, none of which made too much sense to me. Ever-smoking men with prison yard eyes congregated in each corner, their conversations often hushed, their guts like sickly tongues lolling over their beltlines.

I saw an incredible variety of goods arrive and depart, arrive and depart. Everything from barrels of hissing tar to polystyrene caskets of fresh fish, straight from the city markets.

Hickey never seemed wealthy, but the yard must have brought in a hefty income. He was hardly ever there and, when he did appear, every gathered gang of grimacing goons made their way over to him in turn, offering some kind of dumb fealty, expressed in simpering expressions and the offer of thick, brown envelopes, likely full of cash or confessions.

For my part, Hickey arranged for me to shift whatever needed hauling from stack to truck or back again. Crates, containers, barrels, boxes, punnets and sacks, I didn't care what they were, what they had inside, I just moved them from one assigned point to the next. I wheeled the pallet truck, huffed weakly beneath the teetering boxes, held the sacks between whitening fingers.

Cooper was supposed to be working there too, but he never showed up. He and Hickey were spending all of their time together, advancing their monster trap, their wild hunt. I stayed out of their day-to-day entrapments, catching up with them later at the house or, as was the case most evenings, meeting them at The Gladiator for a few beers after I finished up at the yard.

It was a Wednesday, the middle of a meandering week. I turned my key in the door, dropped my backpack, walked into the living room and there, doll-like with her tiny figure, Shanice looked up at me the from the sofa. Cooper was sat in the armchair opposite. Hickey stood over at the window, the fading evening light drawing only his silhouette, his features unknown.

'You know Shanice, don't you, Danny boy?'

I nodded. 'From up the way,' I added noncommittally, not wanting to draw attention to her trade, to where she spent her nights, shifting skin.

'Nice to see you again,' Shanice smiled, then seemed to look over at Cooper for approval, like he was some kind of etiquette teacher.

'That's good, isn't it?' Cooper replied, looking up at me.

I didn't answer, just made my way through to the kitchen, keen to throw something frozen in the oven.

Cooper was behind me before I knew it. The hum of Shanice's and Hickey's voices hid our discussion.

'Listen, Danny,' Cooper whispered, glancing back over his shoulder between each word, 'Hickey and me came up with this idea, right, we -'

I didn't let him explain it. I told him I'd guessed that's what they'd do.

'Smart lad,' Cooper squeezed my shoulder. 'Should've guessed you'd be one step ahead of us, eh?'

'Listen, you think this is a good idea?'

Cooper seemed taken aback. 'She looks the part, could be fourteen.'

'Fuck's sake, Coop, not *that* part of it, just having her around to begin with? She's a smackhead.'

'Keep your voice down!' Cooper moved closer, his breath was sweet with recent cider, 'She's got it in hand, working it out, you know. She doesn't want to be on the street with those other tarts. She just had a bad run. She's twenty.'

I said I didn't care. 'Your business, mate.'

'Our business,' Cooper's face hardened, 'you're in this as well, Danny, or are you forgetting about Big Barry.'

'One kick doesn't make me a nonce hunter, Coop.'

'You tell Hickey that. He reckons you're integral.'

'I haven't done anything.'

'He reckons you'll be essential as things grow.'

'Grow?' Grow *how?*'

'Look, now's not the time, Danny boy. Hickey thinks there's far more to come, plenty more we can do with this.'

I turned away, back to whatever frozen shite I could pry from the solid fog of ice in the freezer drawer. We hadn't defrosted it in months. Even the chips needed excavation.

When I turned back, Cooper had gone. He was back in the living room with Hickey and Shanice.

I ate my dinner at the dining table, over by the window to the back yard. I watched the evening birds settle across the fence tops and phone wires. They quickly became little more than silhouettes as the night came in. Inked to outlines, the birds seemed so organised, so well assembled there. High above, they made me feel like they were an audience to our behaviours, there to judge us, gathered at an unreachable periphery, their own distant city.

I tried to ignore the conversation across the room, but it became impossible.

Hickey remained quiet as Cooper explained our divine mission, the work being done to root out all of the world's dirty bastards, its real monsters.

Real monsters. Little could Cooper have known.

'You see, we've already nailed one filthy sod. Thought he was meeting a fourteen-year-old at the bus station. We took care of him.'

'I hope you battered him,' Shanice sipped from her lager, 'fuckers like that don't need to exist.'

'Exactly what we're thinking,' Cooper beamed. 'Gotta do what we can, you know. Get em out of circulation, put the fear in them.'

'Fear is the master,' Hickey added coldly from his chair. 'When you can control that, you can achieve everything.'

Neither Cooper nor Shanice replied, they just looked at Hickey, then carried on talking.

'So,' Cooper rubbed his hands together, 'that's why I bought you tea, a few drinks. I, *we* wanted to ask you a favour.'

'Oh yeah?' Shanice suddenly crossed and uncrossed her legs several times, suddenly nervous. 'What kind of favour? You know I don't do two blokes together, right? I already said that.'

'No, *no,*' Cooper dropped from his chair onto his knees. 'Fuck all like that. Forget that shit. We were hoping you'd give us a hand snaring some of these perverts, that's all.'

'How?'

'Photos, maybe even a bit of chat. Change of clothes and you could get away with being fourteen, fifteen. It'll make our profile more legit, help us catch some of the real scumbags.'

'Okay, sure.' Shanice agreed just like that, nothing else required. I guess she had so little happening in her life, so little to love, to enjoy, it made sense for her to do something that seemed useful, that seemed worthwhile. It was pathetic to see.

50

'Atta girl!' Cooper saluted Shanice by smashing his half-drunk can against hers. 'We'll pay you, of course,' he added, standing up and returning to his seat.

'I did wonder. How much?'

'What you make a day, *up there,*' Cooper's face thinned with a disgusted expression as he nodded in the rough geographical direction of the red-light zone, 'or a night, whatever.'

'Hundred, maybe a bit less now it's getting cold.'

'Okay,' Cooper finished his beer, 'I'll cover that, up front. I want you off the streets whilst you're doing this. That's a deal breaker. No hooking.'

'You ain't gonna pay me a hundred a day from today though, are you?'

Hickey leaned into the light, his face savage, a sneering smile like lightning across his jaw. He tossed a roll of notes over to Shanice's feet. 'Couple hundred there, get you started,' he said, then receded back into the darkened corner.

Shanice picked up the money and stuffed it into her little pink handbag. Not real leather, the material squealed as she clutched it to her chest. 'When do you want me to start?' she asked. 'I need to uh pop out for a bit now, but can come back afterwards.'

We knew where she would be going. A glistening spike, the moistened tip of the seedy dropper.

'Tomorrow's fine,' Cooper answered, popping the top off a new can. 'You do what you gotta do tonight.'

8.

The band of bones

HICKEY GAVE SHANICE MONEY FOR adolescent clothes.

She worked her way through the teen stores on the high street, picking up the t-shirts, the leggings, jeans, skirts, the trainers and heels worn by the young girls on the estate, the ones who hung out around the rusted playground by the arcade. They were the archetypes, those apparitional howlers. They were the doomed gigglers waiting to get knocked-up by the first tracksuit gargoyle to ply them with cider by the lockups and forget to bring a rubber.

I always hoped a few would escape, but the noose only tightens. A gilded rope, one simply covered in cheap reflective paper, like chocolate at Christmas. It choked them all the same way. Hoisted upwards, amongst the tower-block gallows, their air pummelled from the lungs, the dreams shaken from their lifeless heads.

Hickey was adamant that Shanice impersonated them. He didn't want to speak to her directly, so instructed Cooper to take care of it. Once more, advancing every day, Hickey plucked at our strings, orchestrated the band of bones.

Working at the yard, I wasn't around to witness the daily machinations. I couldn't see, then, just how much Hickey controlled, how much he ordered Cooper into actions. All I saw were the leftovers, the finished products. I didn't think about it too much then, why would I? As far as I was concerned, Hickey and Cooper were continuing their violent crusade, their *exercise*. They knew they had what they wanted, weeks before. They had power over the seedy underclass, the perverts. They could fool them, wrangle them, beat them, torture them and the pervs could do nothing in return. They could no more go to the police and report Cooper and Hickey than a man carrying the head of his murdered wife could walk into the local copshop and fill out a missing persons form.

I didn't hurry home during those first days. Instead, with a little more pay in my pocket from the yard, I developed a new routine. I would drop into the hospice every few days, sit with my sleeping mother for a little while, then make my way through the bars in the city centre, invariably eating out.

Sometimes I wandered the bookshops, thumbed through whatever took my eye, maybe even picked something up to read at the yard, on my breaks, as the boozy luggers, mean-eyed travellers and hench ex-cons bickered over payments and loads.

Occasionally, I would try to stay off the booze, knowing it would make the gym harder every time, but I had no self-control, no shutdown switch. Even when I picked up a coffee and sat on a bench by some meaningless statute as the office fodder blurred their way home, even then I would only be delaying the inevitable, knowing full well that I'd be three beers deep in the nearest bar within an hour.

It was a better option than heading back to the estate, to where the puppeteers fashioned their marionette.

When I made it home, it was often late. The computer screen and Katie Pop burner phones lit the living room, but Cooper and Shanice would have settled into a film, or some trash TV. Hickey was sometimes there, sometimes not. It wasn't always easy to tell. I could be in the living room for ten minutes before I realised Hickey was off to one side, haunting the unlit kitchen, his eyes swimming in the mass of hair and beard like silver-finned salmon caught beneath the moon.

Cooper would be excited to tell me about *this nonce, that nonce*, the ones they had on the wire: 'You free Thursday, Danny boy? We've got this bastard coming in from Lincoln…from Nottingham…from Warwick…from Dundee…'

I didn't go with them for the first few after Big Danny. I made every excuse I could. I knew it wouldn't last, but I needed to extricate myself, at least physically.

When I asked Cooper how the meetings had gone, he would always grin broadly, mention the shooing he had given the bloke, the way he left him crumpled, folded, flattened, bloody. I would follow with the same question every time. 'Hickey carve that eye on his back?'

'You know our Hickey,' Cooper would laugh, 'he loves leaving that signature of his.'

That signature. The two-pupiled eyeball, the above and below.

One Tuesday, half drunk, I came back to the house and found Shanice dressed in some new teen get-up. Her hair washed, the spike marks on her arms hidden by a jumper with the cartoon face of a bear smiling from her small breasts. Carefully applied make-up hid the blueish circles around her eyes.

'We've got one who wants a webchat,' Cooper announced proudly, 'Hickey's coming round for it in a bit.'

I said it was late. 'What kid's going to be up online at midnight, eh?'

'School dodger,' Cooper was stirring a mug of tea, loudly, 'way we've told it, she's not all there, up top, so isn't heading to school. Mom's working shifts, nights tonight, so our Katie Pop's got the place to herself, wants to chat with…chat with…what's his name, Shan?'

'Marco,' Shanice smiled up from her nail-painting, the smell of the paint saccharine, ugly, 'can't remember the surname. Looks Italian.'

'Looks about fucking fifty and all,' Cooper added, 'sleazy old shit.'

'He'll probably want to show me his cock.'

'They usually do,' Cooper agreed, 'just remember, don't get too close to the camera, eh, might jump out and bite you!' Cooper grabbed Shanice by her side and tickled her wildly. Shanice laughed and fought him off.

A warm gesture, one of gentle, welcome intimacy. It couldn't have been more out of place for what they were doing.

Hickey arrived a little while later. I let him in. 'Wait up a second,' he said as he pulled me to one side in the hallway. 'Everything okay?'

I had no idea what he meant. 'Down at the yard?'

'No,' his voice was soft, cajoling, 'with this, with what we're doing? You're absent most of the time when we meet them, ducking out. I get why you would, but I want you to be a real part of this, Daniel. I always have.'

I wasn't sure how to answer. Hickey's mannerisms, the recurrence of the kinship he had shown me after the beating of Barry, it didn't feel right. 'I'll come next time,' I said, without thinking, cursing myself for my cowardice, for that easy acceptance.

'Good, *good.*' Hickey pulled me towards him, embraced me. His physical strength was bludgeoning, even when he was being gentle. 'You're the biggest part of this, Daniel,' he whispered, 'this and what's to come.'

I asked what he meant.

'In life,' Hickey stepped back and surveyed me with his piercing, unreal eyes, 'for all of us. What's to come down the road. I like to think we'll see all that together.'

I nodded, wondering whether he had dropped a pill on the way, snorted a line from the dash of his van.

In any case, I made myself scarce as the webchat began. Cooper and Hickey flanked the computer screen, Shanice sat in the chair ahead of it. The lights low, Shanice carefully opening and closing her legs as they began to chat. I heard Marco speak only once before I closed the door and went upstairs.

Wanna see my cock, girl?

◊

MARCO HAD A ROOM AT Hotel Dauphin.

A classy monster, it was a five-star hotel in the centre of the city. A molester of means and teens, Marco appeared to be as brazen as it got, as decadent as he fancied. He was trying to meet a fourteen-year-old girl for sex, but wanted to do so in a polished place, a place of desk staff and piano bars, a place of polite coughing and ties for dinner. Marco wanted to defile poor Katie Pop, but he wanted to do it in a luxurious room.

Perhaps Marco was so wealthy that the notion of ever being caught with a child was merely something he believed he could pay his way out of? Well, as he would quickly find out, there wasn't a sum he could offer which would prevent the righteous punishment our band of bones were keen to deliver.

The arrangements were set the previous night. Katie just needed to show up around two and make her way to room 0121. Cooper and Hickey were excited. They always were. The violence hung from the doorways like tinsel. It was a physical thing, something I could taste. It was iron and copper. It seeped from their pores. Yet, even then, there was such a difference between their rages, their violence.

For Cooper, the precursor to his violence was blandly palpable. It manifested in him stretching his arms, his legs, pacing the threadbare carpets of the living room and hallway, talking loudly about what he was going to do to Marco, how he wanted to hurt him. Much of it was pure bravado, huge dialogue extremes, loudly snarled threats.

'I'll cut his fucking bollocks off,' Cooper would march back and forth, occasionally punctuating his threats with uppercuts to the fetid air ahead of him, 'break every bone in his hands, see how he types then, eh?'

The difference between this and Hickey's violence was enormous. They were like different species. Where Cooper raged loudly, the veins on his throat standing like walls around an unkept garden, Hickey remained mostly silent, the violence captured in the cathedral of his flesh, retained there, growing in intensity. Tintinnabulations from bells of fire. Even then, watching them in preparation for the following day, I found Hickey the most frightening, the most appalling.

Then, I could have no idea why this was, but instinct told me that there was so much more depth to Hickey's bloodlust than Cooper's.

As for Shanice, I could see the malignancy growing in her too.

Just like that, as quickly as the light from a match fades to scentless smoke, Shanice had become Katie Pop and Katie Pop had become a scheming thing, a vengeful thing, a malicious entity conjured from the mind of hateful men and the uncleaned keyboard of a computer contained in the bowels of one more council estate, indiscernible from the next one and the next one and the thousand after that.

We arrived at Hotel Dauphin late on a Thursday morning.

I didn't know exactly why I was there. I knew I wouldn't attack Marco. The disgust I felt for the kick I had planted on the first rube still hung in the air around me. I didn't want to add to that load. Something was pulling me down towards the gutters as it was. A grimacing anchor, a burden on the muscle of my heart. I believed that if I added further weight to the gnarled iron, it would tug me down into a sewer from which I would never escape. With that in mind, my presence was merely as a camera, a recording device of flesh and twitching nerves. We filmed nothing for real, so perhaps I was only onboard to help Cooper and Hickey recount their red successes, later on, when they were too drunk to remember every detail.

We sat in Hickey's van, the engine running.

The plan was simple. *Katie Pop* would head in a little after the time she had arranged to meet Marco. He would be waiting in room 0121, likely rock-hard on blues – according to Cooper – ready to force a bottle of fizz down a young girl's throat before he went to work on her body. As soon as Katie Pop was half inside the door and, we guessed, Marco twigged she was older than she had seemed on the grainy and purposefully distant webcam when they'd chatted, Cooper and Hickey would barge their way in and reverse the gruesomeness, turning their flesh on Marco's, protecting the dream-child of Katie Pop from the abuse which would have followed, had she been real to begin with.

It was all there, as clean as it gets.

Time to kill, we wandered into a nearby pub. What a quartet we must have seemed to any of the early-morning drinkers not yet soused enough to become blind to everything beyond the pumps and optics.

Hickey bought the round and we sat in the snug, huddled quietly, chewing the plan.

Hickey stayed outside of the conversation. He sat at its border, eyeing the discussion from his own, invisible republic. Eyes in dark bracken, something bone-white in the night-woods. An echo of things to come.

As Cooper and Shanice giggled and japed, I looked around the morning pub. God-rays through the unwashed glass, spotlights on the doomed.

The usual crowd, the fag-lipped limpets clinging to the sides of their sanities. Newspapers crinkled, mostly copies of the free Metro. Intermittent belches punctuated the heavy silence around the loan drinkers. Each of them seemed to wear a cowl of bees. Their faces swollen with stings that came from within, their sagging cheeks peppered with white bristles from bad shaves, their hands shuddering with withdrawal. I wondered what brought them into the centre of the city, what strange instinct drew them there, away from their decrepit terraces, their identikit newbuild galleys, their perfect prisons of addiction.

I supposed they were counting the moments, or trying not to. They were corralled, wrangled by their hidden masters. They were herded here by the forces that pummelled them. They were owned and manoeuvred at will, little more than shuffling cattle moving towards the abattoir.

Watching them, I was struck by that same dream, that thundering nightmare, the images of cities above and below my own. I was ushered back to that troubling ether, that impossible horror of realisation. Something gnawed at me, even then. Something insisted through my marrow, demanded I pay attention to what was there before me, the tableau positioned by weightless hands, by the shadows who look back at the bodies who cast them. I shook it off, too frightened to pursue the idea.

Before I knew it, Hickey was telling us to drink up, pointing at his watch, pushing Cooper and Shanice towards the door, telling me to get a shake on. Suddenly we were in the street, the unending lines of furious traffic a metal canal. We were sidling through them, edging between bumpers, making our way to the hotel lobby, our measly band of bones.

9.

Marco

HICKEY USHERED ME AND COOPER into the bar at the left side of the lobby.

He had already told Shanice to make her way to the reception desk and say she was here for Room 0121. A smart move, I suppose. Hickey figured a pervert with the kind of cash Marco seemed to have likely had eyes on her arrival. As far as Hickey was concerned, Marco probably slipped the reception geeks a hundred a piece to give him a nod if the fish looked sick.

'Can't be too careful,' Hickey grinned maliciously as the barman poured us three small whiskies, 'we have that scumbag lipping the lure, almost ready to pluck him out the pond and gut him in the grass. If we fuck it up now, we likely blow the chances of Katie Pop catching any more freaks online.'

'Shanice,' Cooper corrected Hickey, 'Shanice, not Katie Pop.'

Hickey's face lit up with amusement. 'That little slag is whoever we tell her to be. Katie Pop, Mother Theresa, Margaret Thatcher, Minnie Mouse, *whoever the fuck we tell her she is.*'

'No,' Cooper sneered a little, thumbed his glass across the bar to where it hit the polished plastic of a spills tray, 'her name's Shanice and she *isn't* a slag, okay?'

'Sweet on her, that it?' I could see Hickey turning the blade, tickled by Cooper's sudden defence of Shanice.

59

'She's working with us,' Cooper said calmly, staring at Hickey, 'she's taking a risk too, she's part of the group, at least as far as I'm concerned.'

'Part of the group?' Hickey licked the silver edges of his lips. 'Only difference being we have to *pay her* to be here. You aren't getting paid, I'm not getting paid, Daniel here isn't getting a fucking penny.'

'Cheers,' I tried to end the discussion as quickly as I could, 'now that we've all established that we're making nothing from this, can we draw a line under Shanice's involvement and get this shit done as quickly as possible?'

Cooper shrugged. 'Fine with me'.

'Same.' Hickey finished his whisky and nodded at the doorway.

We turned and saw Shanice trying to get our attention, pretending to look into her make-up mirror, but nodding towards the stairs, an indication the desk had given her the all-clear to make her way to Room 0121.

'We give her a minute or so, then we head up via the stairs at the back, understand?'

Hickey had it all worked out. Cooper and I agreed, the air suddenly electric around us, the frisson of confrontation buzzing on our skin.

Through the lobby, Cooper offered a confident smile to the receptionist who looked up, the phone pressed to their ear, a black plastic mollusc absorbing their full attention. Thick carpet beneath our feet, plusher than my finest clothes. Occasional faces staring out from the wire mesh of their office windows. Echoes of laughter from tinpot kitchens. We found the service stairs and made our way up.

Into the hallway of the 01 floor, the addition of the zero before the one like some kind of self-appointed honour, a gift of greater numbers, of more property.

We walked quietly along, waiting to intersect with Shanice before she knocked on 0121. The doors at either side of us seemed, at least to me, to loom outwards, to be crushing us as we moved. I could hear the murmurs of hidden shenanigans. They sounded sinister by proxy, those muffled conversations, the spasmodic laughter. Almost muted entirely, almost undersea, more like moans and growls that human language.

I wanted to get out of there fast; I asked myself over and over why I was even there. I felt part of something inglorious, beyond malicious, beyond repugnant. There was no effort to seek justice, just a perfect target for the violence Cooper and Hickey were keen to shed from their bodies.

We found Shanice leaning casually next to Room 0121. Faint music pulsed from behind the door. An omnipresent reek of aftershave made the acids in my gut boil.

'Shall I knock now then, or what?' Shanice asked, her small face casual, amused. 'We gonna raid our Marco, or stand here catching flies?'

Cooper's eyes glistened as she teased. I could see his affection for Shanice, for Katie Pop.

Hickey gave the signal, silently.

We cloaked the outer frame of the door, out of sight. I could feel the palpitations of my heart, that frantic morse code, pleading for me to run away.

One plimsole shoe arched child-like against the back of her other, her hair in pigtails, her painted lips pursed in an air-kiss, Shanice knocked at the door.

The following moments played out like sudden theatre.

Marco opened the door. From where I stood, I saw one damp arm, the skin pocked with dark hair, reach out and take Shanice by the shoulder, an attempt to lead her into the perfumed room as quickly as possible. From the opposite side of the doorframe, Cooper burst in behind Shanice and then, feeling the rush of his movement, Hickey barrelled past me, one lingering fist clutching my shirt behind him, tearing me into the hidden world of the hotel room.

In that same moment, we moved as a group from the hallway into the room.

I froze as the others went to work.

Along with the cloying stink of aftershave, there was the disparate percussion of some throwaway pop music from a nearby speaker. In the shadow of the flailing Marco, I saw the bed, its sheets peeled back, an armoury of greased dildos and vibrators lined up on the mattress. Marco's laptop fluttered with pornography, the figures half-pixilated by bad wi-fi, their bodies dehumanised in every conceivable way.

Next to the bed, rocking on the tray as Marco was hurled against the wall behind them, several bottles clinked and rattled. Vodka, coke, then two smaller, brown, medicinal bottles. I guess they were maybe GH or amil nitrate, perhaps even a Roofie for Katie.

I felt solid, fastened to the carpet. I was the audience, the theatre rocking and shattering around me.

Marco tried to speak, but Cooper punched him straight in the gut, collapsing him, causing his towel to fall away, rendering him breathless and naked. An instantly pathetic sight, like Big Barry had been, the middle-aged Marco wheezed and tried to cover his genitals with a trembling hand. Cooper's punch was so hard that I heard his fist travel through the air towards Marco before the inevitable, car-crash impact when it landed.

As Marco folded, Cooper followed through with another punch, catching him above his right hip, deep in his kidney. A dull sound, wet dirt in a binbag, the punch paled Marco instantly, drove him half out of consciousness.

On his back, any pretence at covering his crotch disintegrated, Marco looked cadaver-like, meat-like. He had the appearance of a slaughtered pig, delivered whole, its butchers standing over the abattoir kill wondering where to begin.

As Marco gasped, his lips peeled back in an ugly plea, Cooper mounted him and, snatching a pillow to cover his moans, dropped a succession of heavy elbows onto his face. Standing, Cooper pulled the wet pillow away, the underside bright red, waxy with the blood from Marco's flattened nose.

Without invitation, Shanice stepped past Cooper and kicked Marco in his naked balls. Three, four times, Shanice's thin foot ploughed into Marco's private flesh, the impact of each kick wetter than the one which proceeded it. Marco pissed himself. Like a new-born, he lay there feebly, unable to speak, struggling to breathe between the sobs, the arcs of piss landing on his shuddering belly.

'Now, now, Marco,' as Hickey walked to Marco's head, took his dyed hair in his fist and lifted him to the bed, 'you've been a terrible boy, haven't you?' Hickey pressed Marco back against the headboard, seated him there. The man's eyes rolled with pain and shock. He was bewildered by the notion of capture, of recompense. It must have never dawned on him, never struck him as a possibility. Marco must have seen himself as a superior species, as the farmer casually wrangling the lamb.

'We're here to punish you, Marco. It's as simple as that.' Hickey revelled in his role as organiser, in his dream of judge penitents and executioner angels. 'Are you frightened, Marco?'

The man nodded violently, his jaw bloodied, a beard of fallen roses. Marco gurgled something, an offer.

'Say again?' Hickey leaned in, cupped his ear comically, 'You'll give us what?'

Marco sputtered, licked away the clotting red from his mouth.

'Ah, money.' Hickey turned back to Cooper and Shanice. 'Our friend, Marco, says he'll pay us to go, *whatever we want*. That's very kind of you, Marco,' Hickey laughed, his teeth like chalk amidst the matted black of his beard, 'but that won't help, I'm afraid. We were always going to take what we wanted anyhow. That's not really the point.'

At this, without any further instruction, Shanice and Cooper began gathering Marco's laptop, his watch, rifling through his wallet, taking cash, snapping his credit cards. Cooper even bent his car-key.

'This *isn't* a robbery,' Hickey continued, 'this is a sacrifice.'

With that, his face burning with malice, Hickey began to strangle Marco with his left hand, letting the man writhe, airless, until his lips blued, then released the grip, only to repeat the same action immediately.

Weakened, putty-like, enfeebled by fear and violence, Marco barely resisted when Hickey turned him onto his stomach and, reaching beneath his shirt, pulled the Stanley blade from his belt. It was time for the eye, the omni-eye, the two-pupiled eye, the eye able to see the cities above and below.

Before Hickey left the confusing signature, Cooper read some of Marco's chat logs aloud, his shoulders straight, his head held high, his voice a mockery of a judge, an executioner.

'I'm going to cream in you,' Cooper sneered. 'Send me a photo of your cunt', 'I've been doing this a long time, I know how to handle young girls, don't you worry about a thing, sweetheart…'

When Cooper finished, all I could hear was Hickey's breathing. Deep, animalistic, the air released from his nostrils and grimacing mouth seemed to have weight to it, seemed to carry the stink of freshly turned soil, of autumnal decay.

'You see, Marco,' Cooper leaned in, Shanice joined him, her eyes wide, entranced, 'we have everything on you, every stinking comment you've made to our little Katie Pop. We're taking what we want, doing what we want. You try and sound the alarm and we'll fuckin ruin you, wanker. Understand?'

Marco couldn't answer, of course. Hickey had gagged him and, even if he hadn't, so much of Marco's face was obscured by the pillow in which his face was rammed, he could barely have uttered a word through the clotting red of his battered face.

I noticed that Cooper withdrew a little as Hickey slid out the untouched, shimmering blade from the Stanley knife. He didn't seem to want anything to do with the ritual. Shanice though, she came closer, her teeth bared, her smile almost frantic, almost wild.

Hickey didn't hurry. He traced the outline of the eye with a finger, pressing it deep into Marco's sodden back. Oiled to a ludicrous degree, Marco's skin had some kind of culinary quality to it. This was the chef teasing his customers with the finest cuts.

Then, the shape fading slowly as Hickey withdrew his forefinger, he began to cut.

Marco's stifled screams sounded like distant traffic. The roar, obscured by glass, the engines dulled to an incoherent murmur. That was how Marco sounded, as if he was screaming back into himself.

Hickey's face shone as he sliced away at Marco's flesh. The blood trickled down either flank of the brutalised man, massing on the ruffled white sheets at his sides, spreading hypnotically until Marco seemed to possess wings of crimson, unfurled in the mattress, unable to carry him away from there.

I felt no sympathy, no love, no care. I was comfortable in the shock I knew I would feel again. It was like a familiar shirt, misshapen by years of use. I wore it as my eyes became cameras, as the reels rolled behind them, as the latest violence occurred ahead of me.

It didn't take Hickey long to cut the eye into Marco's back. With a few moments, Hickey was stepping off the bed, wiping the blade on the sheets between Marco's legs. I didn't realise, but Hickey wasn't finished.

From a pocket in his jacket, Hickey withdrew a small, plastic bag. The resealable kind, the type that dope comes in. I could see white powder. I wondered whether Hickey was going to snort some kind of celebratory line off Marco's body. One more decadent celebration of brutality for the day.

He didn't. Instead, as Marco shook and begged, Hickey opened the bag and, Marco secured with a firm knee, poured the power across the bleeding shape. Marco stiffened with agony, then began to writhe against it. The powder began to bubble and burn. A sudden bitter stench, a chemical smell. It filled the room and made us all cough.

As I stared at Marco's back, I could already see the eye being seared into the meat, scolded into it.

Half intrigued, half horrified, Cooper asked what was in the bag.

'Little treat,' Hickey wiped his face and surveyed his bubbling work, 'bit of bleach, lime, salt. Something to ensure the eye never fades, that's all.'

We were back on the street minutes later. Hurrying pedestrians paid us no mind, yawning drivers paid us no mind, the absurd gods of conventional religions paid us no mind. We hardly existed. We were just graffiti on a crumbling wall.

❧

THAT WAS THE FIRST NIGHT I heard Cooper and Shanice have sex.

My room was near to Cooper's, just down the hall. We had never had partners in the time I had lived there. Cooper had spoken of old girlfriends, of loves lost, of atomic arguments with wild-eyed women from every corner of the city, but I had never seen Cooper with a woman.

Similarly, I had never taken anyone back to the house. In fact, I hadn't had a relationship like that in years.

What I remember most about that first night was how gentle it sounded, their sex. Seeing Cooper, his strength, his size, the way he carried himself, I expected some kind of thundering fuck, some wall-clattering melee of flesh and teeth. It wasn't like that at all.

I heard them laugh a little, talk in that husky whisper lovers use. I heard the bed move, its rhythm gradual, almost soothing. I heard

Shanice moan, sigh. I heard her breathing rise and fall. Finally, more like someone trying to supress a cough, I heard Cooper finish.

Laying there, hearing their quiet conversation in the hours which followed, I almost felt jealousy.

I was envious of Shanice, of the way she experienced a part of Cooper I never could. That tenderness, that hidden space, that private ledger of a man I saw as something more than a friend, perhaps even something more than a father, a brother.

I think back to that night now, as one more expanse of glistening stars appears above me. It recurs in the darker moments. The romance of it somehow feels both clean and vile, both fresh and decrepit. It occurred before I knew where humans stood, where we were corralled and by whom. Still, regardless of the tender ugliness of their lovemaking and the relationship spun out of that spidery muck, it makes me wonder whether Shanice and Cooper could have ever had a life together, if they would have been able to carve something valuable from the trauma they knew.

A stupid thought, a moribund idea now. The damned have nothing more than fruit machines and lottery tickets, mortgages and theme-parks. They are restrained by their Saturday nights and their new sofas, bought on tick. They are gratified by orgasms and Ovaltine, by trendy cocktails and branded shirts. Best they only think in those terms. Best the universe opts not to reveal its terrible face to everyone.

If the walls of the slaughterhouse were transparent, the cattle might flee the trucks.

10.

The waltz to end them all

THE HOSPICE CALLED AND TOLD me to hurry, but Mom was dead by the time I arrived.

They led me into her room, to where a nurse stood at her side, looking down at her, then up at me, over and over.

Death seemed to have taken even the tiny sliver of a body Mom once had, even before she was sick. Death had taken everything from her. It had burgled her flesh, her thoughts, then finally her heart.

I walked over and sat in the chair by her side. Her nearest hand lay on the embroidered blanket. Her fingers were curled into a fist. I tried to unfurl them, to hold her hand, but they felt unnatural, phoney. They felt like green twigs, somehow brittle, yet impossibly immovable.

I didn't know what to do. I simply sat there and let the nurses watch me. I suppose they wanted to speak to me, to classify the death, the destruction of the hardening woman in the bed. I suppose they had a waiting list, someone else on the conveyer, someone who needed to take a seat before the furnace rendered them to whimsy.

Eventually, the awkward moments ebbing weightlessly away, one of the nurses led the other from the room, leaving only me and the cadaver of my mother.

I couldn't cry. Tears weren't there. It was insane to me. I had sat at the bus-stops at the edge of the estate and sobbed wildly, uncontrollably into my shuddering hands. I hadn't understood why but, that morning, sat next to the dead body of my only remaining relative, I couldn't summon a tear at all. I wonder whether it was shock, whether I just hadn't taken it in, whether I hadn't understood the depth of the scene ahead of me. Moreover, I wonder whether I had expected it so often before then, that I had already rehearsed my poses, stylised them in my thoughts. I wonder whether I had dreamed my reactions before that day, whether my face was performing them weeks or months before the moment they were required.

In any case, I simply sat there, still, waiting as the moments tumbled around me, as the city and all cities cranked and groaned, twisted and yowled.

What I did think of then, what I believe I may even have seen, was the white stag Mom had mentioned in her somnolence that morning a week or two before. I didn't see it in the air ahead of me, or through the slim opening between the curtains, through the wire-meshed window that led to the model garden. No, I seemed to see it at the edge of my vision, off where the skin meets the dark. I saw it, but didn't see it. It was more like I *knew* it was there, that I could summon some kind of mental image, even invent an odour. A reeking, earthy, forest-floor stink, like wet earth, musty, rotting, yet fresh and unmistakeably the marrow of the planet.

I sat and thought of the white stag, saw it at the peripheral point, the apex of my understanding. Then, I saw things like that as apparitions of the mind, as nothing more than fancies, as dreams, as something necessary and melancholic, as religion.

I don't know how long I stayed there, for how long I chased the picture of the white stag in the forest of my eyes. Eventually, her living hand like a tired moth on my shoulder, an older nurse shook me gently from my thoughts. I turned to face her and licked my lips, moved my tongue, both of which had dried up completely as I sat there agape, lost.

'I'm sorry, Daniel,' she said quietly, sincerely, 'she was a real fighter.'

I agreed. 'Did she ask for me? Did she say anything?'

'No,' the nurse smiled warmly, 'this came to her in her sleep. We checked in on her, noticed that she…that she was paler and was moving in her sleep.'

'Moving?'

'This happens sometimes, when people pass away in their sleep. I suppose they're dreaming, but they move, their body twists, they writhe, slowly, painlessly, dreamily.'

'Dreamily,' I repeated, 'their last dance. The waltz to end them all.'

The nurse said something else, but I didn't hear it. I was already stood up, already zipping my jacket, already on my way out of the door.

'Her things?' The nurse asked, a little panicked by my sudden exit, 'should we collect them?'

I said yes, but knew I didn't want them. The funeral was already arranged, Mom had seen to that. Simple, humanist, her body set in cardboard, something else which would decay easily, which would present her to the soil beneath the silent grass.

The nurse was still speaking when I left the room. I had nothing to say, nothing to add. The stag had taken my mother. She was in a woodland of underlit wonders, a place that shone from the dark.

At night, white bracken.

◊

AUTOPILOT TOOK CARE OF THE following days.

I was there, but wasn't there. A wall of clouds existed between me and everything else. I stared at the world ahead of me from the wrong end of a telescope. Where people and objects were once near, they now shrank into an impossible distance, barely visible from my window.

Cooper, Shanice and Hickey came and went. They spoke to me and, like something on wires, some kind of impeccably operated marionette, I performed responses, acted like the Danny they knew. I laughed at their jokes, cracked some of my own, took the joints passed to me, handed them back, sipped drinks that tasted of nothing, ate food that felt like pebbles in my mouth.

I washed, I pissed, I dressed and undressed, but I wasn't there for any of it.

In those immediate days, before the funeral, I lived in a small container, in a safe. The box was in a cabinet, the cabinet in a cellar, the cellar at the base of the house I wore. I didn't need to come out. A facsimile of me took care of all the pleasantries, ticked all of the empty boxes.

I knew the three of them went out to assault other targets during those subsequent days.

It was a set routine now, a day job. They were locked into it. Sometimes, hung at the corner of the living room like a spider, I watched as Shanice became Katie Pop, as she giggled into a webcam, occasionally opening her legs to show impeccably white underwear, or teased down her t-shirt to show a new bra, unwashed, starched, perfect for the slavering goon on screen.

Laying there in the dark circles of night, I listened as Shanice and Cooper made love. Their wet reverie, the orchestral oohs, the thud of flesh in the void. I felt nothing. I may as well have been an empty shirt, some forgotten shoes.

It was only on the day of the funeral itself that I began to wake up, to come around from the glue of the shock.

Of course, Cooper and the others knew nothing about my mother, about her death. They hadn't known about her beforehand, whether she had been well, or ill.

I woke up just after dawn, unzipped my only suit from the bag in which it hung and made my way into the city centre to kill some time before I had to be at the cemetery.

I could have been a city worker then, a commuter. Suited, shaven, I slid into that herd without the least suspicion. Just as we had wandered into the shoppers and aimless strollers after the scene with Marco at the hotel, I joined a wave of echo people, of mildly different hairstyles and conversations from the hundreds who walked alongside them.

Sat in a coffee shop, the central train station across the road, I watched the ebb and flow of faceless throngs, the grey tide. I returned to my dream of cities above and cities below, and began to see the clear distinction between us and the inevitable others, the unhuman puppeteers, those in undoubtable control. The animal behaviour manifest in yawning workers, that irrepressible mammal routine, the desire to acquiesce to the familiar, to find your flock, to recognise and follow.

As the coffee cooled on my tongue, I half expected the street to rip in half, the tarmac to peel apart like the stained teeth of smokers and, with the carcinogens of the world's core wheezed outwards, the smouldering nothingness below us all to swallow everyone and everything.

That didn't happen. I simply finished my coffee and, my tie straightened for the benefit of absolutely no-one, I made my way to the next train, the train to the cemetery.

Brandwood End, Crematorium and Cemetery.

I arrived early, Mom's slot was a little while away.

The crematorium sat at the centre of the place, the assorted graves and monuments moving away from it, concentrically arranged. A marble artefact. I wandered between the headstones and the myriad flower arrangements in various states of decay. A fitting gesture, the adornment of beheaded flowers, the delivery of something already dead for the benefit of display.

That was us all over, human beings, that was all we were. From the second of birth, that first stolen breath in the bleached nothingness of the delivery room, we were severed from our root, held up and inhaled like the August rose. We gradually decayed, gradually faded until, our petals curled inwards, our vibrancy rusted away, we returned to the soil.

When it was time, I walked slowly over to my mother's plot.

I was the only attendee. There was no priest, no vicar, no guru, no shaman, no liar. It was just me and the trench, with one solemn worker keen to fill in the hole.

The cardboard coffin was already in there, already in the cool depths. I leaned over the sheer angles of the grave and looked down at the box. It looked like unconstructed furniture, like a flatpack wardrobe delivered by fat-bellied men with rosacea and high blood pressure. I didn't know why, perhaps just because I had seen it on TV, but I picked up some of the soil, rolled it around in my hand, then scattered it on the coffin, listening as it clattered loudly against the cardboard. I thought the box would be almost hollow, so little of her had been left after death had raided the cupboards.

I nodded to the attendant, who replied with a simpering expression, one likely well practiced from decades of that dead-heavy daywork. I stepped back into the glooms cast from a windless willow and watched as the man stepped into the small digger and started it up. He had moved

71

half of the soil into the grave before I noticed the figures at the very edge of my sight.

Like the white stag Mom had mentioned, the apparitional beast I thought I had seen when sat at her deathbed, these figures existed beyond my conventional eyes, observing the ritual.

I felt terror, I felt excitement, I felt madness.

My assumption was simple, that I was in the midst of a nervous breakdown. I stood there as barely discernible figures stuttered to be seen, shimmering in and out of focus, refusing to let me draw any definitive detail on them, existing like sunspots. I wondered whether my guilt had created these ideas, the tonne-weight of angst I felt for my part in the activities of Cooper and Hickey. That, along with how infrequently I had been to see Mom, they gnawed at me. Maggots in my thoughts. I had pushed them all down into the depths and, I assumed then, they were smashing at the door, trying to escape, appearing as fantastic creations, as ghosts, as lies.

I had seen nothing. I had seen enough.

I left the cemetery quickly, my life as a human being with living family over.

11.

A snowflake couldn't change its course

I SPENT LESS TIME AT the house then ever over the fortnight that followed.

I worked all hours at Hickey's yard. I did whatever I was asked to do, moved whatever needed moving, swept whatever needed sweeping, ignored whatever scams, illicit chatter and inferred violence I needed to in the few minutes I took for a break, or when I found myself at the border of a hushed conversation. It was easy work for a ghoul, easy work for the absent hearted.

I moved crates of stolen car stereos, badly repackaged to look new. Other car parts too; catalytic converters yanked from polished vehicles in high-end suburbs during the night. Snotty youths in tracksuit battalions brought them to whichever wrangler was working that day. They came in their droves, early in the morning. Almost ceremonial, they prayed at the feet of the cash-in-hand messiah. A black-eyed mass of sweat and fake watches.

I didn't get involved with any of the scams, I just hauled the goods. Chop-shops, protection rackets run from the local gyms by men with amphetamine hearts. Every trope you could imagine, melded together on that intersection, that underworld sewer.

The main thing was to allow myself to hide. I didn't want conversations then. I didn't want to be involved with anything Cooper and Hickey were doing. I didn't want to be at the house at night, inhaling the sour perfume of Shanice and Cooper's intimacy. I didn't want to eat with them in the mornings when they sat on the sofa ahead of the morning news, their bare legs intertwined, wrapped like ribbons around the bone. They spoke to me, I was polite, but I just moved into the fog for a while, out to some kind of hinterland of vague existence.

It all worked out okay until one night that changed everything.

I finished early at the yard and made my way home. I hadn't slept well in days. It had caught up with me. I felt gaunt, burned up, hollowed out. My head throbbed, my eyes too.

I made it back to house and everyone was out. I crawled up to bed, slid beneath my hardening quilt and was asleep almost instantly. A dreamless sleep, the mindless dark, I don't know how long I slept, but when I woke up, Cooper was sat at the foot of my bed, his eyes lit by the lampposts on the street.

'Wondered when you'd come round,' he said huskily, 'thought you might never wake up.'

My mouth was dry, I edged up to a seating position and fished around on the carpet for my water. I took a deep gulp as Cooper continued.

'We've got a real monster, a real piece of work.'

'What?'

'The latest nonce, Danny boy. He's a fucker alright, make no mistake.'

I told him I wasn't interested. I didn't want to know who they had on the hook next. I was out of all that.

Cooper laughed. 'Ain't that simple, Danny. Isn't a case of him being *on the hook*. That's been and gone. Fact is, we snatched him up. We've got him.'

My thoughts were murky, sleep-sodden, I didn't understand.

'We took him,' Cooper slapped my leg through the covers, 'kidnapped the cunt.'

I didn't know what to say. I just stared at Cooper through the glooms. He was purple with night. My whole room was. Everything looked rotten.

'I know what you're thinking,' Cooper continued, 'I can tell you think this is nuts, I get it, but hear me out. We've been watching him for a while, had Shanice giving him the Katie Pop treatment online. He was cagey, took a while to reel him in, you know?'

'Groom him?'

'Cut that shite out.' Cooper stood and began to pace back and forth, his figure monochrome, then invisible, monochrome then invisible. 'You know as well as I do that these bastards have it coming.'

'Sure.' I swung my legs out of the bed, rubbed my face with my hands.

'Anyway,' Cooper looked out through the curtains, spoke with his back to me, 'Hickey got the notion this pervert is in some kind of ring, maybe even the boss of it.'

I asked how he knew that, 'Mate of his?'

'*No*,' Cooper was agitated, excitable. 'The way he spoke, this fella, the caution he showed, some of the things he said, it…it all made sense, that he was some kind of, I dunno, some kind of boss.'

'Fuck's sake, Coop,' I started to dress, eager to get out of there, 'it's one thing catching someone at a bus station, giving them a hiding, taking their wallet, that shit, but now it's kidnapping? Taking a fucking hostage? All that and Hickey carving that weird eye in their backs like it's normal*?*'

'We needed to get him somewhere we could question him. Tactical necessity.'

'Tactical necessity? You're not at war, Cooper.'

'Maybe I am. Maybe *we are.*'

I didn't know whether he meant us against the beasts, or me against him. I repeated that I didn't want anything to do with it, especially now. 'Just keep me out of it,' I snapped, searching the rug for my missing trainer, wondering whether I should move out.

'That's not going to work, Danny boy. Hickey has plans for you.'

'Plans? *Plans?* I'll tell Hickey where he can put his fucking plans.'

It was only then I realised that Cooper and I weren't alone in my room. From the thicker, meaner shadows by my wardrobe, obscured by the broken door that hung from one hinge, Hickey stepped into the silverlight, next to Cooper.

I was frightened, livid. 'Fucking hell,' I slung my quilt against the wall, 'how long have you been stood there, watching me?'

'That's not important, Daniel,' Hickey said soothingly, like some second-rate hypnotist trying to get an audience member to meow on command. 'We waited for you to wake up naturally. Didn't want to disturb you.'

'Well, if I wasn't disturbed before, I am now.'

'Listen.' Hickey stepped forward and put a heavy hand on my bare shoulder. 'Daniel, please, just give me a minute or two to explain. I promise, it will make sense afterwards, okay?'

There was nothing I could do. I could have stormed out of the room, out of the house, but what then? I would have had to return, to come back, feebly, lost, out of options. The money I had came from the yard work, the house I lived in was Cooper's. Even if I planned to get gone, I needed time to do it.

I sat back on the bed and Hickey sat beside me. Cooper remained a heavy-breathing monolith by the window.

'Theo Watkins,' Hickey began, 'that's who we're talking about here. His name is Theodore Watkins, otherwise known as *Uncle Feels* or *Free Meat* online. He's a vile specimen, Daniel, a real insect.'

'One of how many?'

'Exactly.' I could see Hickey's wild black hair and beard move in the darkness. 'That's the whole thing, Daniel. *One of how many.* More than we could ever pick up one at a time, half arsed. That's why Watkins is more important than the others we've lured in so far. I believe, no, I'm certain that Watkins is part of a ring, maybe even the head of it.'

I asked what made him think that, how he could possibly know. It just sounded convenient to me, unprovable.

'His reluctance,' Hickey began, 'he hid away, ignored the DMs. He had feelers in the water, but the vibrations backed him off. We practically had to have Katie Pop's fanny pressed against the camera to get a rise out of him.'

Cooper hissed at the window.

'Maybe he's just shy?' I rotated my neck slowly, listened to it clunk and snap. 'Maybe he's new to all this, a tourist.'

'He's got chat hits dating back five years, Daniel. He's a veteran, make no mistake. We noticed that he was pally with loads of the other nonces on the logs, especially FishTank. They used odd language when they commented to each other, something that looked almost coded to us, didn't it Cooper?'

'Coded,' Cooper agreed, 'no doubt about it.'

I still didn't get it, didn't understand them taking him prisoner. 'So what, you just went and fucking kidnapped him.'

'Escorted him to a safe location.' Hickey sounded professional, measured. 'I wouldn't call it kidnapping, Daniel. It's just a case of having a chance to…interrogate him, that's all.'

Hickey hung on the word *interrogate*. I had no doubt he meant torture.

I asked where he was. 'He's not downstairs, is he?'

Hickey laughed a little, Cooper too. 'No,' Hickey stood and stretched, the weave of blue veins around his neck and shoulder muscles caught the fleeting streetlight and stood out vividly, 'he's down at the yard, in one of the lockups.'

'Aren't you worried someone will discover him?'

'Nah, I've fastened the gates, closed the whole thing off for now, put a sign up saying we're shut until further notice. The lads'll just think I've been busted, so no worries there.'

I could see what was coming, the reason they wanted to talk to me.

'Thing is, Daniel,' Hickey squatted ahead of me, wolfen in the glooms, 'we need you to keep an eye on him.'

'Me? Why the fuck would you need me to keep an eye on him.'

'We can trust you, Daniel, that's why. Trust you to do a good job, whilst we work it all out, get our feelers back out there, that's why.'

'That's right, Danny boy,' Cooper joined Hickey, kneeling before me. The only time either man felt shorter than me. Yet, squatting there, close enough for me to feel their breath, they both seemed coiled, poised to leap at my throat. 'Also, hope you don't mind me saying, mate, but you've seemed, well, out of it recently. Shanice thought you might be on the smack. You aren't, are you?'

'You know I'm not. Just had a few things on my mind, that's all.'

'Well, we all do,' Hickey stood again, 'but you'll be fine, Daniel. Just have to swallow these things down and move on. There's more at stake than you think.'

I didn't feel like I could refuse, like I could escape.

'I'll pay you the same daily rate,' Hickey continued, knowing it was agreed, 'cash in hand. All I need you to do is drop in, give the weird cunt some water, something to eat. Slop out his buckets, job done.'

'And your…interrogations?'

'We'll get to that.' Hickey's teeth lit the blackness of the room as he smiled. 'Let's just let him sweat for a few days, eh. That's the best torture of all, the not knowing. We'll keep him braced at the lockup, make him feel like he's doomed and, if he won't talk then, well…'

I was just glad to get them out of my room, to hear the door close behind them, the security of the latch. I sat back on my bed, listened to the speeding cars of the estate, the unending race to oblivion. I weighed the situation, turned it over in my thoughts.

I didn't want to get caught up that mess, but I couldn't stop them, I couldn't persuade them to let Watkins walk. There was also a part of me that wondered whether Watkins was some kind of pervert kingpin. For all I knew this was a sequence of imprisonment. We had him shackled in a garage, maybe he had some whimpering child shackled in another garage. There was a chance, I told myself, that them getting something from Watkins could protect others, could bring down a few more fiends.

Did I believe it? It didn't matter.

An anchor doesn't question where its dropped, a snowflake couldn't change its course. I knew I would be at the lockup the next morning.

12.

Theodore Watkins

THE YARD WAS DESERTED, NOT a soul in sight.

Nobody ever came looking for Hickey, or tried to find out why the place was closed down. It was obvious why. There was almost no legal operation at the yard, everything was a racket, under the table. The notion that someone had been busted, especially Hickey, was a red light, a starting pistol. They would keep their distance, find another site to move their hooky fags, their sawn-offs and patchwork cars.

Watkins was in Unit 14. Hickey made sure he was as far away from the main road as possible, tucked right at the back of the snaking lot.

I procrastinated for almost an hour. I flattened crates, checked the padlocks were all fastened, even swept up some broken windscreen glass from a neighbouring unit. I didn't want to meet Watkins, to talk to him. I knew once that had happened I would be locked into the melee, part of the swirl. The moment he saw my face, spoke to me, I would become the contact, the conduit for his survival, or the conveyer for his torturers.

Still, it had to happen, I was sure of it. If I could have run, I would have gone already.

I unlocked the heavy door and slipped inside. It was pitch black and there was a strong smell of urine. I had a torch in my side pocket and didn't knew where the main light was. I thumbed the torch on and shakily scanned the lockup ahead of me.

It was strange. I knew someone was there, felt that fission of one human near to another, but it took longer than it should have for me to find Watkins, as if I had checked every other inch of the room before I simply aimed the light forward.

A pallid face, gaunt and gagged, Watkins' eyes thinned as the light hit them. He didn't make a sound, he just wrestled his head from side-to-side, avoiding the intensity of the torch.

'Sorry,' I said without thinking, overly polite, patently nervous, 'I'll find the switch. Hold on a second.'

Clumsily, thumping my knee on every surface I passed, knocking over empty paint tins, chairs with broken legs, tools, I eventually found the switch to the strip-light above us and lit the room.

Watkins' grey hair was wild, his frame thin, tiny. He looked like someone's grandad, like some old bloke at the library, busy in the archives. I stood behind him for a moment, unkeen to make eye contact with him, to see him properly.

I had thought about wearing a balaclava, a mask, but there didn't seem to be a point. No matter what Hickey and Cooper were wrong about, they were right about those characters not being able to go to the police. All that mattered was not being seen by others, not having my face recorded by some inquisitive dawdler wandering in from the street.

Besides, the way things worked out, it wouldn't have mattered anyway.

As I emptied my backpack of essentials, I tried to avoid Watkins' eyes. Piercingly blue, metallic, they circled independently, watching every motion, every movement I made. There was something instantly childlike about the eyes, yet somehow melliferous. I couldn't explain it to myself then, I couldn't have known what they held; the rot, the decay, the meat-stare.

When I had unpacked, I moved over to Watkins and, careful to make sure his hands were still tied behind his back, I lowered his gag.

Watkins didn't speak at first. He rotated his jaw, opened and closed his mouth, licked at his rag-chapped lips and searched the lockup with his cobalt stare. Eventually, eyeing the bottle of water, he nodded towards it and asked me to pour some into his mouth. 'Please,' his voice was plummy, educated, the kind of voice which belonged to a jaded English lecturer at a redbrick university. '*Please*, I'm terribly thirsty.'

I obliged, carefully tilting the opened bottle to his mouth, watching as he greedily suckled the spout, guzzling the water until it spilled in rivulets down through the deep wrinkles around his mouth and chin.

I placed the bottle down and pointed at the sandwich and crisps, 'Hungry?'

'Listen,' Watkins breathed deeply, coughing up some of the water that pooled in his cragged neck, 'There's been a mistake, a dreadful error. I…I shouldn't be here. I haven't done anything wrong.'

'You weren't talking to kids online?' I asked tonelessly. 'You weren't trying to meet them? There's no way you'd be here if you weren't. Believe me.'

'What? Look, it isn't *like that*. I…all I was doing was…all I was doing was talking to a young lady on the computer. That's it.'

'Maybe that's enough. Enough to get you here.'

'Hardly.' Watkins' face twisted angrily. 'If bloody thoughts and idle chatter were crimes, we'd all be breaking rocks, wouldn't we?'

'Not all of us.' I pulled over a stool and sat opposite Watkins, careful to keep at arm's length, just in case he was able to free himself, to lunge at me.

'Besides,' he continued, 'I didn't even want to say those things to that Katie girl. She was the one who pushed it. Or should I say you and your gang of loonies were the ones who did it. The ones fishing for me.'

I wanted to correct Watkins, to tell him I wasn't on the other side of the screen, it wasn't my hands that dragged him into a van, made him a prisoner. Yet, somehow, I felt in saying that I would have been betraying Cooper, even Hickey. I wondered whether my keenness to provide distance between myself and their crimes would have given Watkins some kind of hope, some idea that I would free him.

I wanted to clarify my role there, though, to ensure Watkins knew I was low in the pecking order, a mere pawn ahead of vengeful bishops and a queen in pumps and leggings. 'Listen, all I'm here to do is feed and water you, let you take a piss and so on. That's what I'm here for. Just that. You can plead with the others when they come down to see you.'

'The ones who kidnapped me?'

'The ones in charge,' I nodded, happy to at least draw some kind of line between us, even if it was just inferred.

Watkins asked if I had done this before: 'Take perfect strangers hostage?'

'What does it matter?'

'It matters to me. It happens to matter a great deal.'

'I wouldn't worry about what went before, I'd worry about what's to come.'

'My god.' Watkins' bottom lip trembled, his eyes became wet, tears hung there, trapped by an invisible dam. 'I'm…I'm frightened. Terrified. Are they…are they going to hurt me?'

I couldn't help but want to reassure him, to calm him. I didn't know Watkins, I had no idea what he had done or said to Katie Pop. All I had was what Cooper and Hickey had told me. I questioned myself, wondered where the truth sat, where facts slid away from lies, from exaggeration.

'Listen, Mr Watkins,' I looked around the room, expecting to see other figures, knowing none were really there, 'I don't think the others want to hurt you. Honestly. They're just after information, that's all.'

'Information? What kind of *information* do they think I have?'

I told him that they – we – thought he was part of a ring, maybe even its head fiend.

'That's preposterous!' Watkins was indignant, amazed at the idea. 'I'm…I'm just some old fool whose feelings got the best of him one night! Please believe me.'

I remembered Cooper and Hickey saying that Watkins' chat logs went back years, that he communicated with other men in the rooms, that he seemed to know them, used coded language. I didn't want to tell him I knew that. I didn't want the debate. This wasn't even my scene. I was just mopping up the tears of someone else's tragedy.

'If that's true,' I assured Watkins, 'then all you have to do is explain. They aren't unreasonable people,' I nodded, knowing full well they absolutely were.

'Reasonable people don't kidnap strangers, dear boy.' Watkins seemed resigned then, unable to push the point further with me.

'Do you want the sandwich,' I asked. 'You should eat. I don't know how long you'll be here.'

Watkins agreed. I peeled away the plastic and held the triangular sandwich to his mouth, watching like a zoologist as he chewed piece by piece, as his moistened lips eventually reached my fingertips, freezing there for a second or so in some bizarre kiss.

After Watkins had eaten, he wanted to piss. I nudged a steel bucket over to the space between his feet. It was only then I realised that I would have to either untie him, or help him.

I mithered for a while, paced the floor. I didn't want to unzip him, to hold him. The idea was horrible, some kind of violation to both of us.

'I really need to pee,' Watkins insisted, 'please, I'll wet myself otherwise.'

I searched the drawers of the workbench in the lockup and, far from ideal, found some thin rubber gloves, *marigolds*. They were speckled with paint, likely from some chop-shop touch-up, but they'd do. With them pulled tightly over my hands, I unzipped Watkins' fly and fished him out. I looked away. I held it over the lip of the bucket and listened to the loud pings of wet on metal as Watkins relieved himself.

When he was done, I zipped him up and tipped the bucket's contents down the drain at the corner of the room.

'What about when I need to poop?' Watkins asked, somewhat maliciously, a slight curl of amusement at the corner of his mouth. 'Are you going to *take care* of me then too?'

'Maybe I'll let one of the others sort that out for you,' I snapped, 'doesn't seem fair for me to have all the fun.'

'Look,' Watkins' face fixed, his eyes wide, sincere, pleading, 'I have nothing to bargain with, of course. I have no way of persuading you to free me, I understand that. I don't know how long I'll be here…I don't know if your friends will kill me. My requests will likely fall on deaf ears, on ears of those who believe I deserve nothing but hatred, torture. However, I…I have a cat, at home. I have a cat and she's locked in my house.'

'So?'

'So,' Watkins eyes moistened again, 'she will starve to death in a few days. This is already the second day I've been gone. I know how you must feel, but is there any way that you could at least go back to my home, let her out, give her a sporting chance?'

'I...I don't think so' I replied, the immediate image of a thinning cat already horrible, appalling, 'that's not a good idea. I have no idea what would be waiting for me there. The others wouldn't like it.'

Watkins continued through gritted teeth, the urgency real, immediate. 'The only thing waiting for you there is Dora Lee, my tabby. She's done nothing to you and your *militia*. Why should she die on account of this idiocy?'

I explained it wasn't as simple as that. 'Try to remember the situation we're in.' I attempted to be reasonable, to help him see it objectively. 'You're a captive and, however it works, I'm on the other side of the bars. How can I just wander into your house. What if a neighbour saw me?'

'I have a back door,' Watkins' voice became raised, almost shrill, 'I have a key, there's an entryway, you can go through the garden without being seen. *Please.*'

I didn't want to continue the conversation, not a single second more. Feeling my heart palpitate, sweat gathering on my forehead, I snatched at the gag, pulled it back over Watkins' mouth and, knocking over the remaining water, left the lockup.

♦♦

I RETURNED TO THE HOUSE and found Cooper and Shanice on their usual shabby throne.

They were laid out on the sofa, Cooper spooning Shanice's comparatively tiny figure, the television blaring ahead of them. Some kind of home improvement show, the pair of them giggled at some distraught imbecile whose reclaimed wooden doorframes were lost in transit.

'Aye up, Danny boy.' Cooper turned slightly to face me as I passed them both and switched off the TV.

'We were watching that,' Shanice protested.

'Well, you can fucking well watch me,' I snapped, waiting until they both sat up and paid attention.

'What's up?' Cooper asked, as cool and comfortable as if I was about to ask which of them had used the butter with my initials on.

'*What's up?* How can you even ask that? You know very fucking well what's up. I've just been down the yard, at the lockup, holding your prisoner's prick so he could piss in a bucket.'

Cooper laughed, Shanice too. 'Shouldn't be giving favours like that to a head nonce, Danny boy,' Cooper added through a smirk, 'he's supposed to be having a rough time of it, not a weekend in Ibiza.'

'This isn't right,' I began to pace the threadbare carpet, kicking discarded clothing when I found it, 'there's no way you and Hickey can keep him captive there, no way.'

'Why not?' Shanice asked, her tone bold, defiant. 'He's the one what did it to himself, ain't he? If he weren't online chasing littluns, he wouldn't be tied up down there, would he?'

'That's not the point, *Katie.*' I felt my face contract into a sneer as I spoke. 'You lot have every opportunity to turn him over to the police, the evidence too.'

'Not this again,' Cooper stood and approached me, lowered a hand onto my neck. 'We've been over this, there's no point passing that ponce to the pigs. Waste of time, you know that.'

'Don't tell me what I know, Coop.' I shook off his hand and moved away, created more space between us. 'Like I said before, it's one thing to shake them down at a bus station, take their cash, terrify them. It's another to kidnap them.'

'Hickey has a plan,' Cooper yawned, stretched, sat back down, cuddled Shanice, 'he's cool about it.'

I told them Hickey wasn't the one down at the yard, the one dealing with Watkins.

'You've only had one shift with him,' Cooper tried to calm me, 'it'll be better tomorrow, you watch.'

'It will be, Danny,' Shanice added, nodding affirmatively, eliciting a warm smile from Cooper, 'I'm sorry we laughed,' she added, genuinely. For the first time, I saw the kindness in her then, just a flicker of it, but something tangible, some string of light, the glint of a silver coin at the bottom of a well.

I sat down in the chair, rubbed my eyes. There was no end result to the discussion, no way of persuading them it was a bad idea. Hickey had them hooked, Cooper most of all. There were talons in Cooper's shoulders, even then. If I listened carefully, I could hear the flesh tearing as he was swung by the grim puppeteer.

'We were about to have tea,' Shanice said gently, 'Chinese, most likely. You want somethin?'

'Sure, thanks.' I was hungry.

As Shanice got up to search through the library of takeaway menus tucked into the magazine rack, I suddenly thought of my mother, of the only other woman I had ever known to offer me a meal.

A strange thought really, Shanice and Mom had nothing in common, except for perhaps their height, their build. It was just a transitory thought, a sudden jolt, something basic and almost arbitrary. It was their femininity, their inherent calm, their godliness. I had ignored Shanice, thought of her as some pixilated entity born of Hickey and Cooper. I had only genuinely seen her once, back by the empty factories, the redlight district. I had taken her in then, noticed the ruin in her. She wasn't the same now, she was fuller, more well, somehow partially repaired, reconstructed.

Maybe it was the retaliatory power of affection, of love. Maybe that's what they had then, Shanice and Cooper, maybe that was love. I don't know. What I do know, what I am unable to unsee, is how it ended.

It ended as raw meat, as trails of blood, as skin-kindling for a final fire.

It ended as bone memories in the dead earth below.

◊

I TOOK A WALK AFTER we had eaten. I had the sense that Cooper and Shanice wanted to be alone.

I began to understand that I was an invader now, a ghost of Cooper's yesterday.

He would never say it to me. Cooper was, despite his choices at times, a kind friend, a caring human, at least to those he valued. I had the idea that, no matter what happened with Watkins in the days that followed, it wouldn't be long before my escape from the clutches of that rotten time became a simple ejection, a gentle nudge into the night.

I walked through the estate, my head down, my hood up.

I moved along the periphery of the fencing, the car-crushed walls, the rusted arcade shops; their windows flowered with shattered glass. I avoided the eyes of the yowling youths, of the gangs who made the night their own. They mostly knew me, or at least they knew I was with Cooper. The gangs wouldn't jump me, but they still screamed incomprehensible threats and skimmed bottles in my direction. I heard the glass explode a few paces behind me. I heard the screech of BMX wheels as they circled, as their riders eyed the meat they wished they could skin.

I found myself on the canals, meandering along the towpath, the city centre to the South, its infinity of electric lights turning the night-sky lilac. Stars were lost, polluted by the melee of bulbs beneath them, by the unending traffic; the headlights like a heatless pyre carrying the dead to the long barrows of their bedrooms.

Before I knew it, I had arrived at the redlight district, the place of Katie Pop's physical birth.

The working girls looked skeletal in the spotlights cast from the lampposts above them. A quiet night, I watched as a handful of cars drove up, slowed, cruised the kerbs creepily, surveyed their options, then sped up and drove away, sometimes with a girl, sometimes alone.

They women seemed anchored there, mere statues in the concrete. Their addictions, their hungers, their lack of options; they kept them there, on that street, the oil drums burning in the arterial alleys around them. They were corralled, their ribs raised, their flesh sunken, their faces looking only into the darkness, waiting for it to end.

I couldn't watch them for long; it turned my stomach, pummelled my heart. I have never been much of a sentimental person, but the sight of a starving dog would see me sob. They were the starving dogs of us; forgotten, chained, beaten, left to scrounge around in the dirt for dinner.

I moved around them, taking the fly-tipped pathways that snaked through the factory units.

Sporadic drunks and derelicts too broke to even afford some poxy flat on the estate sat around their fires on filthy mattresses, their beat faces lit by the flames. Ugly, drink-pickled urchins, they sucked on gas canisters, stood with ruined gaits from smoking spice. They huffed soiled bags of solvents and laughed maniacally as the highs starved their minds of oxygen.

I kept my distance from them, eventually finding a walkway so dark, so devoid of any life that I felt sure I was only person there.

How wrong I was.

I heard his breathing before I heard his voice.

The night was thick there, like a forest of crows. The light struggled to find even an inch to shimmer. I passed a doorway, some jagged hole that led into a workshop stripped of copper years earlier.

Perhaps it was instinct, but my hackles rose. I knew someone watched me, closely.

I felt that sudden spasm of fear, that survival pulse, the notion I would need to fight. My fists clenched tightly, my enemy invisible, I waited for the attack and, when it was Hickey's voice I heard, I felt something beyond relief, something close to euphoria. The familiarity of the demon I knew.

'Lovely place for a wander, isn't it?' Hickey emerged from the doorway as he spoke, his silhouette almost lycanthropic. 'Great minds.'

'I…I was just trying to avoid the nutters,' my mouth was dry, my words empty, 'it's rough as arseholes down here.'

'That it is, Daniel, that it most definitely is.'

I asked Hickey what he was doing there, why he chose to walk around the dead factories so late. 'If I've got a fucked-up idea of where to take a stroll, then we both have.'

'I like the rot,' Hickey answered casually, his face clearer in the slither of a light from an unbroken bulb above the doorway. 'The complete degradation of it all. It makes me feel, I don't know, *righteous.*'

'I don't know if I understand.'

Hickey laughed, 'I'm sure you do. Come through here, take a wander with me.'

Hickey turned and walked back into the gutted factory. I followed.

The space was enormous and bleak. A bombed-out place, a hollowed hub of industry, forgotten, reamed, vacuumed to death. I could hear the swoop of bats from the rafters, the rustle of wings, the movement of somnolent birds.

Skeletal machinery remained; mechanical husks too heavy to steal. Instead, like beached whales, they had been gutted, eaten by maggots, the copper thieves. I'd seen them a thousand times, the flatbed trucks, so like funereal processions. Peopled by boilersuit boys, their mean faces lit by unending cigarettes, ducking into places like that factory, burning off the plastic and rubber, sliding out the malleable metals, hurrying off to the scrapyards to get their prizes weighed. Pennies for industrial intelligence, beer money for broken bones of lathes and presses.

What I noticed most, though, what shook me as we strolled along the concrete floor was what appeared to be the shadows of people, their movement at the walls of the factory.

I couldn't see them, couldn't make out anything more than a shuffle, a shrug, the wave of a silent arm. I could hear breathing, something raspy that echoed through the gardens of litter. I could see the silhouettes of gnarled heads, of swollen shoulders. Yet, it wasn't seeing anything that mattered, it was *sensing* them, knowing that whoever they were, they watched us from their dark corners, from their empty webs.

'More tramps?' I asked Hickey, hurrying to his side as I spoke, keen to be nearer to him.

'Maybe,' he lit a cigarette and I saw the right side of his face; stark, orange, the rumour of a smile curling into his lean cheek, 'maybe not.'

'Maybe not?'

'Maybe they're just like us, Daniel. Just souls who struggle to rest. I wouldn't worry.'

'You mightn't worry,' I spoke in a whisper, keen not to rile anyone at the edge, 'but then I doubt you worry about much.'

'I worry you don't like me,' Hickey stopped and turned to face me, his thick black hair like rainclouds over the faintly lit hillocks of his eyes. 'I worry that I've offended you, made an enemy, things like that.'

'What?' I couldn't believe he'd said it, that he would give two fucks whether he meant anything to me, whether I existed as anything beyond an underling, something trodden into place.

'It's true, Daniel,' he continued, offering me a few drags on the cigarette. I accepted, but didn't know why. 'I get the feeling maybe you even hate me. Do you?'

'No. Of course I don't hate you.'

'But you hate what we're doing, Cooper and me. You hate that, right?'

'It's not like I don't understand why you're doing it,' I lied, 'I just don't see why…I don't see why you have to torture them, you know. I especially don't get why,' I lowered my voice, 'why you kidnapped Watkins.'

Hickey placed a hand on my shoulder, his right, my left, 'I think you *do* understand, Daniel. I think you understand a whole lot more than Cooper, than that bitch, Shanice, or most other people for that matter. I think you see things for what they are. For what they really are.'

'I don't hate you,' I repeated then, like some weird acknowledgment to the compliment Hickey had given me. It felt like church then, like the prayer from the vicar, the answer from the pews.

What Hickey said then, the way his words cut through those glooms, it wouldn't make sense to me for days to come, but it landed like an anchor in my chest.

'I know about your mother,' he said calmly, 'about her death.'

I felt rageful, incredulous, disgusted. I felt like a secret had been stolen from me as I slept. 'What the *fuck?* How'd you know about her? You been following me?'

'Relax, Daniel.' Hickey held his palms up to me. 'Pure happenstance, that's all. Believe me.'

I asked how he knew again, over and over, my annoyance palpable in the tremolo of my words. 'I need to know, Hickey. Right fucking now.'

'A friend, that's all. I have a mate, spends a lot of time there, at the hospice. I'd told him about you and Cooper a few times, mentioned some of the things we've been up to, nothing too detailed, but enough that he cottoned on when he saw your name down as a visitor for your ma. Not too many Solomons around here. He twigged a couple of weeks back, relayed it to me. I was sure you'd have mentioned her to Cooper, you two being pretty close and all.'

It felt like dark machinery was moving, as if the dead engines of the factory had been brought back from oblivion. 'Spying on me then,' I shook my head slowly, pendulously, 'you come down there too, watch me through a crack in the door.'

'It's nothing like that,' Hickey's tone was warm then, even caring, 'I wondered why you hadn't said anything, what you must've been going through. It's why I threw you the yard work, kept you out of all the shite Cooper and me have been up to. I figured you wanted distance, time to yourself. Believe me, Daniel. I have no reason to lie to you about this, do I?'

I couldn't think why he would lie, what benefit it would give him to know my mother had died. There was no apparent win there for Hickey. I had to believe him. I asked if he had mentioned it to Cooper.

'Not a word,' he said, beginning to walk again, with me in tow. 'The way it seemed to me, Daniel, you had a reason not to bring Cooper in, not to let him know what you were going through. I'd have likely done the same thing. A person needs that space, that bone space, you know? The privacy of the skull. If you don't want to spill, then why should you? These things are sometimes all we have.'

'I couldn't bring it up, you understand. I didn't have it in me, the energy to talk about it. There was too much to cover, her illness, where she was. I didn't want to open that up.'

'You didn't want to open up, full stop,' Hickey answered.

I asked why I should open up, why I should share anything about myself with him or Cooper.

'You shouldn't feel like you have to.' Hickey stopped again, a rustle of figures nearby, which he completely ignored. 'I just want you to know, I'm here if you need to talk. That's all.'

'That's all?'

'I've been around, Daniel. Seen a lot, know a lot. You might think Cooper has nothing to offer in reply, but I might.'

'I don't think that,' I panicked, 'about Cooper. He's a mate, my closest mate. I just didn't…it wasn't the right time to tell him about Mom. It wasn't.'

'Fair enough, Daniel,' Hickey lit two cigarettes, passed me one, 'it's your business. Clear as day. Secret's safe with me.'

I couldn't explain why but, simply, that discussion, its setting, the way Hickey sounded as he spoke, I felt a sudden sense of loyalty, of brotherhood, as though him knowing about my mother and me knowing about his work with Cooper unified us somehow.

I had disliked Hickey enormously, his sinister looks, the sheer muscularity of him, his swaggering terror, all of it but, like Cooper, something drew me to him also. It was some kind of safety, maybe even a desire to be like them, to be with them, whilst also wanting to run as far away from them as possible. I was reviled by their behaviour towards the blokes they caught online, but I was also tempted by it, excited by and disgusted at myself for feeling that.

Everything blurred at the edges, nothing felt defined, nothing felt clear. All of the shapes of my world were carved by a blunted blade.

We came to the other doorway to the factory. It had been smashed open, just like the entrance we had walked from. It brought us back onto the strip where the prostitutes patrolled their purloined pavements.

'So,' Hickey was clear now in the electric light of the street, 'you okay to keep watch over Watkins for a few more days.'

I couldn't say no.

'Good lad. I knew I could trust you, Daniel. You see between the cracks,' Hickey laughed loudly enough for the working girls to stop and turn towards us, 'you know what looks back at you, right?'

I nodded in the direction of the women, 'White Bracken,' I said, with no idea why.

'White Bracken,' Hickey repeated, laughing again, elated by a reply I didn't even feel like I'd said, 'that's perfect, Daniel. *White Bracken.*'

We parted there. Hickey turned and walked back into the abyss of the ruined factory, his shape fading to nothing after only a few paces.

I pulled my collars up tight around my face, the needling cold stung at my cheeks, my nose.

I had wanted to tell Hickey about Watkins' cat, just to share that too. I didn't, of course. In not doing so, I turned the next cog, gnashed the teeth of the gears, moved the juggernaut onwards, towards the fire.

13.

Lens is viewer

WHEN I ARRIVED AT THE lockup the next morning, Watkins was sobbing.

Inconsolable as I pulled the gag away from his blubbering mouth, he immediately started up about the cat again, his dear Dora Lee.

'She'll be *desperate,*' he wept, 'terrified. You're torturing her, not just me.'

I tried to ignore him, to focus more on the acrid stink of his piss-hardened trousers, the pool around his feet. 'She's a cat,' I tried to assure him, 'they're canny, she'll find a way out.'

'*A way out?*' he screamed. 'She's not a lock-picker, you idiot! You're sick!'

I backhanded Watkins. A clean strike, one neither of us expected. 'I'm sick? You're the fuckin pervert tied to a chair. *You're* sick, Watkins. Through and through.'

I felt immediately awful, nauseated by the feeling of his jaw against my knuckles. Like the kick I'd given Big Barry, it seemed to doubly hurt me, to wind me and leave me reeling.

Watkins tried to stem his crying, sniffling like a toddler. 'I'm...I'm just w-worried about her,' he stammered, 'she's just a cat, can't you see? She hasn't done anything.'

Perhaps it was the guilt of the slap, or just the terrible idea of a cat slowly starving in some suburban nowhere, but I began to play the scenario out in my mind, eventually saying it aloud. 'Maybe,' I began, spittle gathering at the corners of the mouth, 'maybe there's a way to let her out, give her a chance.'

I shouldn't have said a word. A soon as I spoke, Watkins was overly animated, elated, shaking his chair from side-to-side with joy. 'Yes! *Yes!* That's all I'm asking for, please. *Please.* If you do that… if you help my lovely Dora Lee…I'll…I'll try and help your friends, tell them what they want to know.'

I turned away, I couldn't look at Watkins then. I felt like he was grooming me, persuading me to show him something dangerous in exchange for a reward. All over a fucking cat. He had told me what a mistake it was, what an error it had been for him to have been scooped up by Hickey and Cooper, how he had nothing to do with that scene, how he was just a silly old man at a computer. Now, when the prospect of the cat came up, suddenly he was willing to talk, to spill information he denied ever holding.

I couldn't think. With Watkins' high-pitched plea ringing in my ears, I left the lock-up and went for a drink.

Some lousy local pub, I can't even remember its name now. An eagle on its sign, maybe a buzzard. Faded, splintered wood, dozing regulars sucking the last remnants of life from the pint they'd nursed for the past hour. Hacking coughs from an unseen snug, the phlegmy rattle echoing through the wordless bar and lounge.

I sat there and stared at pint after pint. I thought of the previous night with Hickey, that strange walk through the abandoned factory, the shuddering figures at the edges of the dark. I thought of how Hickey knew about my mother, of how much more he knew. I ignored that in favour of Watkins' cat, of his *lovely Dora Lee.*

I don't know why the idea of the starving cat bothered me so much. Animals starved on the streets every day, ignored, neglected, tethered to some abusive goon and booted in the guts every time their horse was last past the post. I couldn't understand why Watkins' cat, the cat of a probable predator, affected me so much. I wondered during the following days whether it was quite simply something good, something pure in the human muck. The notion of freeing a hungry cat, a cat I pictured then like some kind of tin-ribbed waif clinging to the net curtains, looking out in the grey morning for Watkins, for the saviour.

The thought of helping that cat escape began to seem essential as I sat there drinking.

The early afternoon grew orange, then brown, ripening into evening, spoiling, blackening, rotting away.

When I got back to the lock-up, it was pitch black. I had to use the torch to find Watkins again. I had forgotten to gag him when I left, but he hadn't been screaming. He was just sat there, chewing his lips, mithering. Hours had passed since we spoke. I could smell the booze on my breath when I told him I'd go to his place and free his cat.

'Thank you, *thank you,*' he repeated, over and over again. A mantra, something to cling to in his dark hours, I supposed.

I fished through his belongings, found the keys.

'You're sure I can get in, through the back door? I won't be seen?'

'No, not at all. My house is at the corner of the cul-de-sac. The entry runs down the left-hand side, along the side of my garage. There's a security light at the back door, above it, but I'm not overlooked, my house is detached. There's high privet, elms, ash trees, thick with dog roses. Nobody can see you there.'

'An alarm? You setting me up?' I remember slurring a little as I spoke, adamant something was up, that there was a trap waiting, some violent partner in the shadows.

'I *promise,* there's nothing of the sort. No alarms, no cohabitors, no curtain-twitchers who could make out anything other than your outline from across the road, especially not at this time of night. You are going now, aren't you?'

I nodded. Watkins seemed sincere. He had no real leverage, at least none that I could see. I'm fast, I thought I could run if there was a sign of trouble, if someone stuck their head out.

Dulled and bold with booze, I took the keys, Watkins' address and left the yard.

❧

THE STATION WAS DEAD. I was the only person leaving the train.

A gossamer fog had settled on the suburbs. It pixilated the pavements, the living room windows, the litter bins, unspoiled cherry-red post-boxes and carefully positioned benches, along with the merry-mowed verges on which they sat.

I didn't know Harborne well. It was never an area I had spent much time in. Post-graduate academics, affected thinkers, those who wanted their children to attend Montessori nurseries and understand the stock market before their adult teeth came in: Harborne was for them. Not me.

I passed a tennis club, the courts lit brightly, evening players decked-out in their spotless whites, prancing between their rackets. Guffaws from the clubhouse, new cars gleaming in the carpark, polished to oblivion, their metal like rolled gold.

The smell of open fires, of crackling embers winking yellow from the grates. The perfume of dried wood, sliced evenly, stacked on the restored brick of a Victorian fireplace. I could see families as they ate late dinners. I watched them from the street as I walked.

Mothers and fathers swirling red wine in oversized glasses, precocious progeny in theatrical poses, their adenoidal adolescence played out perfectly, just as the family had planned. Preened pets sat in their corners, on their pillows, watching the imbeciles who fed them as they loafed, laughed, leered.

One after another, every single home on those streets projected the same film, the same gouty reel. It was as predictable as the estates were. An indictment of the individual, a demonstration of the paddocked person, every single type of the species exactly where they needed to be. Only I was the interloper, the gnat on the houseplant. Only I was the scumbag wandering their swept wonderland on my mission to save a starving cat for a pervert. Not to help him, simply because of him.

I reached Watkins' cul-de-sac just before eight pm.

The Victorian homes had faded, replaced by their modern equivalent, the bungalow land of carbon copy homes, their front gardens demonstrative of their owners' wealth and power. Every flowerbed and preened tree a testament to their disposable income, to how well they had suckled the right tits.

Watkins' house was, as he had said, at the top of the cul-de-sac.

I spied the gate to the entry, verified how it snaked along the shuttered garage, around to what appeared to be his back garden. There was no immediate neighbour, no way that someone next door could see me as I made my way into the house. Still, I didn't try the gate straight away. Instead, my hood up, a scarf covering my face below my nose, I walked down the cul-de-sac, no hurry, as if I was comfortable there, like I belonged there.

It was an extremely long cul-de-sac. Like some concrete teardrop, it ballooned more the further down I went. At its centre, there was a small green. Benches, a covered seat, even a board with some neighbourhood information. I didn't stop to read any of the notices, but slowed a little as I rounded the green, just to make sure there was nobody around, no unnatural eyes on my back.

It was clear; every resident's eyes were glued to their enormous televisions. Supine, full of pudding, the citizens of Watkins' cul-de-sac didn't care about me. They never had.

I opened the gate quickly, flicking the latch and edging into the entryway before it had time to land back in place.

I stood there in that dark gulley, my breathing fast, nervous.

I could smell autumn on the rotting hedgerows. Earthy, sour with putrefaction, I inhaled deeply, my face twisted with disgust. I must have stayed there for two minutes, maybe more. Just a figment in the dark, afraid to move forward, afraid to leave. Eventually it passed and I edged down the entry, towards Watkins' garden.

I moved onto the lawn, the shapes of carefully tended trees skeletal with their withering leaves. A dog barked in the middle distance, its owner shouted a muddled name and the barking stopped. I heard a back door open and close a few doors down. I smelled cigarette smoke, its stench carried on the night air. Someone sniffed, finished their fag, went back to their sepia evening.

There were no signs of another person in the house. The glass of the back door was frosted, but there were no lights on, nothing to indicate anyone was waiting. I tried to look through the kitchen window, but the blinds were down. I thinned my eyes and could just see between the base of the taps, a small gap at the bottom of the blinds. Again, there was no movement – not even a cat.

I fidgeted for a while, wringing my fingers, the buzz of the earlier booze worn well away by then and, with it, my earlier indifference, that boldness booze brings in buckets.

I took out the keys. Watkins was an organised man. The back door key was labelled. I slid it gently into the lock, somehow frightened to hear the muddle and clank of metal on metal. The key moved perfectly, sat silently in the lock. I turned it, heard the latch give and, the key pocketed, I lowered the door handle and pushed my way in.

I suppose I expected the cat to come dashing out, to sprint between my legs, into the night, her freedom assured. There was nothing like that, no such hurry, no sign of Dora Lee.

Watkins had said that turning on a light was fine, that it was nothing to worry about. I didn't want to risk it. I was risking enough already.

Once inside, I closed the door behind me and tried to adjust my eyes to the dark. Sure I was alone, I called for the cat. *Pssss, pssss, pssss, Dora Lee, come on then kitty, pssss, pssss, pssss.*

No movement, no sign of the cat.

I worried she was already dead, starved in less than three days. That seemed impossible, though, unless she had no water either. I remembered how aloof cats were, how she was likely perched on a chair, hidden beneath a table, eyeing me from a black cowl. I moved forward, treading carefully as I went.

Into the hallway, I ignored the photographs on the walls, keen to keep Watkins' humanity at a minimum.

I worried that I couldn't even smell cat shit, or the acrid piss they were so happy to spray. I questioned myself as I hung there like a spider coming in from the cold. A litter tray upstairs? Maybe there was a cat-flap to the garage? I hadn't asked Watkins any of these things. My decision seemed more idiotic by the second.

I could see the arm of a sofa through a door left ajar, a living room beyond. Increasingly edgy, keen to be out of the house, I decided to check that room and make it my very last stop, to leave immediately if there was no sign of Dora Lee.

It was a mistake I would never be able to fix.

As the door moved inwards, I heard a mechanism engage, the loud click and thud of something in the darkness. Suddenly, violent with the speed they came on, every light in the house burst into life.

I reeled, half-blinded by the sudden brightness.

I covered my face, expecting someone to be there, in the living room, charging at me, the snare triggered. Sunspots, I blinked for clarity, I blinked against the shock, everything blurred around me.

Stepping back, clattering my right shoulder against the doorframe, I saw my enemy, my captor.

On every surface, every tabletop, every shelf. Mounted on the walls, leering out from the plaster, even sat in the corners of the rooms on emaciated tripods. *Cameras.*

The lenses seemed alive, as if they were leaning towards me, their glass eyes bulging.

Lights flickered on the sides of the lenses, illuminated those sinister monocles. They were clearly recording me, perhaps even live. One, purely for stills, clicked wildly as it took snap after snap after snap. I backhanded it and ran out of the room, back into the hallway.

Previously obscured by the darkness, I froze with horror as I realised there were more of them there, again on every tabletop, next to the telephone, propped behind the door, swinging from the light-fittings like plastic primates, their faces fixed on mine, their irrefutable truth screaming that lens is viewer.

I sped into the kitchen, fell into the table, knocked over a vase. I watched in slow motion as it rolled from the dining table, as it crashed to the floor. A camera set near to the kettle seemed to catch the whole thing. Their mechanical sounds, the fizz and gurgle of the servos, seemed to be laughing at me, giggling as I flailed around, lost, levitating with shock.

There was no cat, no favour for the kidnapped man. There was a trap and, like the unsuspecting fawn that wanders into the sight of the silent shooter, I was caught.

I ran from the house, the door open. I moved into the entry way, barrelled from side-to-side, kicked the gate to the street open wide, heard its hinges yowl and snap.

Then I was gone, back through the suburbs, my legs burning as I ran.

I WANTED TO KILL WATKINS.

By the time I arrived back at the lock-up, my clothes soaked with sweat, stuck to my skin, hardening with the late cold, I was flush with hatred, with vengeance. I picked up a spanner from a nearby step before I unlocked the pervert's cell, my teeth bared, my skin taut with fury.

I was ready to hammer the snivelling bastard, to smash his face to pieces.

Yet, when I hit the switch, lit the room, sought Watkins on his chair, there was no snivelling man to be found.

Where earlier there had been a beaten man, a sobbing man, a shrunken man pleading for the life of a cat that never was, now there was something else completely. A steely man, a tranquil man whose eyes glittered with success, with control.

I lifted the spanner, Watkins mouth still gagged. He didn't flinch as I held it there, above him.

No, he winked at me.

The fucker *winked* at me.

I hurled the spanner across the floor of the lock-up. It clanged loudly against the workbench, the echo of metal on stone like tintinnabulations between us.

Knowing I was defeated, I snatched at Watkins' gag, pulled it down and towards me, rocking his malicious head as I did so.

'I see you've met the cameras,' he licked his lips, spat some cotton on the ground. 'Very good. Very good *indeed.*'

'You bastard,' I panted, 'you filthy bastard. I was trying to help you.'

'Oh, shut up,' he snarled, gleefully, 'you silly, imbecilic young man. Trying to help me? You've had me tied to this chair for days. That, I assure you, isn't *help.*'

I tried to feign indifference, which didn't work one bit.

'Don't try that with me,' Watkins laughed, his frail face a sudden lantern in the glooms, 'I can see how unnerved you are.' He licked his lips and leered at me. 'It wouldn't be the first time someone has been shaken by the camera, believe me.'

The insinuation disgusted me. It was as if the devil had let its mask fall to the floor.

I asked Watkins what he wanted.

'Oh, let me see,' he began sarcastically, 'how about untying me from this bloody chair and letting me go?'

I knew I couldn't do that. Not until I had spoken to Cooper, to Hickey.

I tried to explain to Watkins. 'I have to check with the others. It isn't as simple as just letting you leave, trust me.'

'Trust you? How amusing. The fact you need to have a conference call with your gorillas is, like the fact my cameras have caught you, entirely *your* problem.'

'I'll see them now. I'll go right there.'

'As you should,' Watkins smiled. A syrupy, ogling smile, one which suggested he was almost aroused by my discomfort.

I tugged Watkins' gag back up across his mouth, without looking at him.

By the time I was back out in the night air, my heart was beating wildly, spasmodically. I was in the grip of panic, ruined by it.

I sat down on the cold concrete of a step and tried to control my breathing. I couldn't think clearly at all. For a moment, as much as it went against my true feelings, I genuinely thought of killing Watkins. The yard was deserted, the units free of onlookers. There were chemicals, barrels. I saw myself wandering in behind him, a lump hammer, a makeshift noose. I could have done it quickly, dealt with him. I could have burned him.

The thought appalled me. I shook my head furiously, tried to shatter the idea, to dissolve it.

It wouldn't have helped me, murdering Watkins. I was likely held there, captured on the easel of his lenses. Whatever we did to him then, there was every chance someone had my image, as clear as day. A shocked idiot in an alien living room.

There was nothing else for it. I had to see Cooper and Hickey.

◈

COOPER AND SHANICE WERE SAT on the sofa, eyes fixed on junk TV. Hickey reclined in the armchair, eyeing the estate night through a crack in the blinds.

I said nothing as I walked in. I just went straight to the TV, turned it off at the wall.

'Hey,' Shanice struggled up to a seating position, 'we were watching that!'

'Yeah, Danny boy,' Cooper agreed, 'could've just lowered it down.'

I ignored them. I needed to get straight to the point. 'Listen,' my throat was dry, hoarse, 'it's about Watkins…'

Cooper stood up, stretched, didn't let me finish. 'Our Dan's right, Hick,' pulling Hickey's attention away from the yowling engine of the evening, 'we've left that noncey fucker with him for too long. Time we went down there, started squeezing his neck for info.'

'*No!*' I shouted, 'Let me fucking finish, *please.*'

Cooper looked shocked by my outburst. He held his hands up, sat back down. 'Okay, sweetheart, go for your life.'

'What is it?' Hickey asked, his tone caring again, soft, like it had been the previous night.

Their faces, the shards of concern for me, it made it so much harder to tell them what I'd done, the mistake I'd made. Sitting next to the television, feeling as wiry and fleshless as an old ariel, I explained everything, right from the first time Watkins has mentioned the cat.

I expected Hickey to be livid, to pummel me there and then.

I couldn't believe it when he smiled, when his eyes grew bright, when he stood, walked over to me and rested an arm around my juddering shoulders. 'Nothing for you to worry about, Daniel,' he said in a fatherly way, as if he was pleased with a lesson learned, but knew I was punished enough already.

It was Cooper who was shaken. 'What the fuck do you mean there's nothing to worry about?' He was back on his feet, pacing the carpet, his thick arms flapping at his sides. 'I'd say there's a fair whack to worry about, Hick. Fuck's sake.'

'Nonsense.' Hickey walked to the dining table, refiled his glass from a waning bottle of scotch. 'It's pretty much what I expected.'

'How's that?' Cooper, like me, seemed to find Hickey's calmness more disconcerting than anything else. Rage would have been a blessing, peace was a curse.

Hickey sipped his drink, swirled what remained in the glass, 'We knew that Watkins was deep, a kingpin in the sleaze. It makes sense he would have something like that planned, an out. Maybe the cameras go nowhere, maybe they do. What I'll guarantee is if the feed links to anyone, it'll be some other poxy fiend. Watkins is the real deal, a prime sicko. You think they were there for the benefit of the police? In case we decide to snuff the cunt?'

'You aren't going to?' I asked feebly, my voice thin with worry. 'I'm the one on film.'

'Nah,' Hickey took another sip. 'Likely it won't come to anything like that.'

'Likely?' Cooper looked at Shanice, then back at Hickey, their eyes communicating some private arrangement, a line they wouldn't cross. 'I...I didn't think we were in the market for digging graves in the woods, Hick.'

'We aren't, mate. Christ.' Hickey sat back in the armchair, opposite me. When he spoke to Cooper, he kept his eyes on me. 'Funny you should mention the woods though, Coop.'

'Eh? Joke's gone right over my head,' Cooper replied. Gallows humour.

'Not a joke,' Hickey continued, 'just happenstance you bring up the woods. See, I've never mentioned it, but I've got a place, a cottage like, right out in the middle of nowhere up North. As remote as it gets. I've been fixing it up, here and there, when I have a few days.'

I asked what that had to do with us, with Watkins.

'Well, Daniel,' Hickey's smile widened as he spoke, 'I reckon we should take ourselves a little holiday. All of us. I think we take Watkins out there, out of sight, out of the city. There's an outhouse, we can strap the bastard up in there, torture him, get everything we want from him *and* keep clear of any friction from the cameras whilst we're at it.'

'Some fuckin holiday.' Cooper poured a drink for him and Shanice. I walked over and poured my own.

'I've got contacts all through the city,' Hickey was rolling, 'I can check in with them every so often, make sure Daniel's in the clear. I've got eyes all over, don't you worry.'

'Not really the weather for it,' Shanice added innocently, as if we were simply discussing a trip away, a few days on the coast before the summer faded to grey.

'Not quite the deciding factor, my dear,' Hickey replied without taking his eyes from me, 'but we'll take it onboard.'

'And it's a decent spot?' Cooper asked, quickly warming to the idea.

'It's perfect,' Hickey added, 'not a person for miles. Just woodland, mate, forests all around.'

Maybe I knew then, as Hickey reclined in the chair. Maybe I already saw that the escape, the move to The Red House, to the wilderness, perhaps I knew it was just another gear in the roaring engine, the machine ignited by me, driven by Hickey. Yet, if I did know, if I felt something gnaw at me, I pushed it down into my gut, down there with everything else I couldn't stand to believe.

Regardless, the plan was quickly agreed, the concrete set around the steel.

Within an hour, we were packing our things, with only our living luggage, Watkins, left to collect the next morning.

14.

Spiralling descents

WE SET OFF AT DAWN the next day.

Still gagged, now hooded, Watkins was bundled into the back of Hickey's van. His protests were cut short by several hard digs from Cooper. They rocked him into silence.

Neither Hickey nor Cooper covered their faces when we arrived at the lock-up to get Watkins.

They didn't seem to care, especially Hickey. I could never have fathomed why then, could never have even chanced my wildest, most unhinged guess, but Hickey was absolutely merry when we snatched Watkins. Hickey whistled, hummed, tapped his fingers against tabletops and walls with some inherent, private rhythm. He was abuzz, awhirl with our escape from the estate, the city.

Despite my general unease, I enjoyed seeing Watkins' smugness wiped from his face by Cooper's fists and the general indifference of the group. Shanice even laughed in his face. It was grotesque, but Watkins had manipulated me into this. It was a train of manipulation, of control. If Watkins was guilty of his perversions, then he was a high-end fraudster of gentle flesh. Hickey, Cooper and Shanice had manipulated him thereafter, trapping him with his own wet noose. Then, sealing the triangle, Watkins had fooled me.

A sequence of human ruin.

I hadn't packed much. I didn't have much to pack.

It wasn't the same for Cooper and Shanice. They were treating the trip as a regular holiday. It didn't seem to matter that we had Watkins gagged and chained in the back of the van, that the purpose for taking the journey was so sinister. No, they appeared to see it as their inaugural break, their first time away as a couple.

Shanice asked Hickey relentless questions as we packed our luggage. They bugged him massively.

'No beaches nearby then?'

'No.'

'Clean bedclothes? A good telly?'

'Take sheets. There's a TV, not sure how well it works.'

'Nice walks and all that?'

'You can walk where you like.'

'But *nice ones* though, like on the front of magazines?'

'How the fuck do I know whether they're nice or not?'

'It's your place, that's how.'

'Alright, then the walks are *nice fucking walks,* alright?'

Even Cooper got in on the act, 'Got a DVD player there, Hick?'

'Hey?'

'Got a bunch of classics I wanna show Shanice. You know, she's never seen *Predator, Double Impact, Once Upon a Time in America.*'

'I couldn't give a shit, Cooper.'

'Alright, alright, keep your pinny on. Just want to make sure there's stuff for us to do. Hope it ain't too cold.'

'There's a generator, open fires. That okay?'

'Ooh, listen to the *hotelier,'* and on they giggled.

Hickey didn't perk up and become truly happy until we picked up Watkins and had him fastened in the back of the van. Then the sun came up, his face grew lighter. The engine growled, we pulled out of the arches, out of lock-up land, out of the slums and onto the motorway.

The van was large and wide. There was space for all four of us in the front. Hickey drove, Cooper and Shanice whispered and canoodled against the opposite window. I was stuck in the centre, like a toddler.

With Cooper and Shanice distracted, I took my chance to apologise to Hickey.

'Sorry? What for?'

'For this bollocks with the cat. I shouldn't have been so stupid.'

'Look,' he turned away from the road slightly, the early traffic still sporadic, the road yet to brighten, 'If I didn't think you had more power in your heart than me and Cooper, I never would've asked you to take care of Watkins. That's why you were there, Daniel. Try and understand that.'

I didn't understand it. How could I? What they had been doing was the furthest thing from care, from heart. It was violence, terror, intimidation, so what did it matter whether Watkins was cared for? It didn't mean anything to me then.

I thanked Hickey and let him get on with the driving, content to stare out at the roads, the scenery. It had been so long since I had left the city, everything beyond it seemed like fantasy. With the radio turned up high by Hickey, I relaxed back into the seat and watched the universe as it bled into a blur.

It was such a strange sensation, leaving the city, especially the tiny, grey segment I had occupied for what seemed like my entire life.

I thought of my mother first, of her telling me about her dream; the unreal woodland, the white stag glimpsed at the treeline. It was strange to me then, when she said it, that she had spoken about forests, woodlands. In my life, first as a child with her, then as an adult alone, we had never travelled anywhere like that, not even briefly. We came from nothing, the poverty line, or as close to it as Mom would ever let us get.

In between Mom working two jobs, sometimes three, there were few opportunities to travel anywhere. When we did, it was the standard community centre coach trips to some candyfloss coastal town, its pier rusted, its beaches hard with stones and the leathery phlegm of dying jellyfish. Daytrips, three-quarters of the day on a coach, a couple of hours for me and the other ragged-kneed kids to scream in the cold waves. If I had ever seen woodland, it was in passing, as I did on our journey that day. A green wall, leaves sewn into one another, impenetrable, alien.

Like watermarks against a cliff, scars from varying tides, so each stage of leaving the urban landscape felt like a fading pointer, a ring within the trunk of a concrete tree.

I had the feeling that I was leaving there forever, even before I knew what awaited us.

From our manic estate, the morning already loud with yowling babies and tethered dogs, through the ring of ruined industry that surrounded it, we made our way from the City's hellish ring roads, onto the motorway. Those strips of road scythed through the country, through every country. The one we took was no different. It parted the suburbs and postcodes like a torpedo, edging us into unknown places.

Power stations, disparate call centres, hulking warehouses with piddling forklift workers, the outskirts of the city housed every sinister secret of the human race. Away from the citizens, the mechanisms still clunked, the gears still rusted. Even before we reached the emergent farmlands, the sight of cattle was clear, painfully so. Some fodder was farmed on two legs, some on four.

Cooper and Shanice slept against each other, their mouths open, their NHS fillings charcoal as they snored. Hickey was entranced, silent as he drove. I didn't stare, but glimpsed his expression as the engine roared, the wheels spun. Barely blinking, his mouth carved into a grin, our ersatz general pushed us onwards, to oblivion.

I felt a mixture of terror and elation as we began to move through the rural voids.

It was very much that, the *emptiness* of the world around me. There was something instantly frightening about an absence of tower blocks, shimmering office monoliths, brutalist carparks, cloned terraced houses, barking bulldogs at the windows. There was a fleeting sensation of loss, almost of bereavement for the dreadful shopping precincts, the tracksuit thugs and their BMX circuits, even for the rotting hookers who lingered around the destroyed factories near to the estate, spitting their gnarled miseries into the litter-finned canal.

It was ridiculous, but it felt like a kind of birth, as if I was being regurgitated from a sickly stomach, as if I was being spat out onto the tarmac.

I felt the kind of unease I imagined those adrift in the sea might feel. The shipwrecked loners, the thirty who cling to shards of their boats, hoping some godly searchlight will find them. I knew the names of some of the small towns and outposts we passed, but had never been to them.

We moved through the outskirts of Worcestershire, Herefordshire, circumventing the chugging cities I knew, rattling through the neon chicane, a wilderness of emerald outcrops speeding past us as we moved.

In the smaller towns, constructed around their stolen churches and bingo halls, human archetypes paraded through their planned routes, grimacing, giggling, mooning. From the older couples, their matching waxed jackets like lawns on their backs, to the young parents, their precocious toddlers marauding along the pavements, coiled litter carnations at their feet.

Monuments to old wars, bronzed soldiers with bayonets erected on poppy podia. Proud gardeners, neighbours at the edge of their drives, envious, complimentary, phony, bored. The opening time regulars waiting for their doors to open. So like all boozers, like those from my estates, their rheumy eyes watched the clock inside their chests, the mucky ticker. Their thin lips chapped, licked dry in anticipation of the first of the long pints.

Hickey took each road as though he knew them intimately, and maybe he did.

Then, as we made our way to what we would come to know as *The Red House*, I knew so little about Hickey's past. The towns he had lived in, the people he had trodden, even the universe he looked out on. An pseudo leader, a hulk with more brains than Cooper, Hickey played the tune and us rats scampered upwards from the sewers, following his melody into the night.

The towns soon changed to villages. Intermittent homes of matching stone, their ornate doors bright, ringed by flowers. *Luxton Oak, Bugle Under Moss, Hedley, Scupper's Run,* every little conurbation was alien to me, their names like songs from a medieval past. Well-bred dogs peered out from privet hedgerows and heavy gates, their noses wet, healthy. Their eyes seemed to follow the van as we carved our path through the curves and creases of their land. Their heightened senses told them we were something else, spun from somewhere else, something alien, perhaps something to be feared or hated. It didn't matter to me. It still doesn't.

From the villages, we passed through uninterrupted farmland, with the only homes being those of the farming families. Industrial cowsheds, corrugated kill-rooms well away from the roads. I could hear the sounds of the cattle, their doom-songs, those guttural shanties they shared and remembered. The sheep were fallen clouds, the grazing cows like mighty pups.

Occasional pheasants sprinted towards oncoming traffic, their bred-for-shooting brains depriving them of even a sporting chance at survival. Hickey ran over three or four north of an area called *Lawnton Marsh*. He didn't even react when they registered beneath the wheels. I felt them die in the wheel arches. Snapped and clattered, their feeble bodies meeting the oncoming machine, nowhere near ready for what lay ahead of them. I can empathise now. I can feel the momentary terror of the thundering monster they could not outrun.

It's funny...I can remember a fleeting idea then, during that part of the journey, an idea that has since become essential to me.

As I had seen cities above and below cities in my nightmares, so I now saw how every human stratum looks at those below theirs as a hallow. To those straddling the average, the middle-classes, estates like the one on which we had lived were hidden places, places to be feared. They were places of night creatures, of the wretched and the bizarre, the hungry and the violent.

Above them, for the wealthy, so the environs of suburban landscapes were hallow-like. They were places of intrigue, places that shimmered, places to investigate for kicks, for a feeling of terror, or excitement.

Cities were hallows to those who lived beyond them. Every level below, every cavernous nowhere was something to be feared, peopled by goblin-men, ethereal hags with hypodermic fingernails.

I saw then that there was a spiral, a chute down which we were all sliding and, when it mattered most, all that separated us was fear of what awaited us below and the rungs on which we could firmly grip, just long enough to watch others vanish first.

Cooper and Shanice began to stir after a couple of hours' kip.

When Cooper spoke, his voice was deep, thick with sleep. 'Where the fuck are we, Hick?' He stretched, yawned, playfully held my head under his arm, then relaxed his grip into a hug. 'You alright, Danny boy?'

I nodded, twisted his arm a little. 'Just taking in the scenery, plenty to see.'

'Plenty of fuck all,' Cooper replied, then asked Hickey where we were again.

'North,' Hickey said blankly, his eyes never leaving the road.

'Well, that clears that up,' Cooper laughed, leaned towards the windscreen, eyed the countryside. 'How long till we get to where we're going?'

'You sound like a toddler,' Hickey half-smiled, 'do you need a wee-wee?'

'I could certainly use a piss, mate, sure. We need food and booze though, so we'll have to stop somewhere before we get too far away from the real world.'

Something about how Cooper said that, *too far away from the real world*. There was a tremble of uncertainty in his voice, fear even. I hadn't thought until then, but seeing Cooper away from the tiny galaxy of the estate, a place in which he occupied some kind of celestial significance, was strange for him, as if he had been stripped of rank, dishonourably discharged from his status as concrete magnate, the wrangler of the rotten.

Now he was just a passenger in a van, no more control or understanding than me.

'We cut back onto the motorway in a while,' Hickey assured Cooper. 'There's a service station before we move back into the wilds. Probably the last big spot we'll have before we start to get right out there, into the sticks. We'll stop off, have a breather, stretch our legs. Plenty of shops there, we can stock up, maybe get a meal.'

'Oh, hopefully they've got a Mackey's, Burger King or somethin,' Shanice said, perking up, 'I'd kill for a whopper about now.'

'Dirty bugger,' Cooper pulled a silly face, drew a giggle from his girl.

Hickey looked at me through the rear-view mirror, his eyes humourless, suddenly like rivet holes in the brick.

❡

HICKEY PARKED THE VAN AT the edge of the service station carpark.

There were hardly any cars around. Those parked nearby were empty. With a nod to Cooper, Hickey went to the back of the van, unlocked the doors and checked on Watkins.

It had almost been easy to forget he was there, *the prisoner*, trussed-up in the dark, gagged, invisible. I could hear the low mumble of words exchanged, but couldn't make them out. There was a sudden thud, something hit the inside of the van. Silence followed.

When Hickey stepped back on the tarmac, he was opening and closing the fingers of his right hand. 'He won't be bothering anyone for a while,' he said, 'we'll get him something to eat later on. We'll have to pull over when we get back out there, let the miserable cunt relieve himself.'

A strange mixture of people haunted the service station as evening arrived.

Salesmen sulked over Styrofoam dinners. Their sunken shoulders and ageing faces made them seem partially melted. Catalogues of their brands sat next to them on their tables, demanding to be revised, memorised. Bathroom fittings, living room sets, cleaning products, a thousand types of hammers, they were out there on a rotting catwalk, pushing their junk to indifferent clients.

Elderly couples paused mid-holiday, their retirement years allowing them to become motorhome ghouls, prowling the roads for sites and shower-blocks. Some seemed happy, almost giddy. Others were silent as they ate, barely casting an eye at their partners. I hated that, one of the things I really despised about people was the way they could discount those they shared their lives with, the way they could treat them as coldly as the grave they would eventually occupy. These people would talk more to the tombstone of their deceased on summer Sunday mornings when they turned up to refresh the flowers. It was silly, facile, an example of human beings' misunderstanding of time.

Cooper and Shanice ran into one of the arcade kiosks, laughing riotously as they pushed coins into a game with two plastic machineguns. They were blasting zombies to pixilated oblivion by the time me and Hickey ordered a coffee and took a seat.

'Feeling better,' Hickey asked me, 'lighter?'

I didn't know what he meant.

'Pressure's off,' he shrugged, 'Watkins won't be anything to worry about now.'

'I don't know about that. Whatever happens to him, mine's the face on the videos, the photos.'

'That doesn't mean a thing,' Hickey paused, thanked the waitress as she brought the coffees, sliding a fiver into her crinkled hand. He waited until she had gone, then continued, 'No matter what he was threatening us with, Daniel, he'll be too shook up to ever follow through with it, believe me.'

I drank my coffee, offered Hickey a quick smile, tried to look like I believed him.

Cooper and Shanice eventually joined us at the table, their cheeks red from laughter, 'You wanna have a crack on that shooter, Danny boy, proper laugh, isn't it, Shan?'

'Oh yeah,' Shanice agreed, looking more like Katie Pop than ever, her eyes childlike, lit with amusement. 'Except your man here can't shoot for shit.'

'Eh? I was blasting zombies left, right and centre, love.'

'If you say so.'

'Let's eat.' Hickey was impatient. 'We've got a long way to go, trust me.'

'Fair fucks,' Cooper grinned, 'I could murder a burger.'

'That right?' Shanice winked at me. 'Because you couldn't murder a zombie for love nor money.'

And so it went, the playful couple, the focused, thunderhead driver, and me.

We ate burgers, chatted like we didn't have a care in the universe. Cooper and Shanice began to start a shopping list, before we stopped at the little supermarket at the far side of the service station. Roles were being developed, right there and then. We didn't have to say anything, arrange a single thing. Hickey watched, listened, okayed the couple to buy whatever they thought we needed. 'I'll cover it, no worries,' Hickey said, as he wiped his mouth. 'Money isn't an issue at the minute.'

Cooper and Shanice added more booze to the list after Hickey said that.

'You sure?' Cooper paused, asked Hickey again.

'Definitely,' he smiled, 'I'm the one who's dragging us out here, aren't I? Least I can do is make it as fun for you all as possible. Like I say, stock up on whatever you want. There's nothing out there, where we're going. You could walk for days without finding a loaf of bread.'

'How long are we gonna be out there, Hick?' Cooper twigged that Hickey wasn't exaggerating. I could sense his recurrent trepidation, like a moth on my cheek.

'As long as it takes,' Hickey answered coolly. 'Few days, a week or so, however long we need to squeeze Watkins' throat enough.'

'Fair fucks,' Cooper repeated, comfortable with the phrase and happy enough with Hickey's calmness.

The surety of Hickey was mesmerising in a way, almost attractive. He was unshaken, relaxed, certain. He led the line. It hadn't happened immediately, but he had grown into the alpha. We all knew it. Cooper may have hulked over him at the gym, but Hickey was stronger. Leaner, his muscles cut and squared, rather than bloated, Hickey had assumed the head of the phalanx after the incident with Big Barry, the first time he had carved the eye on flesh. Since then, whether Cooper was louder, whether I tried to protest, what Hickey said went. That journey was no different.

When Hickey had finished eating, he stood up, nodded over at the relentless sliding doors of the service station's entranceway. 'Let's get a shake on. Get the supplies. Daniel and I will check on Watkins, make sure he's tied down firm enough for the ride. It'll be dark when we get there, I'll need to fish the spotlights out of the lockbox too. We don't want to be veering offtrack when we get near the cottage. It's deadly.'

Cooper and Shanice hurried off to the little supermarket, their fingers linked, Shanice's head against Cooper's billboard shoulder. The perfect holidaying couple, candyfloss and neon smiles. I can still picture Hickey watching them, his expression genuinely curious at first before, as was his way, returning to a resting, leering, self-amused position.

We walked out to the carpark, heading for the van. Before we reached it, Hickey stopped me, his hand on my waist. He turned me back towards the service station, to where the intermittent travellers bustled, yacked, laughed, argued.

'Circle after circle,' he nodded, 'all following their assigned routines, not a free thought in their heads, Daniel. Not a single unlimited idea, a notion of the land on which they walk.'

I asked if we had free thoughts, or just a pervert in the back of a van.

'Both,' Hickey laughed, 'I can't explain just yet, but we're operating *outside* of all this, Daniel. We are moving away from shoddy conventions, moving towards the realisation.'

'I'll just be pleased to get as far away from the police as possible.' I found myself looking in every direction, wondering when Watkins' camera trick would kick in.

'The police,' Hickey laughed again, louder this time, 'they can't touch us now. Shit, if they tried, their fingers would move right through us.'

With that, Hickey opened the van, jumped in, towering above the prostrate Watkins. I watched as Hickey lowered himself to the tethered man, then the doors slammed shut, Hickey keen to speak to Watkins in private.

Cooper and Shanice took almost an hour. When they returned, they pushed three trollies, all full to the wiry brim; two with food, one with booze. Cooper handed what was left of the cash back to Hickey, who didn't even look at how much they'd spent.

'Got everything we'll need for a few days,' Cooper said proudly, winking at me as he did so, 'stocked to the roof, don't you boys worry.'

'Yeah,' Shanice thumbed the mountains of plastic-wrapped trash, 'meals for days, snacks n'all.'

Hickey wasn't interested in what they'd bought. 'Just get it loaded up sharpish,' he growled, 'we've still got a long way to go and we're gonna be hitting the worst part in the dark now.'

Shanice sang some shitty pop song as she and Cooper loaded up the van, completely ignoring Watkins, around whom they stacked the bags and bottles.

'And don't you think about wrecking any of this,' Cooper warned Watkins. 'Don't wanna give me an excuse to use broken glass, do you?'

Watkins ignored Cooper, closed his eyes, retreated into the thicker shadows at the bulkhead of the van.

We reversed out of the service station, into the deepening purple of evening, the sky above us clear, cold, already bright with an audience of burning planets.

The remaining daylight faded quickly. The roadsides splintered, changed from something tangible, to smears of fleeting blur. The distance beyond the roads became impossibly dark. Streetlights disappeared, the motorways a distant memory. Alien highways, an end to other vehicles.

In the time I had before the light vanished completely, I noticed a different landscape, a barren, haunted world.

Forests loomed from the clouds, ringing the horizon like bitter mourners. Gone were the paddocked fields, the uniformed crops and cattle of the farmlands. Instead, dug into the rock of emergent cliffs, only occasional animals looked out at the lonesome, unaccompanied van that chugged through their landscape, its engine sounds a grizzled song for the wilderness.

I quickly felt a sense of terror, one I tried to swallow. There was a weight to the wilderness, a chorus of crushing voices, all of them bellowing intangible words to me. As the darkness grew, as my field of vision narrowed only to the headlit road before us, so I was unable to shake the feeling I was being lowered into an abyss, cast into the fetid guts of some well, a place far from empty, far from human.

I couldn't have known what was to come, not in a literal sense, but that feeling I had, that choking notion, should have told me that the soil was being shovelled over our heads.

Eventually, there was nothing of the world around us to see, only the potholed tarmac beneath the headlights, the winding roads, the occasional bracken, silver-lit, alive with feral eyes.

We were all quiet, even Cooper and Shanice.

I think back to that journey now, that final part of it and, somehow, it is impossible to comprehend the route we took through the heavy dark, the roads which may have led here. There was a rollercoaster sensation, a notion of climbing great heights, an occasional parity with winter-white stars beside us. There were spiralling descents, stomach-rolling lows.

Hickey's eyes stared everywhere as he manoeuvred the van along tracks, wide-open roads, back into narrow trenches of dirt. The map seemed to be chiselled into the interior of his skull, carved like a brail motorway.

In terms of where we were, how far North we had travelled, that too was a mystery and any questions shot at Hickey were just ignored. The enormous and silver-skinned lakes of Cumbria had passed by hours earlier, not long after the service station. Already night by then, all I had been able to discern of them, or what I thought was them, was the occasional reflection of the night sky, a trickery of two moons, both full and clean.

Thereafter, it was guesswork and nothing more.

I tried to map the route on my phone, as did Cooper, but there was no reception, just dead, black plastic in our hands. I had to assume we had crossed the border, that we were in Scotland, but still very much on the mainland. We had left in the morning, the smoking Midlands behind us, northern towns and cities peering gloomily from between the chimneys of refineries and power stations, their cathedral spires and high-rise homes little more than needles in a grey nowhere.

Thereafter, once we had moved into total darkness, the evidence of other people, other homes became beyond sparse, almost totally non-existent.

I remember there was a small hamlet, some tiny conurbation, no more than three buildings, just before we reached the Red House.

I couldn't see the detail of the buildings, but cubes of orange light stood like framed fires in the dark. I had to believe they were homes, because furnaces or crematoria had no place on the tundra.

Sweat poured from Hickey's face as we approached the final decline, swirling down a thin and heavily uneven track. The van rocked badly, everything about it seemed suddenly rickety, as if it could fall apart at any moment.

'Cooper, the spotlight,' Hickey ordered.

'Gotcha,' Cooper obliged, lifting the spot from the footwell. He wound down his window and lit up the ground ahead of us. Deep, almost impossible trenches in the dirt. Hickey slowed the van to a crawl, easing the wheel from side-to-side, trying desperately to avoid letting the van slip into one of the ditches, something which would have been impossible to extricate ourselves from, especially in the dead of night.

'Fuckin hell, Hick, where you brought us, lad?' Cooper struggled to keep the light on the ground as we shook and rocked, staggering along the smashed track.

'Don't worry about anything other than keeping that light on the road.' Hickey was pressed against the steering wheel, his knuckles bone-white, 'Not much further to go.'

Shanice was silent, her face pale enough to light the interior of the van. I must have looked the same, just as neon with fear and unease.

Occasionally, shaken off course by the movement of the van, the spotlight lurched upwards away from the road, affording us a glimpse of what lay beside us. Gnarled, fierce woodland, matted and machine-like. Only momentary pictures, monochrome, barely discernible, but what I saw frightened me. The eyes play tricks, the forest is a witch.

Just as I thought our luck had run out, that the van would surely topple into one of the moat-like voids around us, Hickey killed the engine. We had arrived.

'Alright, listen.' Hickey turned to us for the first time in hours, 'The Red House, our place, it's about two-hundred metres east of here. Get what you'll need for tonight together and we'll get the rest tomorrow. It's dark, it's cold, the going's tricky underfoot, forget the rest of the shopping and all that, just what you need *now*.'

I asked about Watkins. 'Where are we putting him?'

'Fuck him,' Hickey said as he stepped out of the van, 'he can stay in here tonight. We'll get him when it gets light.'

Shanice said she was cold. 'Will we be able to get a fire going?'

'Yeah,' Hickey spat in the dirt, cleared his throat, 'but the jenny'll have to wait until sunup.'

'Who's *Jenny?*' Shanice asked, innocently enough.

'The fucking *generator.*' Hickey slammed the door and walked to the front of the van.

'Miserable sod,' Shanice muttered, as she collected a few things and eased out of the van behind Cooper.

I was last out.

As my feet touched the dirt, there was an immediate change of atmosphere, something I hadn't experienced before. As if gravity had increased, I felt so much pressure that my ears popped. There was a terrible weight to the air, along with a strange, rotting odour, a perfume of absolute decay.

'Stinks here,' Shanice confirmed, covering her nose with a sleeve.

118

'Yeah,' Cooper agreed, 'what's that about, Hick? Shit-pipe gone south?'

'Don't worry about it,' Hickey hissed, 'just the reek of dying trees, undergrowth. We're right out in it now. Maybe even a dead deer. You'll get used to it.'

It was more than that. I knew it. There was something that throbbed in the dark, something which licked at us. We were isolated in the intangible night. Imposters, the blind, the rubes. We couldn't see what looked back at us yet, the faces that stared back from the shadows. We wouldn't see them for days to come, but they were there. They were always there.

I slipped first, my right foot turned over the edge of one of the trenches. Hickey caught me under my arm, lifted me up like a featherweight. 'Easy, Daniel.'

'What's with these fucking drops?' I spluttered, getting to my feet.

'Irrigation,' Hickey answered, 'we're in a valley here. You'll see when it gets light. Risk of flooding, got to protect the house.'

Then, as if summoned by Hickey's mention of it, The Red House came into view. At least its outline did. A stone cottage, twice as long as it was tall, a couple of outbuildings barely visible beside it. There was little to see beyond its moonlit shape, the way the glooms were sharper from the jagged rocks.

Hickey fumbled with the keys. He dropped them and they rang out loudly on the stone doorstep.

Something seemed to reply far behind us, a cry of equal pitch. We all turned to face the direction from which we had walked, the origin of the sound.

'Watkins can scream all he wants,' Hickey said, picking up the keys, 'nobody out here to pay any attention to his shit.'

The door groaned open, musty air welcomed us in. We could make out basic furniture, the tableau of a simple kitchen. As Hickey marched into the shadows, the rest of us stood there, just inside the door, no idea where to go, what was ahead of us.

Hickey worked quickly. We could see his busy arms in the glooms beyond the kitchen. He knew where the fireplace was, the firewood beside it. A sound of dry newspaper, of kindling. The percussion of livid wood being places upon it, echoing in the stone maw. The first yellow eye of fire winked at us from the black. We made our way towards it. I felt immediately calmed by the familiarity of warmth, the security of fire. Quickly, hungrily, the flames took hold and the fireplace was suddenly alive, the room ahead of it lit.

Two sofas, two armchairs, a naked coffee table between them. There were lamps, but no electricity. I could see curtains at the windows. They were open. I drew them, wanting to retain the heat the fire produced. I could see the vague interiors of framed pictures, landscapes, a few books scattered on the surfaces, the uneven large tiles of the floor beneath my feet, but little else.

Hickey pushed the sofas towards the fire. 'Get a seat, warm up,' he grinned, his pumpkin-jawed jagged smile beamed like a lantern as he spoke. 'No point sorting the bedrooms tonight, they'll be freezing. Let's just get some grub down us and snatch a few hours' kip here, in the warm. We'll take care of everything else when it gets light, alright?'

'Fine with me,' Cooper yawned, 'could use a slash though. Where's the pisser?'

'Leave it for now,' Hickey replied, 'piss out front. I need to sort the plumbing first thing.'

'What about me?' Shanice asked.

'I'm sure you've done worse outdoors,' Hickey smirked, then caught Cooper's eye and added, 'like we all have, eh?'

'Just for tonight,' Shanice shrugged, 'as long as we can get the loo working in the morning.'

Hickey took the chair to the far right of the room, barely visible so far away from the fire. Cooper and Shanice took the sofa to the left of me. I was in the centre, sat nearest to the sofa.

I felt shellshocked, completely uneven. I put it down to the journey, the length of it. Also the final hours, the not knowing, the confusion of direction, of location. It all combined, along with everything that had occurred during the days before it, to make me feal unreal, like I no longer existed.

I ignored it as exhaustion. I plunged everything else down to the silent depths, to where it couldn't gnaw at me.

There was nothing to do but sleep. It didn't come easily, but I found it eventually, the room around me fading into obscurity, plunged into nothingness.

15.

A universe away from the City

I THOUGHT I HAD WOKEN first, but when I looked to my right, Hickey was gone.

Dawn light came through the moth-eaten curtains and speckled the stone floor. Pocked by the polka dot sunshine, I could see the occasional dust that covered the granite. The final embers of the fire hissed at me from the gnarled grate, lustreless, spent.

The sofa creaked as I sat up and snorted. Cooper and Shanice were still asleep, wrapped around one another, head resting on head, fingers intertwined.

The room was clearer now, albeit the light was still diluted, unusually green. The furniture was simple, decades old. Dressers lined the walls, odds and ends littering them. Forgotten whatnots, half-mended mechanisms from missing devices, dogeared notebooks, broken biros stabbed through the rings that linked the damp-warped pages.

I stood as quietly as I could, pulled up my hood against the cold. I walked through to the kitchen, back the way we had entered the previous night. Even simpler than the living room. A fridge, a chest freezer lining a bare wall, cupboards in various states of disarrangement, some of the doors broken at a hinge, hanging there winglike, the shelves empty within.

The sink was deep, heavy crock, the taps tall, brass and swan-necked. I turned the cold water tap and the whole system groaned painfully. I didn't fancy my chances of getting anything from it but, after a few seconds and a splutter of dust and muck, clear, incredibly cold water poured out eagerly. I cupped my hands, ladled some into my mouth and cleared my throat.

I needed to piss, so pulled back the front door. Somehow, the notion of seeing what the area looked like hadn't entered my thoughts so, when I stepped into that alien place, the shock of not wandering out into the screeching estate morning hit me hard enough to almost knock me from my feet.

I clutched the door handle behind me as I took in the view.

To try and clearly explain, to illustrate the immensity of what I felt, is almost impossible.

Everything was above us. It was immediately obvious that, wherever we were, we were at the very pit of a crater. Far beyond the floor of a valley, we seemed to be at the lowest point of a huge, verdant basin.

Moving away from the front of the cottage, steep hills on the north and east sides led sharply upwards into menacing garlands of forest. Tightly knit, the trees loomed over the insignificant buildings. Bare of any birdsong, the woodland silence was deafening. Like seawater in my ears, the quiet thrummed and danced. It dizzied me. The sensation from the looming woodland was as if a breath was being held, the air sucked away from me, from the house, lingering in the lowest chambers of some enormous, invisible lungs, waiting to be exhaled.

I hadn't stepped far enough away from the cottage to look behind it, south, to where the sallow sun shone almost sickly on my back.

West, over to my left, there was a sheer rock face, like a quarry wall. Aged fencing hung from its rim, broken, shattered by decades of bluster. Occasional branches grew from the stone. Chewed fingers pointed down at us as the monsters sniggered beyond.

It quickly dawned on me that we must have driven in from the south, as there was no discernible track or road on either side or ahead of me. What I could see though, what gaped far more than I had imagined they would, were the deep, stream-like trenches in the earth. Absent of water, yet muddy and musty at their beds, the heavy grooves wound around the front of the cottage, marrying there.

There was space between them, with no pattern apparent. I remembered Hickey saying they were for irrigation. That seemed likely.

I couldn't see the van. I had no geography to follow. I tied my laces, came out of the doorway, followed the building to the right.

As I turned around the cottage's side wall, I bumped straight into Hickey.

'Morning Daniel,' he chirped, his eyes vivid, awake.

I began to respond, but noticed that he was dragging Watkins behind him.

'Had to get this mollusc out of the van before he pebble-dashed our groceries,' Hickey explained.

Watkins was still gagged and, through the ties of his wrists, Hickey had fastened another rope, with which he led Watkins along on his knees.

I caught Watkins' eyes as Hickey passed me. Glazed over, apparently sleepless, they suggested Watkins was deep in shock, looking out into the unwinding nightmare, unsure what was real, what wasn't.

'I'm going to get him set up in the outhouse, over there,' Hickey continued. 'Once he's sorted, we'll get the shopping, light the jenny, get things moving, eh?'

I nodded, still half-asleep, unable to take my eyes of Watkins as he fell onto his elbows, fought his way up, only to fall again as Hickey quickened his pace.

Once outside the front of the cottage, there in the glare of everything above us, Hickey stopped Watkins and tore the gag away.

Watkins' lips were chapped and swollen, his cheeks sunken around them.

'First thing's first,' Hickey grinned, 'start as we mean to go on.'

I didn't know what he meant, until he pulled the pliers from his pocket. I recognised them from the workshop at the yard, the place where Watkins had been held. I had no idea why I remembered them, unless it was just an attempt to look at anything other than the kidnapped man when I was there, with even a tool-scattered workbench preferable to the bastard's searching, deceitful eyes.

Hickey turned Watkins towards the woodlands above, towards the sheer rockface, to the slavering void ahead of us. Hickey looked up, took in the looming universe above our crater.

Then, almost in slow motion, almost inconsequential and arbitrary, Hickey gripped Watkins' jaw with his right hand and, with the pliers gripped by his left, forced them into Watkins' mouth, to the upper tier of his teeth. Clamping into one of his front teeth, Hickey snapped it out of Watkins' mouth, as easily as he would have broken the shell of a peanut.

Watkins screamed. A terrible, rasping, feral yowl. The noise echoed around us, the shout called back to itself in fading waves.

With blood across his knuckles, Hickey went back for another tooth and, turning it this time, side-to-side, back and forth, eventually tugged out the other of Watkins' upper front teeth.

Another scream, a desperate shout accompanied by Hickey's triumphant laughter.

Watkins folded into the dirt, the two teeth ahead of him, grinning back. Plectrums on the stage.

'Do you see?' Hickey asked, kicking Watkins in the back as he did so. 'Do you see *how alone* we are out here, huh? There's nobody to save you, nobody to listen to you beg and scream. That's just the beginning, Watkins.'

With that, Hickey snatched at the rope and dragged Watkins away, towards the larger of the two outbuildings to the East of the cottage. Suddenly, somehow following Hickey as he pulled Watkins' prone body along, the birdsong returned.

Not like any chirruping, twittering, squawking song I had ever heard, the noise which came down to us from the trees was brutal, baying, baleful. A dawn chorus caked in blood, a love song spewed from serrated mouths.

Stunned, I backed away from what I'd seen, quickly finding myself in the arms of Cooper who, along with Shanice, had been woken by Watkins' agony.

'What's all the fuckin racket?' Cooper asked me grumpily, his eyes gluey with sleep dust.

I told them about the teeth.

'Jesus,' Cooper stretched, 'bit early in the morning for all that lark, isn't it?'

Cooper must've read the shock on my face. 'Come on, Danny boy' he gripped my arm, 'it's not like Hick was bringing him to a spa, was it?'

◊

HICKEY RETURNED A LITTLE WHILE later, Watkins' dried blood freckling his fist.

'Right then,' he nodded to us all, 'let's get this place up and running, eh?'

We went back and forth to the van, collecting the food and booze, the service station shopping. I don't know why we made so many trips, it had only taken one the previous night. I wonder whether it was a sign of the days to come, an acknowledgment there was no reason to rush the mundane, when arcane and rotten things would need our attention first.

I could see a wet patch on the floor of the van. The smell of stale piss hung in the space.

'Leave the doors open,' Copper held his nose, 'best to air to this thing out. I ain't riding home in it stinking like this.'

Riding home... all graves demand a guest.

We didn't talk about Watkins that morning. Not a single word was mentioned by Hickey, no recognition of him ripping Watkins' teeth out.

Cooper and Shanice hadn't seen it, but I had. More so even than the act itself, what struck me, what rocked me, was the sight of Hickey turning Watkins away from me, away from the cottage, the way he faced the woodland above us. He seemed to be presenting Watkins to someone, to something.

I wondered then whether there were others up there, acquaintances of Hickey's. I wondered whether they watched, chuckling as Hickey delivered the brutality they had arranged. I also wondered whether it was just a demonstration, just as Hickey had said; a way for Watkins to know he was alone here, no saviours, no escape.

After we had unloaded the shopping, Hickey and Cooper set about starting the generator. It was the kind of thing Cooper loved, being elbow-deep in machinery, his biceps and forearms engorged in the oily metal.

I had no idea about things like that, practical things, not in any detail anyhow. If I had been here alone, I would've just kept the fire burning, cooked on its flames, slept in front of it, the generator left to rust, to decay.

Cooper and Hickey laughed and chatted as they worked. Football, films, twats they'd known over the last few years. They enjoyed it. It could have been an afternoon at the yard, some decorating at the house. Like the arrangement of the sofas and chairs the previous night, the places we took, where we instinctively sat, we were responding to the same blueprint, as if our positions and roles were mandatory.

Hickey and Cooper had the generator purring in a couple of hours. The freezer hummed, the fridge too. Lamps were tested, winking from their dusty bulbs, ready for the dark.

Hickey showed Cooper where the TV was and, almost unbelievably, Cooper had brought the DVD player, along with the films he was keen to show Shanice. There were three bedrooms in the cottage itself. Cooper and Shanice took the large one, the only one with a double bed. I asked Hickey which of the two singles he wanted.

'Neither, cheers,' he shrugged, 'I'm taking the other outhouse, the one next to Watkins. I put a bunk in there last time I was here. I prefer having my own space, you know?'

I did know.

The bedrooms in the cottage were bare, basic. A bed, a wardrobe, a table with an unpolished lamp.

Shanice and Cooper set about making up their bed, unfolding the clean sheets Shanice had brought along. I hadn't thought of that, but she had brought some for me too. Not for Hickey though.

'Sod him,' Shanice whispered to me, 'probably sleeps in the fucking mud anyhow. Looks like he does.'

'That or the bin,' I joked with her, finding the natural warmth she had the only semblance of humanity apparent at that very moment, 'if he sleeps at all.'

Next was the plumbing. There was a bathroom in the cottage, but the toilet hadn't been flushed in weeks, the taps turned on, the shower or bath run. I didn't know the details, but there was some kind of sump, some filter, some pipe somewhere amidst the mangle of metal angles which needed to be drained.

I walked around the perimeter of the cottage as they worked on that, hearing an eventual successful flush, the patter of a thunderous shower, the applause of gratified men.

I wondered about Watkins, how his mouth must have felt. I had broken two teeth in my life, both near the back of my mouth. They had been taken out by a dentist, the pain dissolved by dope, the experience bleached and cheery. The idea of them being ripped away, tugged out with hatred, was impossible to appreciate, to understand.

More than anything else, I tried to understand my surroundings, to analyse the place, the topography. The forests above were immediately frightening, their darkness, the moistness of their shadows, it was a land I didn't know, every high-rise destroyed, splintered, every neon street deleted completely, replaced by a jungle of teeth, a new world.

There, looking up at the snickering trees, it would have been easy to believe that the cities of my life were imaginary, that they had never existed, that they were merely part of that recurrent nightmare. The first hints of dream realities. The first seeds of the merger between what was, what is and what would come.

I saw then that understanding is an amalgam of perceptions, an admixture of realities; some fixed, framed, others opaque, hovering at the edges of their neighbours.

I recalled my mother's funeral, the feeling that the mourners were something else, something beyond human. I had been alone on that morning, just a thin figure in dark clothes. Yet, I hadn't been alone there, I knew that. Whether a conspirator was watching from the treeline, whether it was Hickey or the other one, I couldn't be sure, but they weren't the ones I meant, the ones about whom I was becoming cognisant.

No, the ones I saw were winter skins and luminous droves. They were the bastards born from my mother's own fluttering death dreams.

◊

I RETURNED TO THE HOUSE and found that Cooper and Hickey had completely fixed all the plumbing.

'Elbow deep in shite, but the flush is working like a charm,' Cooper announced merrily, another box ticked, another aspect of the familiar installed.

Hickey went to shower, Watkins' dried blood like tobacco stains on his fingers.

Shanice made lunch. I helped her. We had barely spoken, but I found that I continued to enjoy it when we did. I listened as Shanice talked me through the tricks of making a perfect sandwich.

'You have to get the spread to the very edge of the slices, you know?'

I nodded, seeing someone different from the skinny waif we met that first evening, or the phony Katie Pop lure spun out for the slavering internet creeps. Shanice was herself now, more colour in her, the drugs apparently gone, or going that way. She and Cooper seemed genuinely happy together, naturally so.

It is moments like that I look back on now, as the ashes pop and snigger and the temperature drops.

'After that,' Shanice continued, her face fixed on the task beneath her, 'it's about doing the same with whatever's going in there. Like here, look, you gotta get the cheese to cover the whole lot too, or the ham. Same thing, no matter what.' She carefully flattened the fillings, edged them out along the bread, almost marvelling at having all the food to hand to do it.

I asked about the salad.

'Oh yeah,' she laughed, 'you gotta slice the lettuce up real thin, like they do at Mackey's and the other burger places. Nothing worse than when you get one of them sloppy whole lettuce leaves, is there? Nah, it's like getting a wet flannel in your sarnie. Soaks the bread n'all, has the whole lot falling apart. Cooper likes his bread dry.'

'He does,' I felt myself smile at knowing that, 'has a real moan if it's sloppy.'

'I worried you might be jealous,' Shanice said out of nowhere, sheepishly. It took me off-guard. She didn't look up from the plate.

'Jealous?'

'It's silly, ain't it? Dumb. I know, but… you and him have been mates for ages, living at the house and…well…it's shit sometimes when someone else comes along, no matter how they do it. Like, I know we weren't just two people meeting in the pub or somethin, what with all the paedo bashing and that.'

'I'm not jealous,' I assured her, 'I like having you about, if I'm honest.'

'You do?'

'Yeah. Cooper was lonely, bored. I could tell. I think it's the only reason he ever suggested that whole online vigilante bollocks to begin with.'

'It's good to get these bastards though,' Shanice turned to me, 'they've got it coming.'

'They're shit for sure,' I sliced a tomato, kept my eyes away from Shanice's, no idea why, 'but there're other ways. Look at us here, stuck out here, Watkins in that shed. I don't know how it'll end.'

Shanice placed her hand on mine. 'It'll be alright, you know. Hickey's scary, he'll get Watkins to fess-up, get you off the hook. Don't worry, we'll be back at the house in a few days.'

'Lucky us,' I squeezed Shanice's hand, gently lifted mine away and returned to the tomato.

'Anyhow,' Shanice brightened, her tiny hands on the wings of her hips, 'just gotta enjoy a few days in the sticks, haven't we?'

'*Oi oi*' Cooper emerged from the bedroom, his clothes changed, 'what's the word on these sarnies, my lovelies?'

'Coming along just nicely,' Shanice brushed Cooper away playfully as he squeezed her waist from behind. 'Hook that DVD player up, pick a film.'

'Ah yes,' Cooper said, overjoyed, 'reckon it's time you met my pal, John Rambo.'

◊

THE SANDWICHES EATEN, I WASHED the dishes as the afternoon sky began to bruise into an early, rural dusk.

Hickey didn't eat with us. He took sandwiches to the outhouse, with one for Watkins. Maybe a break in the torture, or maybe he fed it to him in a fist.

130

I found that night came on quickly without the fever of streetlights and neon.

I stood at the sink and watched as Shanice and Cooper rearranged the living room. They altered the positions of the chairs, the sofas, the coffee table, even a couple of the cabinets. I wasn't sure if they even realised they were doing it but, in no time at all, the room had the same layout as the living room back on the estate. Familiar geography, a tableau that made them comfortable, a nesting hour.

I left the cottage for a walk. I didn't make it far. The darkness at the doorstep was almost impenetrable.

However, above us, in the woodland, it was a different story.

White light cast down from the bracken. Not white by moonlight, but from something at its heart. The moon was opposite and, somehow, I could feel the wetness, the soddening pour of the galaxy itself. I could feel that I was bathing in the seas of the moon, drowning in them.

It was amazing, that first proper night. The moon sat opposite the thickest woodland, perched eye-like, peering. It silvered sheer shards lit the quarry face, but didn't meet the woven trees that mirrored it. They burned with their own neon, the glowing source impossible to discern. The light throbbed, it moved, it played with what I saw. It seemed to be either worshipping the moon, or challenging it. A silent, shimmering war.

Hickey had insisted there was nobody else out here. The light in the woodland suggested otherwise. I didn't want to say anything to Cooper. Maybe I should have.

I didn't have long to linger on the thought. Hickey edged into the night, the lit bulb from the outhouse catching my attention. When I looked back up at the woods, the white light was gone, replaced by a curtain of blackness heavier than all of the boulders in the world.

'A universe away from the city,' Hickey asked as he walked to my side, 'what do you think, Daniel?'

I told him I didn't know what to think. 'I've never been anywhere like this before.' I zipped up my coat against the cold.

'No,' Hickey said gently, 'no, you haven't.'

♦

THE BED ROCKED AND CLANGED, Shanice and Cooper made love and giggled. The noise carried through the dormant brickwork.

I sat on the sofa, rolling a joint I felt too tired to smoke. I could see myself, sat there like they had been earlier, in the same seat I would have occupied on the estate, dressed the same, doing the same thing. It was a mirror image, albeit one soiled by gnarled edges. The situation was almost absurd. Even the rotating logo of the DVD player seemed to be smiling at me from the screen.

The joint rolled, I went outside to smoke it.

The night was heavy, laced with pinpricks of silent stars. My eyes returned to the woodland, the neon pulse it seemed to have. Silver strobes moved along every haggard sinew of the infinite branches. Something burned beyond them. Not fire, not electricity, but a light as earthy and verdant as the trees and understory themselves.

Fascinated, frightened, I exhaled the plumes of dope from my cold lips and waited for something, anything to appear to me.

Appear it did.

I believe I caught my first glimpse of the creature I would soon come to know as *Bone Stairwell* that night.

Within the pulsing light, its outline muscular in the white, a shape moved behind the screen of trees. It walked on all fours, its bulk enormous. From where I stood, having not yet ventured up into the looming forest, I could only estimate the creature's size. The size of a small car, its head mostly obscured, large enough to shift aside branches halfway up the trunks of frowning ash trees, the creature moved easily, slowly.

I had to force myself to exhale, so tightly held was my breath. I coughed loudly as I did so and, I was sure, the creature stopped and turned towards me, peering down from some crosshatched perch.

I waited for a few seconds, the shape lost to me without movement. The hairs on the back of my neck stood like TV ariels. They picked up a frequency I could not yet understand.

I edged back into the house, too afraid to wait for more.

Snores had replaced ecstatic groans. Shanice and Cooper were asleep.

I went into my room, my nook in the dollhouse.

In the glooms, too uneasy to put on a light, I sat there, at the foot of the bed, wondering whether morning would arrive as usual, or whether the meteor beneath me would continue onwards, into the moon itself.

16.

Of a gory well, of its heart

COOPER WAS THE FIRST TO mention Watkins over breakfast the following day.

'Any joy so far?' he asked chirpily, his mouth half-full of buttery toast.

'With what?' Hickey asked, leaning back on his chair, his eyes grey, indifferent to the food, the company, the question.

'With Watkins, mate, *with Watkins.*' Cooper swallowed his toast and slurped at his tea, 'Maybe I'll take a crack with him today, eh?'

'No,' Hickey pulled his chair tight to the table, 'I'm taking care of Watkins. I don't want anyone else in there, understand?'

Shanice and I didn't need to answer, we had no intention of torturing Watkins. Cooper though, he looked as if he was being denied some lucrative work, some cash-in-hand at the yard. 'What?' he leaned on the table too, the pair of them like neighbouring sphinxes. 'I thought we were gonna beat the truth out the fucker? Get what we can as fast as, make our way home.'

'What's the hurry?' Hickey smirked. 'You've reshaped this place into your living room already, what're you missing?'

'It isn't about that, it's about...' Cooper wasn't sure what he wanted to say.

'About what?'

'About sorting it out.' Cooper's brow lowered. He seemed confused by his own reply.

'Anyhow,' Hickey stood up, ignoring Cooper, 'time I got off to the office'.

'The office?' Shanice didn't realise he meant his new day job, the *work* on Watkins.

Hickey didn't answer. He was out of the door in a couple of seconds, his half-eaten breakfast left for us, like some dirty protest.

'He can be a right bloody so and so,' Cooper shook his head, 'it's one thing keeping to yourself, it's another thing getting us out here and leaving us to it.'

'Ain't so bad,' Shanice squeezed Cooper's bear-claw hand, 'we can watch some films, have a drink with Danny. Leave Hickey to it, eh.'

'Suppose so,' Cooper managed a smile, despite being neutered by Hickey.

I began to wash the plates and pans, left Cooper and Shanice to shower. I could see what was happening, what had been happening to Cooper since Hickey had taken control of the Katie Pop game. It was as if Cooper's huge muscles were balloons and Hickey held a pin, bursting each one in turn, until only thin plastic hung from his bones.

Hickey had been in charge since he decided he wanted to be. Bringing us out here was just the ultimate physical confirmation of that. Right down to him driving the van, taking us through such a complex route in the darkness. Our autonomy was stripped away, sawed to a stump. It didn't matter whether we agreed with his plan or not, it was the course to be followed.

I thought about mentioning what I had seen the previous night, but there was no universe in which Cooper and Shanice were the right people to have that conversation with.

Besides, what I had seen was *mine*.

I suppose I believed I needed to have something, some kind of new secret, something which genuinely belonged to me and me alone. My mother's death had been stolen by Hickey and the spy whose loose gob had whispered my secrets to him.

Cooper and Shanice were adrift in their own private well, swirling in their depths, the rest of the world on the outside of the bricks and mortar, locked out, forbidden.

I was alone, assuming my life in the city was paused, or maybe even deleted completely, with Watkins' camera snare enough to see me arrested, tried and locked away for years to come. I knew any court would see me as one more online *nonce hunter* who took it too far. A face for the tabloids, to be plastered across them; something new for the goons and dandies to rage about in the nattering database of every social media scream factory. It wouldn't matter what I said, how I said it. There would be a chance to implicate Hickey, maybe Cooper too, but they figured I wouldn't do that and, hating myself on that morning for being so predictable, my hands shaking in the suds, they were probably right.

I was only a minor exception to the toxicity of my gender. I might have been an echo, fainter than Hickey, definitely paler than Cooper, but I still bared my teeth, released the same howl. Only mine was a littler quieter, at least until these last few days.

Once I had washed up the dishes, I decided to head outside, take a proper look around.

It was a crisp morning. The leaves glittered, their gnarled and angular edges frosted by the early cold. I stood outside the cottage for a little while, just looking upwards at the thick, matted woodlands. At night they appeared to burn with white heart-light yet, in the day, they carried night's darkness within them. Black, impenetrable from where I stood then, it was hard to see even a thin space between some of the trunks, the ribboned branches, the evergreen curtains of interlocked leaves.

Still, that morning marked my first attempt to reach them.

I walked the periphery of the cottage first and, if I haven't yet said, it was also the day that I saw the building's name, *The Red House*. The wooden sign was faded, one side rotted and fallen away from one of the posts that supported it. I found it at the back of the house, the route we must have taken in the van. Half-hidden by thick, toothy holly and assorted thorns, I lifted the sign and pulled it out from its cover.

The Red House.

I turned back to the cottage, instinctively, wondering whether I had missed a feature, perhaps a single red wall, a type of brick that caught the light and created an allusion of redness. There was nothing. The house wasn't red, yet.

I ran my thumb over the indented wording, felt its edges, knew then that it hadn't been carved well, professionally. It was rough, splintered, hacked badly. Even giving the place a name felt absurd to me. There was no way it could receive post, deliveries. It was like naming a lamb moments before slaughter.

The sign fell back in the bushes. I decided to try to find the track we drove down a couple of nights earlier.

For a little while, maybe half an hour, I couldn't find any evidence of a road at all.

The notion of that made me sweat with unease. I couldn't shake the idea that we had somehow *landed* here. I could recall only the barest details of the ground itself, coloured phantom yellow by Cooper's spotlight, as Hickey eased the vehicle between deep trenches.

They were still there, like long graves around the property, but there was no sign of a track wide enough to have accommodated the van.

On the verge of assuming I had lost my mind there and then, I stepped heavily through some feverish long grass and found the only surface that could have carried in the van.

The pathway was gritty, arched. There was even evidence of tire-tracks at its edges but, whether I understood it then or not, the road itself had been almost completely obscured by the surrounding forest since we arrived.

I recognised the wandering weeds that dominated the coverage. Dog roses. We had a neighbour in one of the council houses Mom and I lived in when I was really young, maybe only eight or nine. A hunched man, elderly, his mouth collapsed inwards due to missing teeth. Mr Grieves. I remembered that much because of the sound of my Mom's voice when she would say, 'God, Grieves is gardening again'. Something about the words as she looked through the curtains of her bedroom still rang in my thoughts.

The fence between our gardens was low enough for me to peer over. I think Grieves likely hated that but, given the last tenants were riotous junkies who flung their crushed cider cans into his garden when they were done, Grieves was probably happy just to deal with a nosy kid.

I don't remember much of what he said about his garden as he walked the fence, inspecting it and us, but I do recall him telling me about dog roses. They looked like tentacles to me then and now. They were as thick as my child's wrist and the thorns that grew from their apple-green flesh were like my little fingers. Scimitars that slashed at the bees.

I cut my finger on one of them during some sunny afternoon nowhere of childish dreams and imaginings and, my finger bandaged by my annoyed mother, I went back out and asked Grieves about them.

'They run the place,' he said solemnly, his sunken toothless mouth even more defeated than usual, 'they strangle my cherry trees, my ash. They're bullies, young Daniel. Bullies, I say.'

I asked him why he didn't just cut them down.

'Cut them?' He seemed amazed. 'Because, once a year, they flower in the most beautiful way. Their leaves are redder than the blood on your finger, boy. Redder than any sunset.'

I didn't understand. If it was only once a year, he wouldn't miss them much.

'It isn't just that,' I remember Grieves' voice lowered to a whisper, 'they'd come back and, if they did, they might come for me too.'

I laughed. Some stupid game to scare the idiot kid. Something to keep me away from the fence.

We moved a few months later but, in the year or two that followed, I'd often think of Mr Grieves and wonder whether the dog roses did come for him one night, their teeth bared in a snarl, the beauty of their flowers quickly forgotten as they bit into his flannelly face.

There they were again that morning, the dog roses. They had crossed the track, made it all the way to the other side. I couldn't see any evidence of them being crushed by the wheels of the van, driven over during our arrival. There was no doubting that, however it had happened, the vicious-looking stems had closed us in.

I kicked at some of the nearest vines and they gave in easily enough. I was careful not to tread on the thorns – unsure if Shanice had packed a first aid kit. Above them, covering them, facile, wispy pampas grass lay like a sheet on old bones. I kicked that away too and, after a bit more of a struggle, made it to a patch of clear track.

It wound upwards but seemed far too thin to have carried the van. I had to marvel at Hickey's skill behind the wheel. The fact we had made it down to The Red House at all was incredible. To have done it in darkness was godly. I had the sense then that we had simply been allowed to arrive, enabled by unseen conveyors, cradled by them.

It scared me, of course. To see that track, to remember the sight of something moving in the neon woodland light the previous evening, those things alone were completely frightening.

Yet, even with that, there was something else too, another feeling, maybe even a realisation.

It's far deeper in me now, that giggling hook but, that morning, the idea of there being no life left for me there, away from here, it began to grow, malignantly. I was fearful here, but no more so than *there*.

I continued up the track, as best I could, hoping to reach a high enough point to see some kind of genuine road, maybe even a pall of chimney smoke from some property in a neighbouring valley. It quickly became impassable and, more than that, when I looked back down towards The Red House, it was almost completely obscured, as if verdant gates had closed behind me, ushering me into an obscure hinterland beyond.

I sat on the trunk of a fallen tree and watched a line of ants. They busied themselves with carrying the carcass of a fly. Half-hollowed by the gnawing ants, the body oozed along, carried slickly into some crevice, some burrow.

The ants returned a little while later, passing my resting hand my only a few millimetres. They eased around it, perfectly aligned, their work clear, the destination agreed. A hive mind, a unified effort, no cracks, no splintered loyalties, no secrets.

I walked on after a while, trying to move further up the track.

The pathway seemed to curve frequently. The further I went, the taller the bracken and bushes became at my sides. Eventually, after no more than a kilometre or so, the plants and scrub were tall enough to blot out much of the light, even meeting in a canopy above me, their withering fingers marrying amidst the plush, fertile leaves.

I turned back, my earlier interest tempered by something more intoxicating, maybe even oppressive. I told myself there was no way of getting to a high point this way, a place I could see down into the crater of The Red House. I decided then that I would head up into the woodland the following morning, the forest ahead of the house, to the north.

When I returned to the house, Hickey was in the kitchen, sipping a tea.

'Been for a wander,' he asked with interest, 'up the track?'

'What track there is, yeah.'

'Funny, isn't it. Hard to picture how I managed to get the van down here at all, right?' His eyes lit up, watched me keenly.

'That's right,' I agreed, 'I could barely get a mile or so on foot, fuck knows how you drove that junk down here.'

Hickey tapped his forehead. 'Just have to trust your instincts, Daniel, trust what you know to be true. I have that route carved in the bone, through it, like seaside rock. Take off my arm and the map's inside, you know what I mean?'

I heard the nervousness in my own laughter, 'I reckon you just got lucky' I teased, 'let's see how well you make it when we leave.'

'Right,' Hickey finished the tea, tossed the cup into the cold dishwater, 'back to the office for me. Plenty to do.'

I asked if Watkins was talking. 'What's he saying? Anything about his group, who might have seen me on the cameras.'

'He's a tough one,' Hickey opened his hands and I saw the blood between his fingers, 'he's saying a lot of things, but they aren't real, Daniel. People chatter when they're desperate, but you can't believe the lines they give you. It isn't that easy. He'll need more time, a few days to really feel like he has to be truthful.'

'What if I spoke to him?'

'No,' Hickey's upper lip twitched and exposed his yellowing teeth, 'leave it to me. You just relax a little, Daniel. Get acquainted with the place, explore the forests, take it all in. No hurry.'

I watched as Hickey left the house. He paused between the cottage and the outbuilding. He seemed trapped there for a moment. He turned and looked up at the northern woods, leaned towards them, his head tilted to one side. He nodded, then hurried off, back to Watkins.

I found myself lost in thought, the spell only broken by Cooper's heavy hand my back. 'Can you believe Shan hasn't seen the fuckin *Godfather*?' His face was wide, happy, colourful, 'What about we sit down with her now, pop a couple of cans and introduce here to those Corleone bastards, eh?'

'Sure thing.' I followed him over to the sofa, ready to take my place in that familiar tableau, that transferred arrangement, that dollhouse afternoon.

◊

IT COULD'VE BEEN OLD TIMES, the rest of that day. Any evening, any occasion with Cooper and me back on the estate, just sat there, drinking, laughing at the TV, passing a joint between us. Shanice wasn't a barrier to that. In fact, she may even have been the glue that made it feel so comfortable that afternoon.

They watched the film, I watched them. I couldn't forget what seemed to be leering down at us from the woodlands above, but neither Cooper or Shanice seemed aware of anything like that. They were present, together, immediate with each other. As far as they were concerned, it really was a holiday of sorts. Perhaps the only kind of trip people like us ever got.

We knew a few kids on the estate who worked county lines for the opaque tower-block bosses. A shit business, *going country,* but their eyes still lit up a little when they were on their way to hop a train, their chains tucked in or taken off, their slang numbed to fit in to whatever rural town they were being posted to. It was easy to figure they were stoked for the money they'd make, the reputation they would foster with the trappers passing them dope from the hatches, but I didn't think it was that at all.

For me, I believed they were relieved to get away, even just for a few days, a week or two. They might be in the trenches, mostly locked down in some withering junky's collapsing cottage, but even that, even one small walk of an evening, or just standing in an overgrown garden looking up at more stars than they had ever seen in their lives, *that* was exciting, *that* was a getaway.

A vile truth. One more reason it became easier to see why humans were toiling in the dirt.

There was no sign of Hickey as it got dark.

We cooked and left some food on the side for him. It went cold as the three of us worked our way through more of the cans, chatted about the film, about anything.

Cooper was in a fine mood, weightless, made younger with merriment. 'See,' he was saying to Shanice, 'thing about them is they can't lie straight in bed, too much bullshit, politics, too much messing about. Ain't that right, Danny boy?'

'There's a code though,' I shrugged, 'with that whole thing. Has to be adhered to.'

'Adhered to?' Cooper waved me away. 'The only one who really got it was Sonny, that's the fact.' Cooper finished almost a full can in one long, echoing slug. 'And that's because of James fuckin Caan. What a bloke he was. Shoulders on him. As square as sliced bread. Unreal. Here's to you, Jimmy,' Cooper opened another can and saluted the air, 'to Caan.'

Shanice yawned. 'You and your bleedin toasts. You'd raise a toast to your boxer shorts.'

Cooper wrestled Shanice onto his lap. 'Listen here, my little smartarse, I'll have you know that toasts are an essential act, ain't that right, Danny boy?' he asked me again.

'Under the right circumstances.' I stood up, took my empties to the bin.

'See,' Cooper said proudly, 'and our Dan's a scholar, so he fuckin knows.'

'He didn't agree with you, dummy,' Shanice wriggled free and returned to her side of the sofa, 'his answer was noncommittal.'

'Non what?' Cooper looked over at me.

'Means I was on the fence,' I smiled, 'left you both hanging.'

'You'll get splinters.' Cooper chucked an empty can over at me.

I caught it and tossed it in the bin, 'I've always had splinters, mate. A few thorns too.'

'He's a clever one, eh?' Cooper's face lit up. 'Our Dan. Up for another film?'

'Nah.' I told them I was heading to bed. 'I fancy getting a look up in the woods tomorrow morning. Hickey said there are a few pairs of walking boots out in the storeroom, so I'm hoping some'll fit me. You're welcome to come along, both of you, if you feel like it.'

'We'll see how it goes,' Cooper stretched, yawned, 'but I might have to join Hickey at the office, you know, see what's going on with him and old Watkins.'

'Fair enough. If you change your mind, either of you.'

'Nighty night,' Cooper waved me to bed, affecting a lisp, his bludgeoning campery something you'd see from the cheapest seaside variety act in history, 'no naughty dreams.'

I locked my door and lay in the dark. The frisson from the TV seemed almost physical, pooling beneath the door itself; ethereal, neon blue. It was all I could see, all I could feel.

The curtains at the window didn't close properly, but there was very little out there, apart from the bone-grey of the quarry face, lit eerily by a new moon. I thought about moving my bed, so I could look upwards at the woodlands, but I knew I wouldn't sleep a wink if I saw the movement again.

I didn't need to worry.

That was the first night one of them came to the house.

◊

NOT YET FAMILIAR TO ME, not yet personified by the nickname it wore, not yet *The Milliman*. The creature with a tuxedo of fingers, the aristocrat whose bones chirruped as it stalked, the visitor came to my window in the early hours.

I must have fallen asleep soon after laying down. I'd had more beers that I thought, more dope too. Audial hallucinations played me out. Crooked lullabies hummed by shuddering mouths. I don't remember dreaming at all, but I woke suddenly, my mouth dry, a sensation of a violent shock sent me straight onto my elbows, my whole-body rigid, my eyes immediately lidless on waking.

Gone was the television hiss, the frisson water beneath my door. Instead, something silvered the darkness, something from outside.

My first response was noticing the stink, the utterly cloying soil odour that seemed to fill the entire room. The smell of allotments left to fail, of vegetables rotting on the pavements of the city after market day. It was a sickly smell, wet and heavy. I swallowed against it, struggled to understand where it was coming from.

The silence of the room was incredible. A quiet so deep and airless that it felt almost deafening. The silence of the undersea, the silence of breath held beneath bath water.

I instantly looked around the room for Hickey, remembering how he and Cooper had woken me that night back on the estate. There was no sign of either of them. The room was too bare to hide in.

I swung my legs over the side of the bed, facing away from the window at first. I pressed my hands down onto the sheets and recoiled. They were wet, earthy. I squinted against the darkness, brought my fingers towards my face, close to it. I could see smudges of soil, of claggy earth. I leaned down towards the blankets, but they remained white, as crisp as they were when I laid them. Yet I could *feel the dirt*. I could even see the dirt on my skin.

I half-turned, ready to switch on the lamp, but something stopped me, froze me there.

Through the moth-eaten net curtain at the edges of the window, glimpsed only slightly from the corner of my right eye, a figure was clear.

There was no mistaking it for Hickey, Cooper, even for Shanice. Taller, spindly, slouching, even before I turned fully, I could feel the crepuscular light emanating from its flesh, joining the light far above it, the woodland's throbbing neon.

I couldn't breathe. I felt the shudders rise from my naked feet, through my legs, up into my shoulders, my jaw. I knew the figure was outside my window, close to the glass. I knew it stared in at me. There was no mistake.

I knew I couldn't sit there like that, that I couldn't just wait for it to leave.

I scrunched the bedding in my fists, but felt them plunge into dirt. I saw my breath ahead of me, it too laced with silver webs. I pivoted, brought my legs back onto the covers. I turned fully to the window; my decision made.

The first thing I noticed was the clothing. I didn't know if I had expected it to be naked, for mounds of milky meat to be hanging, udder-like, from its gut, its chest. There was nothing like that. Instead, raggedy, slightly shabbily arranged, the creature was dressed in a what appeared to be a suit, a tuxedo. Standing taller than me, over six feet, the torso was angular, arms at its side, legs obscured by the position of the window.

I stared at the creature's chest for a long time, too frightened to look up at its face.

I could feel soil gathering around my neck, my shoulders. I rubbed it away, but it only thickened. I was sat upright, but every sensation made me feel as if I was lying in a grave, prostrate, staring upwards at an infinity of giggling moons.

The fabric of its jacket seemed to be moving in a breeze, but the universe was silent, airless, condemned to an atmosphere of mud.

When I finally looked up at its face, I struggled to understand what was etched there, emerging vine-like from its collars.

Familiar at first, the throat was thinner than the head, the skull luminescent, chalk-bright, perfectly rounded at its peak. I didn't want to meet its eyes, but they were unavoidable. They swirled within themselves. They pooled in the head, rocked with black tides.

I looked down again, then back up, slowly. I noticed the skin of the throat was bolete, fanned, waxy. Toadstool meat, mouldering at the edges.

Feeling myself drawn back to its eyes, I raised my own to meet them and, as we looked into each other, it did something so unexpected, I almost laughed out of shock. From its right side, it raised a hand and brought it up to its face and there, held by long, twiggy fingers, the creature held what appeared to be a pair of opera glasses. The metal of the glasses instantly incongruous against the understory flesh of the creature itself, the creature pressed them against its face and there, where seconds ago there had been rockpools, there were lenses.

Beneath the glasses, opening slowly, an inconspicuous, toothless mouth shaped into a smile.

With that, the creature began to step backwards, gently, without hurry. With each step, it vanished more, away into the earth night, into the subterfuge of the muddy air around it.

Just before it disappeared completely, what I had taken for its tuxedo front peeled open, the edges of the jacket apparently part of the creature itself.

Folding away to the sides, an infinity of fingers retreated and, beneath them, I was offered a glimpse of mushy sorel, of a gory well, of its heart.

It took almost an hour before the feeling of soil on my skin disappeared, before enough strength had returned to my legs to stand.

I walked over to the window, my hands fluttering at my sides. I peered through the glass, wondering whether the creature would leap at me, smash through, attack me. There was no sign of it, nothing to suggest it had ever been there. Instead, almost blindingly white through the crags and gnarled angles of the ogling forests, the weightless light hung there, fog-like, pulsing, creeping, soaking the earth and trees.

I was confused, frantic. I wondered whether I had lost my mind. I could still feel the dirt on my neck, my arms. I held my skin up to the light from the window. It was spotless, clean, marbled with sweat, but I could *feel* dirt on me. Cold, wet, claggy soil.

Yet, above all else, what surprised me was what I didn't feel. I felt no more terror. That creature, what I would get to know as Mr Milliman, it hadn't threatened me, it didn't seem to want to hurt me. It existed, I existed. We shared a strange moment, one beyond any universe I knew, but it wasn't violent, hungry, brutal. It was curious, interested, alien. We were alien to each other.

I lay back down on the bed. Four-nineteen. It would begin to get light soon enough. I just needed to work out whether to mention any of this to Cooper and Shanice. I didn't have the same question about Hickey. I was already beginning to be certain that he knew what was happening here, that he knew every creature watching us from the looming woods, from the white bracken.

17.

Like the curtains from which I watched them

I DIDN'T SLEEP AGAIN THAT night.

I played the sight of the creature over and over in my thoughts, occasionally returning to the window, to see if it had returned.

I waited until I heard movement outside my door, until I heard the metallic clangs of breakfast. Once I was sure someone was up, I dressed quickly and went out to see who it was.

I found Shanice sat alone at the dining table, her head in her hands.

I said hi, but she didn't seem to hear me. Her small face was hidden in the folds of her fingers, her lank hair cascading over them, locking out the new daylight, darkening her.

I spoke again and Shanice jumped. She peeled her hands away and I noticed that her eyes were heavy, ringed by sleeplessness. Her face was pale, drained, bone-white.

I asked if she was feeling alright.

'Huh?' her voice was faint, almost unbearably distant.

'You okay?' I repeated, 'you look a little wiped out.'

'I don't...I don't like it here,' she whispered hoarsely, 'I don't like it here now, Danny. I want to go. We should go.'

Shanice had seemed fine last night. Relaxed, content with her and Cooper's ersatz home, the living room tableau, the familiar set-up. I guessed maybe she and Cooper had argued, but I hadn't heard anything, not a single raised voice, not a slammed door. Nothing.

She must have seen the creature too. That was my only conclusion, the only reason I could pinpoint for such a sea-change in Shanice's outlook.

'I thought you were enjoying it here.' I sat down next to Shanice, pulled my chair close to hers, 'You have a bad night?'

She looked around, furtive, almost feral, her nerves standing from her skin like knitting needles from balled wool, 'I...' there was a tremolo in her breath, a shuddering fear, 'I thought I saw...last night, I thought I saw someone outside...in the dark.'

I didn't want to say what I had seen, to describe what seemed impossible to me. 'Hickey?' I asked. 'He's enough to put the fear up anyone, eh?' I smiled, tried to ease Shanice's mind. It didn't work.

'No,' she spoke quickly, but seemed laboured, 'no, not him, not Hickey.'

'A dream? I never sleep right in new places.'

'Not a dream,' Shanice seemed to pale the more she spoke, 'something creeping about, in the dark.'

'Try not worry,' I poured some tea, 'it's probably nothing. Besides, Cooper's here, me too. See how it goes later on, eh? Besides, I don't reckon we'll be here for much longer anyhow.'

'You don't?' Shanice perked up immediately, excited by my lie.

'Sure. There's no way Watkins can hold out much longer. We'll be on our way before you know it.'

Quickly relieved by nothing more than my empty words, Shanice jumped up and began to cook breakfast, her mood lighter, even if her face remained chalky, sapped.

I sipped my tea silently. I asked myself why I didn't feel more disturbed by the creature, why I didn't feel the same fear Shanice wore on her narrow head. I suppose I had begun to believe that the creature wasn't the first of its kind I had seen, the first I had felt.

I recalled the cemetery, the moments accompanying the lowering of Mom's coffin, the way things moved at the treeline, peeked between the neighbouring stones. I remembered her telling me about the white stag of her dreams and, through the city, through the estate, along the motorways and carved-out sideroads which had brought me to The Red House, very little had felt real or in the least bit tangible since then.

Mourning, desolation, the fever of a trodden heart, call it what you will, but my universe wasn't the same as it had been.

There was a loop, something sewn into the horizon. I was moving towards it, tethered to a gallows bird, fastened to the unstoppable missile of either magic or madness. Either way, despite the guilt I feel now about how things turned out with Shanice, I had no desire to reveal what I had seen, and even less desire to leave that place then.

By the time Cooper was up, Hickey had also made an appearance.

I could feel the tension over the breakfast table. It wasn't aimed at me, but it sat there, cumulous, sagging in the air above the burned toast and tepid tea. It came from Cooper. A throbbing, wheezing force of boredom and annoyance, all of it aimed at Hickey.

'I'll come to see Watkins when you go back,' Cooper announced. 'I'm tired just sitting about the place here, fuck-all happening.'

'No point.' Hickey didn't look at Cooper when he spoke. 'Not like I can't handle that clown alone.'

'It's not about handling it,' Cooper rotated his cup impatiently, 'it's about us being in this together, yeah? It's about me wanting to move this fuckin thing on as quickly as I can, so we can get Danny cleared, Watkins sorted and get out of here, back to town.'

Hickey listened to what Cooper said, but seemed unmoved. He had no interest in Cooper's assistance. He had everything the way he wanted it. When Hickey replied, he did so bluntly, his tone leaden, straight. 'I said no.' He wiped the end of his nose, stared into Cooper's face, 'Don't make me say it again, Coop.'

Cooper laughed and rubbed the back of his neck. He did that when he was angry. I'd seen it before, over and over. 'That right, Hick? You telling me what I can and can't do? That it?'

'That's right.' Hickey pushed his plate into the centre of the table, between Shanice and me, the spectators, 'That's exactly what I'm saying, Cooper. This is my thing, being out here. I know what we need to do, how it needs to go down. I don't need you slouching in there and slapping Watkins around. That's not how we get what we need.'

'What? And you're some kind of fuckin *artist*, Hick? That it? You're the fella carving weird eyes into the skin of these bastards, not me.'

'So what?' Hickey leaned back in his chair. 'You haven't got the first idea what that means, so don't talk shit about things you could never understand.'

'Hey!' Shanice interrupted Hickey, stared at him hatefully. 'Don't talk to Coop like that.'

Hickey sniggered and ran his hands through the deep black curls of his hair. 'If it isn't little Katie Pop. How lucky we are to have our favourite junky tart onboard for the trip.'

Cooper's chair flew back as he stood. The fury swirled around him like a hurricane. I could feel the heat from Cooper's face as he leaned over me, his jaw tensed, his teeth grinding against each other as he spoke through them. 'What the fuck did I tell you about talking like that?'

Hickey also stood, but slowly, purposeful, not a shred of fear palpable on his face. 'I've been pretty good about your *situation*, Cooper. I've accommodated her, brought her along, I'm even paying to feed her, but I don't want to hear a fucking word from her, *or you*, when it comes to what's happening here, understand?'

'Aye, I understand *you're a cunt.*'

I tried to intervene, also standing, turning to my right, putting my shoulder between them, across the mucky plates.

'Mind out, Danny boy,' Cooper said. 'If Hickey here wants to test my mettle, there's plenty in the tank.'

Hickey suddenly laughed loudly, hysterically. 'Dear oh dear.' He gripped the sides of the table, leaned in to meet Cooper's face with his own, pausing close enough to kiss him, 'You want a piece of Watkins, you can have it. I didn't realise the smell of blood got you going like this, Cooper. I'm impressed.'

'Fuck outta my face.' Cooper straightened, licked his lips, 'Got nothing to do with it. I don't want to lay a hand on that rotten prick, I just want us done here, that's all.'

'Me too.' Shanice left the table and stood at Cooper's side, their fingers quickly intertwined, 'It ain't right round here,' she added, 'weird place.'

Hickey rubbed his eyes. He looked bored with the conversation, bored with them. 'Whatever you say. Pop a film on, eat my food, drink the booze I bought. I'll get through to Watkins today, tomorrow at the latest. We'll be back on that shithole estate before you know it. Happy?'

Cooper didn't answer. He and Shanice walked over to the sofa, sat there together, wordlessly.

There was nothing else to say. Hickey left the cottage and I began to clean up.

The tension had been building between them. It ebbed from one of their granite faces to the other, corroding their cool, rotting away at any pretences they awkwardly wore.

I couldn't tell if it had always been there. Perhaps. Back in the life I knew before we ran from the city, there had been too much interference, too much static for me to see what was happening clearly. I knew Hickey had assumed leadership of our ugly quartet. That had happened instantly, as soon as he decided he wanted in on the righteous violence, that red purge.

Cooper had invited him, back at the gym that day, back when the iron clanged and the sweat greased every muscle. It was bravado then, raucous talk, something to keep the madness away. I still didn't know how it had moved on so quickly, so easily. I could still see Cooper's stoned, dumb face lit in the TV blue, watching that haphazard, shaky-cam documentary about online vigilantes. We may as well have been watching a show about astronauts, or keyhole surgery. It was just background noise for me, just something to sap away the minutes. Not to Cooper though, and certainly not to Hickey. In no time at all, everything had changed.

I washed up and listened to Shanice calm Cooper. Cooing, gentle mutterings, a fluttering of weightless wings. A secret language, a vocabulary of lovers, something which only belonged to them, a foreign tongue to me.

I tried to ignore the heat between them all. I felt splintered, snapped away from what they were. I was becoming something else, feeling a growing vagueness towards them, even to Cooper. Unreality was becoming commonplace. It wasn't that I didn't understand them, just that they seemed increasingly alien to me. Their arguments, the bickering about exactly what type of violence was best for Watkins, the fact we were even there to begin with, all of it faded to a muffled voice at the end of a tunnel.

Instead, my hands in the suds, I looked up at the northern woodlands, wondering if the creature from the previous night was there now too, looking down at the playhouse lunacy of us.

Staring upwards that morning provided me with the first indication that the woodland itself had begun to change.

I couldn't identify how it had reshaped since the previous day, apart from being sure that it was more angular, the branches straightened into emergent squares, the leaves more organised, folded in across one another, like the curtains from which I watched them.

Something was already taking place, something larger than our purpose for being there.

However Hickey had discovered this place, a story I didn't know then but would later learn, however it had come to him, there was no doubt of its immensity, of the gravity the area held. There couldn't have been a greater disparity than the scene ahead of me and the scene at my back. Whereas behind me, in those cloying cottage shadows, there was simply Cooper and Shanice acting out the stylised poses of a relationship, ahead of me, above us all, I watched as a landscape appeared to communicate with me. Its very roots, the gnarled bones of the dirt were reshaping themselves to show me something I could understand. The bracken was a universe of semaphores; I was the plane manoeuvring towards them through an ugly fog.

I didn't want to be around Cooper and Shanice. It was all too personal, too private. I had been an unwilling interloper since day one with them. I was a ghost in that rotten house back on the estate. A third wheel, a crooked wheel. I haunted the hallways of their love, the static of their fuck. I didn't want to be there and maybe I should have left a long time ago. If I had snatched enough bottle to walk away weeks earlier when they began their online crusade, I never would have been around for the snare trap set by Watkins, for the swirl of dead-eyed crows that Hickey had become. It was too late to regret these things, especially given the situation I was now in, the place we had been brought to by Hickey himself.

Even after only one sight of the creature the previous night, I was aware of magic here, of forces I could never have imagined. The moon was in my heart now, my bones beset by lunar rays.

I finished clearing up and went outside. I tripped in one of the deep ditches, distracted by the windless northern woodlands ahead. Mud strewn over my leg, a thick scratch running down my right calf, I cursed my ignorance and kicked out at some mushrooms that were nodding proudly from the dirt.

My attention turned to the outhouse, to where Hickey was keeping Watkins. With the creature from the previous night, with a feeling of impending discovery, with everything else in the universe, I had almost forgotten about Watkins, about the bastard who had used me for escape leverage, or had at least tried to. I was suddenly intrigued, keen to see just how much he had endured at Hickey's hands.

I walk towards the outhouse, but paused as I thought about the argument Hickey and Cooper had just had, about Hickey's insistence he should be left alone to punish Watkins, to drag words from his busted lips. I figured Hickey would lose his mind if I just barged in there.

I turned away, ready to walk back up towards the matted hills, but stopped when I heard the door of the outhouse open.

Turning back, I was greeted by Hickey in the doorway.

He lit a cigarette, took a long drag, exhaled and waved me towards him. 'Pop in for a moment, Daniel,' He sounded light, friendly, as if he was asking me to take a look at a new car, a huge television.

I asked if he was sure, 'I mean, after what you said to Cooper just now, about him not coming over here.'

'You ain't Cooper,' Hickey answered coolly, turning his back to me, walking into the outhouse shadows, leaving the door open.

I recall looking back at the cottage, The Red House, checking to see if Cooper and Shanice were at the windows, just like the estate's curtain-twitching gossips. I couldn't see them, so continued on, following Hickey's invite like a guilty pup.

I didn't know what I expected to see, but Watkins seemed in a worse state than I could have imagined.

His face was horribly swollen, his lips hung out like two new tongues, blackened, sickly. He was opening and closing his mouth, fish-like, to breathe. His nose was broken. Flattened, bent towards his left cheek. Every time Watkins opened his mouth, every time he panted I could see there were more teeth missing. Beneath the sheen of clotted blood, blacker than any night, I couldn't see a single tooth. There was just a raw, gory void behind the ruin of his face.

The only part of his head which seemed untouched was his eyes. Despite his condition, they were as wild and lively as they had been when he realised I'd fallen for his camera gag.

Watkins was fully dressed, but a blanket draped across his lap. His hands were tethered behind him, between the struts of the chair. Beyond the damage to his face, the only other obvious injury I could see was to the fingers of his right hand. They hung at curious, unnatural angles. Obviously broken at the knuckles, maybe dislocated, they were more like lank feathers from an oil-stricken gull than human digits.

Hickey continued to smoke his cigarette, quietly. He didn't seem hurried, perturbed in the least. In fact, Hickey seemed cooler, more at ease than I had ever known him.

The cherry of the cigarette bulging, red with furious heat, Hickey casually walked towards Watkins and ground the end into his cheek.

I winced, the sound of the singeing on blood-wet skin was grotesque, sickening. It was over in a moment and Watkins didn't scream. In fact, beyond odd to me then, Watkins appeared to lean into the fag, as if he was pressing his own ruin into the heat, eager to meet it, perhaps to extinguish it.

Hickey flicked the nub onto the floor of the outhouse, where it sat amongst a hundred others, all of them bloody. 'You see, Daniel, our Watkins here is doing very well indeed.'

I looked down at Watkins, found his immediate, neon eyes fixed on my own, then looked away quickly, back to Hickey. 'Sure,' I swallowed my disgust, 'fighting fit.'

'Fighting's about right,' Hickey agreed, taking a seat on the other chair, 'more mettle than I expected. He doesn't want to give up what I need to hear, so here we are, one step forward, one more tooth to go.'

'Maybe he doesn't know anything else,' I suggested. I wasn't sure why. I didn't feel like I wanted to leave there then. I didn't care what happened to Watkins. It just seemed like the natural thing to say.

'We're past that.' Hickey leaned forward, his elbows on his knees, his face close to Watkins' own, 'It isn't what Watkins knows that matters now, Daniel. The knowledge he has pales into insignificance in the face of…' Hickey didn't finish the sentence, but I was desperate for him to do so. Right there, at that moment, I *knew* he must've seen what I saw, the creature, the shimmering bracken, the whitewoods.

'In the face of?'

'What do you think of this place,' Hickey asked, ignoring my question, 'this area. How do you like it?'

'What's to get excited about?' I downplayed it, all of it, keen for Hickey to be the one who described what we both knew existed. It was the only power I had, the only secret that remained. 'Just woods, isn't it?'

'Dear Daniel,' Hickey laughed, shook his head, ran a hand through his tangled hair, 'are we all here to play games? I thought you were different. I thought you would see right through this farce.'

'Don't know what you mean.' I leaned against the door, watched Hickey's broad face through the weightless snow of god-rays and dust-mites. 'All I've done is sleep and wash up since we got here. If there's something more going on, maybe you should spill it.'

'Something more going on,' Hickey repeated, '*spill it.*' He shook his head again, a flicker of annoyance apparent between the furrows of his forehead, 'It isn't for me to warn you, Daniel. It isn't for me to tell you what you see. It's for *you* to decide what's happening.'

I looked down at Watkins and could see the keenness in his eyes, the interest with which he listened to us, even through the destruction of his face.

Returning my eyes to Hickey, I could see the glitter of kidology on his face, the eagerness of teasing. He wanted me to tell him what I had seen. He knew what I had seen, but needed me to be the one to say it. The realness of my experience with the creature, with old Mr Milliman, it came through that decrepit outhouse like a comet, scorching all doubt, obliterating any pretence of fantasy.

'So?' Hickey raised his eyebrows, smiled at the blood-blackened Watkins. 'What's it to be, Daniel? Are you going to skirt around your true understanding, or are you going to lay it out, in front of us, everything you know?'

'What makes you think I know anything?'

'I can read the books I wrote' Hickey stared into my face, the intensity of his expression drilled his words through my skull, 'I can find this place with my eyes closed. I told you that the night we drove here. This isn't a place you arrive at on wheels, it's a place you-'

Before Hickey could finish, the door to the outhouse burst open behind me. The force knocked me forward, into Watkins. I tripped on the chair leg, went sprawling into a pile of old sacks and stacked wood.

I turned to see Cooper there, his enormous, panting figure blotting out the sun in the doorframe. The tendons on his throat protruded and throbbed. Dribble covered his lips, frothed at the corners, whitening his otherwise black figure.

'Here we fuckin are,' he seethed, 'torturers together. You in on this, Danny boy?' He didn't turn to me when he spoke. Cooper's face was fixed on Hickey's. 'You been coming in here, working at *the office* with our Hickey, whilst I've been back there, playing the idiot?'

I could see Shanice in the background, near the door of the cottage. Her shoulders were lifted, scrunched around her neck. Her face still wore the fear it had when she had tried to speak to me earlier that morning, only it was even more visible now. A pallid veil on marble emptiness.

'That why you're here?' Hickey asked calmly. 'Figure you're missing out on a piece of Watkins? If it means that much to you, let rip.'

Cooper didn't wait for another invite. He stepped forward and, his right arm drawn back, bow-like, released a huge punch. His fist connected with Watkins' face amidst a horrible, smashing sound. I gritted my teeth as Watkins and the chair toppled backwards, over me. Watkins was instantly motionless, completely knocked out by Cooper's blow, unable to defend himself even slightly, his hands still tied behind his back.

'Feel better?' Hickey asked Cooper. 'Feel like you're part of the troop again?'

Cooper stepped back into the doorway, his heavy breathing percussive amidst the gossamer bricks, 'That punch wasn't for him,' Cooper licked his lips, cleared the spittle, 'it belonged to you, Hick.'

'That right?'

'Yeah, it's fuckin right. You've undercut me ever since you came onboard with this. You and your weird eyes, carved into each of the cunts we've braced. I let it go, but I'm done. I'm *done*. We're stuck out here now on your say so, not mine.'

'Stuck?' Hickey stood up, but kept his hands at his sides. 'You've only been here a couple of days and you're already climbing the walls. What do you have to go back to, eh? That rat-fuck estate? Your rep as a big man in hell? You could never understand what's happening here, not in a million years.'

'What's to understand, Hick? You've brought that old sod out here to torture, that's all there is.'

'That's nothing.' Hickey spat as he spoke, seethed. His skin pruned, narrowed, anger ran in channels across his fatless face, 'Watkins, Daniel, they don't have anything to do with what I'm saying. You're just a figment of the dead world, Cooper. You're a moth on the bulb, burning as it glows, unable to pull away, to join the rest of the night. You're right though, *mate*. You're done. You're completely done.'

Cooper took a step back into the outhouse, towards Hickey, 'That a threat, Hick? You wanna do this, right now?'

'Isn't a threat,' Hickey raised his hands, calmed himself, swallowed the vitriol like an aspirin, 'I'm just telling you the truth. You, Shanice, everyone else glued to yesterday's cancerous tit. You're finished. The universe is a mouth. It blows kisses to the righteous, but it swallows the dead. You could've taken the escalator, but you tripped down the stairs. Don't ever forget this moment, Cooper. It was the day you wrote a postcard from oblivion.'

Cooper ran a vigorous hand over his face, rubbed it so hard that I could hear the click of his broken nose. 'I don't have a clue what the fuck you're talking about, but I want out of here, today. You understand?'

'No,' Hickey refused, 'not today, no way.'

'When then?'

'I need a day, maybe two. You and your *lady* want out of here, no problem, but we go when I say. You give me tomorrow to work on Watkins, I'll get us out of here. You have my word.'

'What's to stop me taking the van, getting gone today, huh?'

'You'd never get out of this place. You have no idea where to go.'

'I've driven out of tighter spots than this.'

'Like hell you have.' Hickey's smile returned, 'Besides, if you leave today, you'll have to go without Daniel. Isn't that right?'

They both looked down at me, as if they had just remembered I was there, slumped amongst the rubble of Cooper's fury. 'What's he talking about, Danny boy?' Cooper looked cheated before I even said a word, 'You don't wanna stay here, do you?'

From Cooper's face to Hickey's, I read their expressions through one long, weightless moment. They were aliens. They were planets orbiting a new sun. I didn't want to hurt Cooper, but what I had seen the previous night, what I believed I had seen in the woodland earlier, its gradual amendment in shape, it all seemed too much, too incredible for me to walk away from right then.

I stood up, brushed myself down, spoke firmly, my voice hardened, even to my own ear, 'Hickey's right,' I told Cooper. 'No matter what shit is boiling up between the two of you, it's my neck on the line, I'm the one Watkins has on camera. We need more time. Hickey needs more time. Give him a day or so, Coop. If Watkins hasn't spilled by then, we'll get out of here,' I turned to Hickey, 'with or without you.'

Cooper sulked away from the outhouse. He took Shanice by the arm, turned once to regard me as I followed, then stormed into the cottage, slamming the door before I could reach it.

I stood there, lost in the hinterland between The Red House and the outhouse. There was no birdsong, no harmonious chorus of the untampered wilds. There was only the sound of Watkins coming around, spluttering, groggy, his voice wet with phlegm and new blood. I caught sight of Hickey helping him up in the chair, just before he closed the door and left me adrift on that livid sea between two craggy coastlines.

I looked up at the sky. I pleaded for the first purple blooms of evening, desperate to see whether I was visited again that night.

I wouldn't be disappointed.

AMIDST THE FRACTURES OF OUR relationship, Cooper found enough civility to invite me to eat with him and Shanice that evening.

He barely spoke to me and, as she had been during the morning, Shanice was quiet, monosyllabic, distracted by how this place was making her feel, maybe even by what she had seen. So many words remained locked in her throat.

I ate quickly and watched as the dark drew itself across the woodlands above.

I cleaned up afterwards and did my best to ignore Cooper's searching eyes. When I was done, I nodded a goodnight to the huddled television couple and went to my room. Every moment of that meal kicked at the door of my skull.

I sat in the dark, the back of my head against the cold wall behind the bed. A sheet of unreality covered me. I wasn't afraid, but I was edgy, unsettled.

The conversation with Hickey told me that he was aware of the occurrences here, even then. He inferred they were why we were here, but I couldn't understand how that had come about, how we had manifested here following the issue with Watkins, or even how that itself had acted as the fuse, the spur to move us from one universe into another.

Every episode, every aspect of what had occurred since the birth of Katie Pop seemed interlinked, but I wouldn't know to what extent for days to come. Back then, back on that third night, I just waited for the cloying soil of arrival, for that creature to return, to regard me through my own television screen, through the unwashed window of The Red House.

I listened to the undersea muffle of Cooper's and Shanice's conversation. The words were gluey, inaudible, but the tone was clear. Upset, uncertainty, anger; the words rose and fell like a cadaverous waltz. I knew Hickey was nearby, in the outhouse with his torture doll, likely pulling teeth, toenails, putting out blazing fags on withering skin.

I tried to see everything in the darkness ahead of me, tried to understand my new existence here, the world I was being shown. I stared into the murk for a long while. So long, in fact, that I fell asleep.

Woken by a sense of choking dirt, I lurched up again, felt every bone jolt and snap. All I could smell was wet earth. Almost briny, it crawled with the reek of rot. The soil licked at me, weightless, invisible.

I knew they were here.

The high moon covered the world in two layers of white. A filthy, spoiled, phlegmy white that saturated everything. Above it, silvery, snail-trail diamante, a second, pristine layer. Yet, more staggering than that light, more brilliant, more beautiful, the luminescence which came through the woodlands and gushed down towards The Red House.

Fastened in that momentary lithograph, clearing my throat of dirt which wasn't even there, I swung my legs from the bed and made my way towards the window.

I expected to see him again, Mr Milliman with his tuxedo of insect fingers. I believed then that he was the only one, with perhaps the enormous stag-shape the only other. It's hard now for me to believe how wrong I was.

Whilst that shape moved amongst the bracken, that one I was yet to understand, far more moved outside the cottage, towards my window.

Silhouetted by the shine of the competing lights behind them, a dozen or so figures hunched and rocked at the periphery of the woodland, the point where the high northern woods met the cragged and rock-strewn pathway.

I felt fear then, for the first time in this place. I don't know if it was the realisation of the existence of more than the few creatures I had already seen, glimpsed at the edge of my vision. I don't know if it was the sight of them, cowed there, the sheets of light reflected on the skein of their moist eyes. Somehow, swallowed by the thudding silence, I froze, stuck there, halfway between two universes.

Gradually, moving as one juddering phalanx, the figures began to edge out from the canopy of twisted ash trees and hanging, weeping willows. Caught in the searchlight of the moon, they were, for a moment, incredibly vivid. Approaching slowly, I could see the nakedness of everything below their throats.

Like Mr Milliman, their skin was blue-white, starved of shades, fungal, waxen. The figures weren't tall, but strange, bolete muscles seemed to swell from their frames. Some were unmistakeably male. Their withering pricks and balls clutched tight to the apex of their thighs as they shuffled towards me.

Others, I assumed female, or without gender entirely, remained smooth at their abdomen, into their crotch. Only swollen veins and the ridges of defined muscles were visible on their lithe bodies.

Strangest of all, their faces were covered by hoods, by hoods independent of any clothing. The hoods too seemed like their flesh. They rolled over from the back of their shoulders, looming over their faces almost completely, with only the polished pennies of their eyes apparent.

The creatures stepped over the trenches without looking down. They knew this place perfectly, every inch of it.

I was still framed there, at the window, a few paces between that and the bed. I had the feeling that, to them, I must look like a bad painting, a paused video tape, something grainy, shitty, something manufactured from static.

In the hinterland once more, between the woodland and us, the creatures paused. They huddled together, writhing in each other's grasps, their splinter-fingers jagged, raking at another's shoulders as they communicated. They returned their faces to me, then gathered again. Angsty, disagreeable, I saw one or two push another away, grip their upper arms savagely, claw at them, pull them back in.

I waited, sure then that they would attack themselves, or even the cottage. I looked over in the direction of the outhouse, but couldn't see any movement, any sign of Hickey. Cooper and Shanice seemed silent in their room, not even the putter of their snores audible as I hung on for the next movement of the creatures.

Separating again, the gaunt gang formed a rough circle. They kept looking back to me, the moon reflected in the glass of their canopied eyes. I couldn't fathom why they seemed to check in with me between their actions, what they wanted me to do, to say. As I stood there, I was still overcome with the sensation of wet muck on my skin, in my nose, my throat.

Eventually, almost comically, the creatures squatted and, their legs awkward, duck-bent, they began to move in their ugly circle. One after another, they rode the air, their slender feet digging into the dirt, carving crooked scars beneath them.

Again, as each of them passed, their focus moved from their strange rotation back to me, almost as if they were seeking approval, as if this were there way of trying to speak to me, to make me understand what they wanted to tell me.

I couldn't respond. I was gripped by the night-dirt, hanging in starless space, a lunar zero.

Seemingly frustrated by my failure to do anything, the creatures stopped, grimaces suggesting despair and then, as quickly as a fox bolts from the sound of human feet, they turned and ran, scattering as they reached the glooms of the woodland. The ethereal silverlight cast through the jagged tress also receded.

I managed to catch a single glimpse of the immense stag-shape, high above. Its outline seemed to hold me for a moment, then vanished completely, swept into the nothingness by the retreating light.

The suffocation of dream-dirt disappeared too. My breath returned.

I felt instantly exhausted. My legs were heavier than they had ever been. My arms felt broken, nerveless, dull. I collapsed back into the unmade bed, gasping, reaching for a cogent thought. None came. Instead, as I remember it, sleep came more by collapse than lullaby. The weight of the night soaked me. In a few seconds, I was unconscious.

I stayed that way until Cooper's screams woke me the following morning. With the sun came something else.

Shanice was gone.

18.

Crashing through a chicane of stars

GUTTURAL, HOARSE, DESPERATE, Cooper's cries rang through the crumbling Red House.

He was a sudden enormous bell clanging in its housing. A clobbering force, wild-eyed and frantic.

Cooper threw himself through my door before I'd even had time to gather the few thoughts I had.

'GetthefuckupDannyfuck!' the words merged, clattered into one another. It was a pile-up, spit-sodden wreckage, bumper-to-bumper.

I tried to ask what was happening, but Cooper was already on his knees, checking beneath my bed. He tore the cupboard open, pulled the door from its hinges, left it hanging there when he spun around to face me. 'What's the fuckin matter?' his jaw jutted outwards, his yellowing lower teeth protruded over his upper lip, 'She's gone, Dan, *for fuck's sake*, Shanice has gone!'

I tried to ask where, when, 'What? She went during the night?'

'Course she fuckin did,' Cooper rubbed his eyes, his torso throbbed with panicked breathing, 'something's happened to her, I know it! Where's Hickey, where's that cunt?'

Cooper stormed out of the room and then, right then, I knew I needed to get between them before what had threatened to boil over erupted into brutality.

Knowing Cooper was on his way to the outhouse, knowing that I couldn't catch him by chasing, I pushed the window opened and clambered out, staggering, tripping as I tried to get to the outhouse.

Cooper came barrelling from the front door of the cottage, his face fixed on the outhouse.

'Coop! Coop! Wait, *wait!*' I tried to calm him, to slow him down. 'Don't do anything stupid, anything nuts. You don't know Hickey's done anything, that's he's got *anything* to do with her going.'

'Outta the way or I'll knock you outta the way.' Cooper pushed me aside like a curtain. I tripped again and my foot slid into one of the deep ditches.

Before I could get back up, Cooper had torn the door of the outhouse open, ready to smash Hickey, ready to ruin him before a word was spoken.

Hickey wasn't there.

All Cooper found was Watkins. The reeking hostage, somnolent, cockeyed with torture. He wasn't gagged, but he may as well have been. Cooper grabbed Watkins by the throat, shook him from side-to-side, demanded he tell him where Hickey was.

'Cooper!' I grabbed at his shoulder, 'How the fuck would he know? He's been strapped to that chair since we got here. He hasn't seen daylight for almost a week. Christ.'

Cooper pushed Watkins backwards, sending him and the chair reeling again.

As Cooper turned and rushed from the outhouse, we heard Hickey's voice. We both turned to look and saw him coming from the far side of the cottage, his own face twisted with anger, '*The van's gone*,' he screamed at us, '*the fucking van.* This down to you, huh?' He was talking to Cooper, hurrying over to us. 'This your idea of a way to get at me, Cooper? That it? You'd better tell me where you've hidden it, brother, or we're fucked. You hear me? Fucked.'

Hickey's righteous volley seemed to stun Cooper for a few seconds, to completely silence him. He was ready to blame Hickey for Shanice's disappearance, but found himself caught off-guard, blamed for something else entirely. Gathering himself, Cooper began to pace towards Hickey, his own rage returning. 'Don't come at with me, Hick,' he leaped over the ditches as he spoke, 'Shanice is gone, what have you done to her?'

'She's *what?*' Hickey stopped and waited for Cooper to reach him. Face to face, Cooper leaned in, ground his forehead into Hickey's. Neither man gave ground.

'Gone,' Cooper spat, 'and you know she is.'

'I know? I don't a bloody thing about your tart.'

Cooper lifted his hands to Hickey's throat, framed his neck with bulging, blood-filled fingers. 'My what? Say it again, you bastard. Say it again.'

'You gonna strangle me, Cooper? That it? Go ahead. Turn the gas off. It won't change a thing. I don't know where she is, where the van is. If I have to guess, they're together, she's taken it and done one in the night.'

I could see Cooper shaking. His face narrowed, intense, the sunlight yellowing the muscles of his shoulders and back. 'You're fuckin mental if you think she drove that piece of shit outta here. Crazy.'

'Why?' Hickey leaned into Cooper's hands, adding pressure to his own throat, deepening his voice, turning it into a growl, 'What do you know about her, eh? You saying she can't drive? Can't get in the van during the night, all of us out cold, just get out of here? You don't know a thing about her, Coop. You only met her a few weeks back. What makes you think she gives a fuck about me, you, Daniel?'

'She wouldn't...she wouldn't go without me,' Cooper's voice was breaking. I watched as his hands lowered from Hickey's throat, eventually hanging at his sides, deflated.

Hickey's voice softened as Cooper took a step backwards, staggering with his disbelief. 'She could've gotten scared,' Hickey suggested coolly, compassionately, his tone a thousand miles away from *your tart* a few moments before, 'this is heavy business, the thing with Watkins, everything else we've done so far. We're in the middle of nowhere out here too. Sometimes having too much space comes down hard on city people.'

Cooper listened, but his thoughts were far above, crashing through a chicane of stars. 'Yeah,' he said eventually, 'we are in the middle of nowhere…and *you* barely managed to get that van down her in the dark, so she'd have to be some kind of rally driver to get the fuckin thing out.'

Bolstered by his logic, by a thought I too had as Hickey spoke, Cooper barged past Hickey, towards the back of the cottage, the direction we had entered the night we arrived.

I followed, thinking of the way the weeds seemed to have closed over the rough road behind us, any sign we had driven down that path vanished, utterly deleted. Before this, when I'd last walked that way, they had closed upon us, without a doubt. Curtains of thorns, gnarled, suffocating. When I had seen them earlier, they were an encumbrance, albeit insidious. Now though, now as we headed around the corner of the cottage, there was every chance they had woven themselves into a noose.

Cooper stopped ahead of me as we reached the bottom of the ersatz road.

I couldn't see his face, but could fathom the confusion and bewilderment by the way he just stood there, looking into a wall of choking weeds and branches. Married like old bones in a mass grave, their owners indiscernible in the death crush, in the rot, the trees and weeds to were shackled to one another, more so even than on my earlier trip that way.

Cooper turned to me then, an expression of lostness plastered across his face, 'No way this was the road,' he said blankly, 'is there?'

'That's the way,' I replied, hearing the death's head in my own voice, 'that's the only way, mate, far as I know.'

'Can't be…where're the tracks, the tire marks? If Shan drove this way, even if she could, where's the proof of it? She must've gone another way…if she went at all.'

Hickey appeared then, coolly smoking. I heard his steps as he approached, saw him from the corner of my eye as he stood to my right, also looking at the matted wall, the impassable dam.

'How the fuck d'ya explain this?' Cooper asked angrily, his temper boiling again. 'How did she drive that shit wagon through here without leaving a single bloody mark?'

Hickey looked down at the road, back at Cooper, 'What do you want me to say, Coop?'

166

'I want you to tell me what happened to her.'

'She's gone,' Hickey exhaled, then took another drag of the roll-up before he continued, 'she's gone, the van's gone. This is the only road out, so unless she's pranking us and they're both tucked up in the treeline, *this* is the only way out.'

'But the weeds, the branches and all that?' Cooper turned back, kicked at one of the low-hanging whorls of thorn-backed dogrose, 'It isn't a gate, it's just plants, Hickey. Just fuckin weeds.'

'It's *all* a gate,' Hickey whispered, audible only to me.

'Eh?' Cooper kicked at the dry tentacle again, 'What'd you say?'

'I *said* that you both know what *I* know and that's it.' Hickey flicked the cigarette on the ground, trod it into the eager dirt with his boot, 'It isn't impossible that she made it through there and it snapped back behind her. Take a deeper look. I'm off back to the office. Watkins is still the priority here.'

Hickey walked away, disappeared behind the corner of the cottage. I felt he was still there, listening, but didn't check. Instead, seeing the lack of thought in Cooper, the sheer absence of an idea, I walked to his side and suggested we cut some of the branches away, take a proper look.

'Think it's worth it?' He seemed dulled again, perhaps in shock.

'Sure, mate, let me get my boots, a couple of hatchets, or something.'

I returned quickly and we slashed away at some of the greener branches, at the bustling understory that knitted perniciously beneath our knees. It didn't take long for us to find some tire tracks, evidence of the van's wheels, fossilised in the muck.

I knelt down, scored them with my index finger, 'Van's defo been this way' I confirmed, uncontented. 'No getting away from that.'

'But *when*, though,' Cooper snapped, kneeling at my side, 'these skids could've been from when we pulled in here. Seems mental to think the weeds crawled over the road in a few hours, doesn't it?'

I wanted to agree with Cooper, but I already knew so much that he didn't. I was the one who had seen the creatures, two nights running. I could sense the neon shape moving behind the fracture of bracken in the northern woods above us. I was beginning to understand the reasons we were here, even if I didn't know what being here truly meant then. I opted to remain on the wall, kicking my feet against the paint-scarred bricks.

'Listen,' I laid a hand on Cooper's shoulder, 'aren't neither of us countryside boys, are we? How do we know how shit like this works? I couldn't tell you an oak from an ash half the time, what leaves are which, what flowers grow where. I'd check online, but we have sod all reception here. For all we know, this lot could've snapped back on us in a matter of minutes, right?'

Cooper shrugged. He looked unconvinced.

'I came up here the other day' I carried on, fostering a bubble I wasn't even sure I needed, 'just to pass the time, to take a look. It was like this then, you know. The weeds, the branches, it'd all come back thick and fast, just like this, even though I'm positive we drove the van down here a day or two earlier. I swear.'

'No shit?'

'No shit, Coop. Believe me. It seemed weird then, but not, you know, not *evil*. I knew we'd gotten down here, I remembered the van rocking, the torch in the night, the thick bush and bracken either side. It was dicey then, but we made it through.'

'You go much further?' Cooper asked me, his eyes unblinking, searching my own. 'When you had a look the other day?'

'A little bit. There isn't much to see. The path's thin, just woodland either side. Like Hickey said, we're miles away from anywhere, mate. There's no way of heading off up there. No point.'

Neither of us had noticed Hickey return. When he spoke, we both jumped.

'Look,' he was swirling a cup of tea, 'kettle's just boiled, there's a pot on. I know you're worried about her, Coop, about us being stuck here. I was too. I was furious when I saw the van was gone, but we aren't completely cut-off down here, so don't worry about that at least.'

I asked what he meant.

'There's a bloke,' Hickey sipped the tea, blew on it, cooled the heat, 'a gamekeeper, I suppose you'd say. A bloke by the name of Yando. He manages the land around here, patrols it. Standard stuff for whatever rich cunts own places like this. He comes around here every two or three weeks at the outside. If he sees this cottage occupied, sees that we're staying here, he'll come down, say hello. He always does.'

'So fuckin what?' Cooper snapped. 'Two or three weeks?'

'So what,' Hickey carried on, calmly, '*so what* is the fact that he has a radio, he'll have his motor within a day's walk or so. Worst case we just wait it out until he turns up and we hitch a ride to the nearest town.'

I watched Cooper's face. Thoughts passed by in twitches, in tiny spasms beneath his eyes, above his lips. His expression hardened, the concrete set. 'Okay,' he grimaced, 'okay. If that's what we have to do, then that's what we do.'

'I know you don't like it, but-'

'No, I don't fuckin like it.' Cooper cut Hickey off, turned back to the covered road.

'Tea's ready,' Hickey repeated, before walking away, vanishing once more.

When Cooper turned back to me, the right side of his mouth was curled up in a smile of disgust. 'You believe a word he says?' he asked.

I didn't say anything, I just looked back to the cottage, then back to Cooper.

'Me neither,' he assured himself, 'not for one minute. Maybe that Yando fella's for real, but there's no way Shan drove outta here. I'm sure of it.'

'What do you wanna do, Coop?'

Standing to his full height, his head a reddened searchlight, Cooper surveyed the northern woodland line, the quarry face east, the veritable walls of the creeping well in which we were marooned. 'Fancy a hike?'

'Where?'

'Up there,' Cooper nodded to the northern woodlands, the place of white bracken. 'Something tells me that's the place to look.'

'To look for what?'

'For whatever is happening here,' Cooper nodded. 'Up there, Danny boy. That's the place.'

'You sure?'

'Get a bag together,' Cooper squeezed my shoulder, 'we're off on tour.'

19.

The wreath of doomed faces

HICKEY DIDN'T CARE THAT WE were heading up to the woodlands.

In fact, smirking slightly from the doorway of the outhouse, he seemed almost pleased. 'Sounds good,' he held the door half closed behind him, obscuring Watkins, 'may as well do something useful to pass the time. If it makes you feel better…' He looked past me, towards Cooper, who completely ignored him and, hoisting the heavy pack over his shoulder, continued to walk towards the winding, almost invisible gap in the forest wall to the north of the cottage.

As I went to follow, I felt Hickey's hand snatch at my backpack, holding me there for an instant. 'And you?' he asked quietly. 'You understand what looks down at us from the guts of the night?'

I eased my bag from Hickey's grip, keen to catch up to Cooper, 'I don't, not yet. But you do, don't you?'

'What I know is different from what you'll be shown.' Hickey licked his lips, 'I'm jealous.'

'Of what?'

'Haven't you seen what they're doing for you? Haven't you noticed the reshaping of the woodland?'

'Who?' I was suddenly desperate, shaken. 'Reshaping how?'

'Hurry the fuck up, Danny boy,' Cooper bellowed at me.

'Breadcrumbs for the birds,' Hickey grinned, then backed into the glooms of the outhouse. I saw Watkins' face briefly, before the door closed. It seemed demented, dislodged from reality. He smiled broadly, his shattered front teeth glowing within the underlit bricks.

I hurried off, towards Cooper, towards the haunted deadwoods above us.

◖

NO MAP, NO IDEA, no route to follow, all we could do was carve a way upwards, through clawing limbs. Every branch a yellowed talon, every step finding us ankle-deep in muck.

For more than a few minutes, all Cooper did was walk the treeline, eyeing small gaps, thin crevices within the thorn-walls. I did the same. The incline through the woodland – what we could see of it – was steeper than I thought, even knowing just how high above us the forest seemed.

Cooper didn't say anything, but I could tell he found it unsettling, the way the bracken seemed to hold us off, to forbid us from passing through it, into it. We knew there must be a way in; we communicated that with shrugs and nods.

Occasionally, I looked back to the outhouse, expecting to see Hickey there, in the doorway, his face smug, feverish with righteous understanding, with secrets. He wasn't there, watching us. The door was closed, the side of the outhouse facing the woods remained windowless. Barely audible creaks and groans hummed form inside.

Cooper had a hatchet raised above his head. Mostly blunt, it looked like it would do enough damage to carve us entry but, just as he was about to strike the green, I noticed a narrow entrance through the bracken.

'Hey,' I called to him, 'we might be able to get in this way, Coop.'

Cooper wandered over, sleeving the hatchet, 'Fuckin hell, Danny boy, that's tight. I'll have to edge in sideways.'

'You see a better way in?'

'Not without burning a way through.'

I went first. I ducked into the musk, into the blackness. It was daylight, midmorning, the sun hovered like a floodlight above the cottage but, even as I craned my head into the dank branch-fingered hash, I felt night wrap itself around me.

171

Thorns picked at my sleeves, my thighs. I backed away a couple of times, but pushed ahead again with Cooper's insistence, 'Come on, Danny boy, it'll be teatime before you get both legs through. Jesus H.'

Just when I felt like we would have to hack a hole through the sharpened bracken, the woodland seemed to ease, to give, to relax and let me in. By the time Cooper joined me, ducking his bulk in at an angle, he couldn't see what had taken me so long.

'I worked the space for us,' I insisted, a little annoyed, but more than that distracted by the growing idea that we were being *permitted entry* to the forest's perimeter, granted an audience with the night-freak populous who had wandered down over the last two days, meeting me near the cottage, somewhere between dreams and winter.

My first impressions were almost of another planet. Even so close to The Red House, the outhouse, to the gouged grounds of the property, there was a thick sense of unreality. Feet away, maybe even inches, just ducking into the first shadows of the woodland, it was otherworldly, something I had never seen before.

I didn't know a thing about trees, about plants, even most flowers. I couldn't qualify what I saw with any kind of botanical knowledge. All I noticed were splinters and jagged, leaf-lined limbs. Almost sickly with their thinness, their lividity, but somehow also flourishing sleazily, everything around them waxy; the fanned edges of the leaves glistening like a million wet lips.

At first, as I stood straight, there in the new darkness, it felt like I'd slid into spoiled meat. There was a cloying, reeking stink that led upwards in jagged slaloms. Cooper didn't seem to mind. He stumbled inwards, unborn from light to dark, suddenly at my shoulder, huffing, panting from the initial brawl just to find a basic pathway.

'Fucking twigs,' he groaned, 'cut me good n' proper getting through there.'

I wanted to say that I didn't think the woodlands wanted to allow us in, but just agreed instead.

'You get cut n'all?'

'Here and there. No big deal. Which way should we go?'

'Which way?' Cooper laughed harshly. 'There's only upwards, isn't there? We need to make our way through this shit, up to the main woods, get a proper look about.'

'You can't think Shanice could've driven the van up here, Coop?'

'It ain't about that.' Cooper began to trudge ahead of me, his boots sloppy in the rotting leaves and root-muck, 'First off, I don't think Shan drove the van *anywhere*. Second, if we can get up there, to that height, we'll have a way better view of this whole place than we've had before. Worst case, we can size up the best way outta here on foot. Fuck what Hickey says, ain't no place on mainland Britain a person can't yomp to. Never has been.'

I couldn't argue with Cooper's logic. Getting up high was what I'd wanted to do when I tried to make my way through the broken, weed-covered road a couple of days earlier. The thing was, that road hadn't let me get further than the first bend and I knew this forest would be the same.

The going was hard at first. We zigzagged, backtracked, hacked a pathway only to abandon it almost immediately. Wet branches tugged at our shoulders, our backpacks. The light was poor and increasingly bad. I had the feeling the leaves conspired to screen any discernible route to the main woodland. The entire sloping mess seemed to lean on us. I felt my breath sapped. The temperature jolted and jerked, one moment suffocating, rotting heat, the very next a blast of bone-cold winter-wind, impossible to rationally fathom, yet I was able to feel it through my clothes, my skin.

I had expected a different sensation from something so rural, so removed from the concrete I knew. The beaten-up shopping arcades, the steely faces nestled in bus-shelter glooms. The speeding boy-racers in their pulverising metal, the gossamer drunks stuck in the doorways of their boozers, lips ablaze with crooked fags. That was what I knew. Not the sight of it, but the feeling of it. That anchor of impending danger; the pub-fight flareup, the underage girls lousy on cider, throwing insults at me as I hurried past. All of that was a *sense*, all of it was inbuilt, a blueprint of discomfort drawn on the bones. As hard as it was to believe, I felt it there too, in the first part of the woodland.

As I followed Cooper's bulk, as he bulldozed on, hardly speaking, I began to notice the angles of the trees again. I think they were ash trees, their trunks scabby and gnarled. They were the ones which seemed to somehow be forming into unnatural shapes. Rather than standing tall, or even bending against the angle of the slope, they seemed to be at geometric angles, in an effort to form rectangular lines, something like doorways, maybe even like buildings. As we moved upwards, I was sure they were not only parting to allow us entry but, in doing so, they were becoming a mockery of the streets, pavements and arcades manifest in my own unspoken thoughts.

I pictured the visitors from the previous nights, especially last night. The way they circled, the way their flesh formed into hoods. Were they trying to meet me on a plain of familiarity? Were they locked into impressions of humans, of the beings I saw the most often? I was becoming convinced, almost adamant that theirs was a performance of the hate-kids, the arcade gangs, the park hasslers, the ones who hovered outside Cooper's place, forever circling, lost in empty pursuits.

I found the notion beyond ridiculous, cursed myself for thinking it, for being a fool, hypnotised by dream-idiocy. I didn't even know if what I had seen was the same as I pictured it then, or the next day, the days that followed. Hickey had assumed control of us, down at The Red House. Everything had a purpose. Even his words led my thoughts, led Cooper's actions.

I tried to ignore the idea, to focus on making my way up to the forest with Cooper, on beating back the bleeding bracken. I know now that I should have kept my eyes open, for every second, every solitary moment. Perhaps if they had been able to show me the world then, we wouldn't have needed to be bludgeoned by it later on.

Despite his bull strength and stubbornness, Cooper had to stop before we were anywhere near the peak of the hillside. The treacherous thorns, grasping branches, the sheer sludge we staggered through, all of it a mire, left there in sunless rot. It got to Cooper and he suddenly stopped, turned, leaned his back against one of the trees and looked down at me, his face flushed with effort.

'Hard yards, eh, Danny boy?'

I agreed, clawing my way up to where he was stood. He helped me up to the tree, his strength still such that he could lift my weight with one hand, 'There you go, mate. Snatch a breather.'

I asked if he thought there was much farther to go, 'To get to the main woods' I wheezed. 'This slope can't go on much longer, can it?'

'Nah,' Cooper took a deep drag from his water bottle, swilled his mouth, stared down past me, his face thoughtful, a little forlorn. 'We've been chopping our way up through this mess for a good hour or so now. Must've busted a mile or more. It'll level out soon enough.'

'Good. Wouldn't want to be stuck here when it gets dark later.'

Cooper looked at me, his face broad with surprise, 'Danny, if it takes us *days*, we're getting to where we need to be. I'll sleep out here, you too.'

I didn't want to argue. I knew what Shanice disappearing had already done to Cooper. Anything else then, any other loss, like me turning back, would've been enough to shatter him, to set his temper ablaze.

'Let's hope it doesn't come to that.' I nodded upwards, 'Better get a shift on.'

'True enough.' Cooper snatched up his bag and carried on, into the angles, the endless curve.

It was easy to lose track of time in the woods.

Deep, dank, devoid of daylight, they seemed to exist out of time.

The canopy of treetops became more knotted the further we walked. The waxy tangle, the patchwork of cloying leaves between us and them, it began to sully the daylight and finally to hide it completely. Where the sun should have brightly lit the land around us, we instead found ourselves trudging through a thick and sepia evening light.

I had no direction, I just followed Cooper. His only goal was *up*. Further and further until we made it to the forest proper.

The tangle of spiked trees around me began to feel more like a tunnel, more like the underpasses of the estate. Those circular glooms, places of giggling echoes and hurried feet, the places of figures waiting to pounce. I was already aware that the woodland seemed to be bending towards me, showing itself, switching themes from hacked hoodoo ugliness to benign muck.

I had the fleeting thought that, at any moment, one of them would appear, one of the creatures.

Looking back, I'm not sure why I went with Cooper, or even why I let Cooper go at all. I couldn't have stopped him, of course. It's not like I could've just said, *Coop, there're things out there, in the woods, things that come at night. I've seen them.* He would never have believed me and, if he had, he would've instantly blamed *them* for Shanice's disappearance, storming through the green window, ready to kill. No, I had to go with him, regardless.

I had noticed a growing numbness in myself, a dullness in the drive for self-preservation. Back on the estate, back in the universe of pavement-facing people and the rattling machinery, back there I had been born a zero, lived a zero sum and would never be anything more than a clock counting backwards, waiting to rot away to the nothingness from which I'd scrambled. Only the fear of being pegged for Watkins' kidnap, maybe even his murder kept me onboard with the plan. Only that snare-trap made me a runaway. Without that trigger, without that prompt, I would have still been there, awash in TV neon, in uniform grey. Just an outline lit by the flickering bulbs of a takeaway window.

I saw the first one before just before we reached the top of the slope.

Off to my left, too fast to focus on in the dingy brush, it scrambled by, peering at me from the bric-a-brac of an ash tree trunk.

One of the skin-hooded things, the night figures, it snapped past, almost weightless, soundless on the scabby leaves.

I hadn't seen one in the daylight until then, not that the woodland canopy allowed much light to seep through. A smoky ozone, an ink spill, sunlight blotted purple and rusty.

I caught a glimpse of it, the hooded one. Seeing me seeing it, the creature stopped, just for a moment. I wonder whether I should have been afraid, but that didn't occur to me. I know why now, I know that the expression of its behaviour, then and the previous night, of all of them, wasn't threatening, not to me.

Skin like a jellyfish, pulled taut on jagged bones, the creature tilted its face towards me, allowing me vision of its lipless mouth, of its pinched nipple-nose, of the stab-wound eyes, lidless, gorily carved, no sign of any pupils, or retina, just tiny voids. The flesh hood throbbed above the lineless forehead, juddering, quivering as the creature ducked and looked back at me.

Then, as suddenly as it was there, it was gone.

In the vapour of its leaving, there was the dirt stink, the wet soil odour that choked me last night and the night before. A signal of them, of what I would know as the Undertundrans. Their hallow perfume.

Cooper turned back. He had heard the rustling of the leaves, 'Fuck was that? A deer?'

'I didn't see,' I lied, 'maybe a muntjac, a fox, who knows, eh? This isn't Springwatch.'

'You can say that again,' Cooper turned back, clawed his way up a particularly steep stoop of moss-wigged rock ahead of him.

I followed, certain they were everywhere here, watching us, following us, learning about us with every word we spoke, every inch we moved forwards, into their universe.

The ground began to dry out the higher we hiked. Like a sea beneath us, the tide seemed have taken the moisture back out, down towards The Red House.

It meant the going was easier, and our pace quickened.

Strangely, though my lack of rural knowledge made me an ignorant tourist, soon, even though the dirt seemed drier, we were increasingly flanked by large toadstools. Waxy to the point of dripping, the fungi reddened as more and more appeared around us. Some the size dinner plates, of frying pans, some even larger, they were almost neon in the undergrowth deadlight. They were more like sirens than mushrooms, so bright that you could squint in the face of them and still believe you were looking into a blood-sick sun.

Cooper saw them too, stopped, thumbed a slick, phlegmy line of moisture from one and smelled it. 'Ugh,' he flicked the ooze away, 'bleedin' reeks.' He spat into the scaly leaves, 'Just imagine how poisonous these things are eh, Danny boy? One drop a'that shite'd see you dead as disco.'

I agreed, 'They aren't there for eating, Coop. Anything red means *stay away*, doesn't it? Berries and all that?'

'Suppose so. Reminds me,' Cooper shook his backpack, 'I grabbed plenty of grub like, so we can stop in a while, have a bit of lunch.'

'Nice work.' My bag was mostly full of water, a few bags of crisps and a couple of pasties crushed against the plastic bottles, 'You wanna wait until we level out?'

'Yeah, let's make a little more ground and see what's what, mate.'

As much as I didn't believe we would ever reach the plateau of the forest, we did.

It took another hour or so, both us of silent, only our laboured breathing audible through the knackering ascent. Accompanied by the toadstools, their lids like raucous, laughing gobs, we chicaned, we slalomed, we dragged ourselves up, always upwards, snatching at the ragged roots of teetering trees, at the dirt itself. Then, eventually, with Cooper cheering the success with a *Thank fuck for that,* we found the lip of the slope, the platform of the forest.

I almost gasped when I found myself at Cooper's side, looking ahead at the vastness of it.

A nation of thickly knitted trees, the spaces between them wider than the ascension, I saw confirmation of what I had guessed at, wondered about. I saw the woodland's impersonation of the city. I saw the trees angled into mimicry of the estate itself.

It was staggering, the immediate recognition of the street-shapes, the arcade lunacy, the severity of straight lines, manufactured by concrete and glass back there, but born brilliantly, bizarrely here, in the home of the hallows, at the neck of the Undertundra.

I watched Cooper closely, desperate to see a sign of recognition from him, to see any evidence at all that he understood what the landscape was doing for us, what it was doing *to* us.

He scanned the trees, the thicket, the way ahead, but his lean, fury-furrowed face showed no fear, no surprise. Aware that he wouldn't say anything about it, even if he thought it, I broached the scene ahead of us, the geometric trees, their uniform endeavour to show us the urban lunacy from which we'd escaped.

'Why are the trees like that?' I asked, pulling Cooper's arm, holding him back from walking on.

'Like what?' he asked, still staring ahead, still searching the woods for a sign of Shanice.

'Angled like that,' I continued, 'making themselves look like…like blocks, Coop, like avenues, like underpasses. Can't you see it?'

'What the fuck are you talking about, Danny boy?' Cooper pulled his arm away, 'They're just crooked is all. Natural, ain't it? Woodlands like this, ain't there somethin about how trees bend and buckle, reaching for the sun when it's blocked out, like it is by all them tall ones, the leaves and that?'

'No,' I pulled at Cooper's arm again, my annoyance manifest in my tone. 'No, it's not fucking natural, Cooper. It's as *unnatural* as it comes. Just take a look, please. Just stand back, look ahead of us, mate. Think back to the estate, the playground outside your own house, the shapes of it. The underpass, the takeaway, even the bloody Gladiator. Forget the details, the paintwork, the broken pavements, the shops, just *look at the outlines*. The edges. Look at what the trees are doing, *please*.'

Cooper sighed, but didn't answer. He laid his backpack down, rolled his shoulders, scanned the land from left to right, slowly, carefully.

I could see it. I needed him to see it. We were walking into insanity, into an unfathomable place. Spun out, cast upwards by Shanice's disappearance, we had no idea where we were going, what we were stepping into. I was desperate for Cooper to realise this, to see it at least, to believe it. I thought if he did, then maybe I could tell him about the visitors.

Cooper lit a smoke. He didn't have cigarettes often, only when he was under pressure, when the stress hit. It was a tell, a certainty that something was on his mind, troubling him. Nicotine blues, he would say. *Pass the fags, I got worries*.

I hoped this was the moment, the dawning of his realisation, the agreement that we were no longer residents of a world we knew. I was wrong.

'Nah,' he said eventually, exhaling the drag, his hand shaking slightly as he did so, 'can't see anything like that, Danny boy. Just coincidence, eh. Trick of the light, that kind of thing.'

I chose not to argue it with him. If he couldn't see it, then perhaps they were doing it just for me. If he could see it and didn't want to admit it, then it was his decision, his private pathway. I thought of the cigarette, the way he smoked it quickly, nervously, the way it burned to the filter in four heavy tugs. I believed it was because he *could* see the morphing forest, its impersonation of our home. I believed it completely, but I also knew that Shanice vanishing, her fictional runaway, was enough to send cracks through his core.

'Come on,' Cooper dropped the nub, ground it into the dirt with his boot, 'let's find a clear spot, grab somethin to eat, eh.'

Then he was gone, striding forward, ahead of me. He meandered into a sun-freckled forest, but I saw something else. I saw him walking down Maddox Crescent, down the alleys between The Precinct and The Gladiator. I could see the undulations of underpasses ahead, of the crisscross of tandem walkways known as *Dagger Alley* by the locals. With each step Cooper took, I saw the trees change their shapes in unison, forming a place of familiarity to us, a place they seemed to extract from our very thoughts, the estate.

◆

By the time Cooper slung his bag down and stopped, it was late afternoon.

No phone reception, no link to the world outside of the woodland, but the digital time seemed to have kept itself straight and correct. *1545.*

As Cooper searched through his swollen backpack for food, I knew there was no way we would be heading back to the house before night set in. We were there to stay. We were there until we found Shanice, or at least found a place that looked out over the land around us. A place which would satisfy Cooper's certainty he would be able to either see the van, or see a way out of there on foot.

I suggested we make a fire. 'Isn't like we're getting back tonight, is it?'

Cooper stopped mooching through the bag and looked at me, his face childlike with apology, 'Yeah, you're right, Danny boy. I'm sorry about this. I know you didn't want to be out here overnight, but...'

He didn't need to finish the sentence. 'Don't worry, Coop, it's cool, honestly.'

'You're a mate,' he said gently, a *real* mate, you know that?'

I offered a smile, but it felt thin and forced. An expression so light on my face it could have been a fly.

We weren't outdoorsmen, or members of those tedious families who grin bleached teeth as they strap tents and pots to the racks of their SUVs. I had no idea how to start a fire, it was just something I said, something which seemed to make sense. Thankfully, Cooper was more practical than me.

He set about gathering up dry wood. Some trees looked long dead, stood between more verdant neighbours, sickly, trying to hide. Cooper broke branches from them, some as thick as his arms. They came away easily, but the resonance of their snapping resounded like a backfiring car through the birdless forest.

I bludgeoned us a clearing. I kicked the dried leaves away, booted dead toadstools into the understory. I made a circle, laid out a couple of blankets from Cooper's backpack, used them to surround the emerging pile of wood at the centre.

Thinking ahead, apparently realising he was never going to get us back to The Red House that day, Cooper pulled old newspapers from his bag, fistfuls of them. Yellowed from years of being stacked in some airless shed. The frontpages were faded, the faces accompanying the headlines were worn away, ghostly with sapped ink. It didn't matter. If I squinted, they could have been headlines and people from that very week. Any week.

Energy crises, government corruption, scandals of disgraced TV stars caught snatching skin backstage. The tabloid blame lottery of every downtrodden, wretched, lost member of our underclass. It was exactly the same.

As Cooper tore those papers to shreds, stuffing them into the yawning gaps of the firewood, the past echo of the headlines further reminded me of the world we had left mere days ago and, more than anything else, why I didn't feel like I'd left anything worthwhile, why there didn't seem to be anything to go back to.

I felt like the perfect vessel for being there, in those figure-haunted woods, in that bizarre, unfolding universe. I felt like I was made for it, brought here on a tickling tide, flanked by eager waves, empty of love for the human land, blindly searching for something else, finding it against my will.

The kindling set, Cooper lit the fire easily. The flames licked out from the gnarled twigs, catching them, scorching them. As the newspaper continued to burn, so then did the historical con and horror of human Britain, with every grizzling bastard face scorched into oblivion.

Cooper really had planned on a few days away from The Red House. His backpack was rammed with food, water too. He knew I had a few bottles, but I could tell he was thinking of at least two days out here, maybe more. I wonder if I should've been unsettled then, knowing he had tugged me up into the place which seemed the most ferocious, the most overpowering of the directions available to us. I knew what I'd seen. I didn't know if Cooper had even glimpsed a twinkle in the night bracken, or whether the idea of finding Shanice surpassed any nerves he may have had.

Fire cures fears, allays the immediate terror. Something about that glow, something which resonates through every person, a kind of comfort, a state of surety, familiarity. As soon as the singe became a roar, we both settled down, almost relaxed.

We ate quietly, neither of us noticing the opaque curtains as they drew around us. It hadn't been genuinely light throughout the entire trek up to the northern woods. The conspiring leaves had seen to that. Yet, as a counterpoint to the emergence of fire, as soon as it began to burn, so too did the night arrive in blots and bat-winged blackness. It covered everything around us, above us.

I studied Cooper across the dancing flames. The furrows of his face deeper with the odd light, the roundness of his eyes thinned against the smoke. I couldn't read his thoughts, but I could see them as they passed from one side of his skull to the other, almost visible, like worms on his forehead. I ate my food. It was cold and dry. I watched Cooper thumb his pasty, pick at it, but not eat it. I could have spoken first, but I waited for him.

When Cooper began, his voice was so different; its usual boom and bluster replaced with a supine gentleness, oiled by a lightness of tears inside. 'I'm sorry,' he began simply, 'I'm sorry about all this, Danny boy.'

'It's not so bad out here,' I offered, knowing he didn't mean the forest at night.

'I mean everything, the whole lot. Everything's that happened since I started this shit, all the online nonce hunting. Everything since then.'

I didn't say a word. I wanted him to continue.

'I shoulda never've gotten you into it, mate. I shouldn't. Shanice too. We'd never be here if it weren't for that. I know it now.'

Cooper fidgeted, crossed and uncrossed his thick legs. 'I know you stuck with me, Dan, all through this. I know what it's cost you, what with Watkins, what the fucker did to you. It's my fault.'

'Hickey called the shots,' I replied, knowing it was time for Cooper to realise how manipulated he had been. Even then, when I said it, I didn't know the half of what Hickey had done, the length of the wires on which we hung. 'It's not all you, Coop. It was Hickey who picked up Watkins, his idea.'

'Maybe, maybe not. I was into it n'all. If I hadn't been, I could'a stopped it. That's the fact. No getting away from it. If I had done, if I'd have had the bottle, the stones, we'd be back home now. Shanice too.' Cooper's voice broke a little at the mention of her name.

'You wouldn't even have known her if it wasn't for all this.'

'Woulda been best if I didn't though, if I'd never've met her.'

I couldn't argue, so didn't respond to that. Shanice had been plucked from that red-light pavement, tugged away from a firing squad of drunken pricks, all of them ugly, randy, toothy with low-end arousal. It had seemed better for her to be taken away from there, a notable improvement on her death sentence but, as we sat there, it appeared little more than a stay of execution.

Cooper continued, his voice hardening, the anger with himself apparent and granite-like, 'I'm a fuckin nobody,' he seethed, 'just some square-headed cunt from the estate. All this, all the paedo stuff, I just wanted to let it out, to have a go, to crush the faces of some horrible bastards but...'

I waited as he swallowed sentiment, vitriol.

'But...but I'm a bastard too, aren't I? Eh? Come on, Danny boy, tell me what I am.'

I struggled for words. They were like peanuts under my tongue, hurting me, refusing to budge. I wanted to tell Cooper that he was right, that he was a bastard, that Hickey was a bastard, that they had woven this nightmare from disparate strings, that they had fashioned their work into a noose and we were all hanging from it, rotting in the breeze. But I couldn't. I couldn't let him hear my agreement. I thought he saw my friendship as the final rung on the ladder, the only thing which stopped him falling away, into blackness.

'You couldn't have known,' I said finally, 'you couldn't have seen what would happen, Coop. Nobody could. You started out doing something you thought was right and, even though I wasn't onboard with how you did it, catching people like that, outing them, it make sense, somehow. Hickey made it uglier, took it further.'

'You reckon?'

I nodded, 'Course. You wouldn't've even met that Barry bloke if it wasn't for Hickey, most likely.'

'I dunno about that, Danny boy,' Cooper knitted his fingers, stretched them, cracked the knuckles, 'I likely would've, maybe.'

'None of that matters.' I kicked at the fire, manoeuvring a smouldering branch back into the orange heart, 'What's done is done, Cooper. It's what you do now that matters.'

'Yeah. Finding Shanice, getting outta here, that's what matters most.'

We were quiet for a minute or two, both staring into the fire, listening to it hiss and cackle. I jumped a little when Cooper continued, so lost was I in the meandering flames.

'I'm sorry for you most of all.' He licked his lips, moistened the words, 'You should never have been dragged into it. I know you didn't want it, mate. Like you didn't want the gym, like you didn't want to be boozing six nights a week. You're different to me, Danny boy, you've got a future, something better down the line. I've blown everything, every chance, every option, I've sent em all down the river, down the drain.'

'You can do better,' I smiled, but it felt like a disguise, 'You can do something else.'

'Thing is, I just wanna settle down with Shanice. That's all. I never thought I'd give a fuck about another person like that, a woman. I…I've been happy on my own, with mates and that, with you. I didn't feel like I needed someone else, but she's been…she's become so important to me, Dan. I just wanna know she's safe, you understand? If she has gone, if she fucked off the minute she got a chance, if she just wanted to get away from here, from us, from *me*, I don't mind, you know? I just wanna know she's okay. I can't stop until I do.'

I told Cooper I understood that the situation had gotten out of hand, that we were somewhere we couldn't have ever expected to be. I said everything I felt needed to be said. I pressed the red button on the conveyer belt and moved the machinery forward. It was just a process. I was beginning to understand. Maybe I already understood it completely.

What I noticed most, as Cooper continued to talk, what I heard loudest of all, because I *didn't* hear it once, was that Cooper was only sorry now, only sorry once Shanice had disappeared. He had told me that he was sorry he had *gotten me into this,* but he could have apologised about that at any point in the preceding weeks, any time when we were sofa-shackled, monged on cheap beer and daytime television. Cooper was sorry now, not then. The sorrow came in the destruction of *his* life, not mine.

I couldn't say that destroyed my affection for Cooper, only that it rounded the edges of the bullet with which I had already been shot.

'We've been back and forth, going nowhere...' Cooper was more reflective than I'd ever seen him, ever known him. Something had opened up. I didn't know if it was the place, if it was a symptom of what I was feeling also, what I had seen. It could have just been the vanishing of Shanice, the emergent distrust of Hickey, the lostness of being away from the familiar grey vascularity of the estate and its perpetual routines, but something had changed in Cooper. Circumspection had arrived in a flood, existential wonderings coming like bile from a meth drinker.

'Thing is, way I see it now,' he continued, 'I ain't been good for you, Danny boy. Sure as shit. I might be a little cunt-struck with Shanice, as my old man would've said, but I ain't too blind to know that I'm no kinda partner for you, no kinda pal.'

I told Cooper that was silly, that it didn't matter. 'What's that got to do with anything, Coop? Mates are mates.'

'No,' he shifted around in the dirt, leaned towards the campfire orange, his face stark and wild in the light, 'you've got somethin in you, bud, somethin I ain't got. Ain't about years, about you been younger an' all that. Nah, it's more, it's different. I said it before...you've got a future, somethin down the line. I've got…I had Shanice, that was my turnaround, the fork in the road. That's why she means so much, y'know? It ain't just about settling down, fuckin laying out the tablecloths and polishing the brass on Sundays, it's about finding somethin that makes the rest make sense, makes it easier to live with.'

I understood what Cooper was saying, of course. He was talking about the golden root, about mainlining happiness, plugging into the heart-box and finding fulfilment where he could. I understood it completely. It was something he would never have said if we weren't there, lost in the upper woods, huddled around a shoddy fire, looking for a girl who couldn't possibly be up there, at least not in the way we'd last seen her.

Beyond the crackle of the firewood, beyond the flood of Cooper's words, beyond the night-sounds of feral things and whirring grubs, beyond all of that, I could hear their movement in the blackness. Large and deliberate, then smaller and skittish, I could hear the coming of white bracken, of the moon things, the night wanderers.

I didn't say anything to Cooper. I had the feeling that they would show themselves to him if it was him who needed to see them. It was a bold idea, a foolish one. It wasn't arrogant, it was just a sensation, like tiredness or arousal.

I listened as Cooper ran through our shitty jobs, the dumb nothing-work we had grimaced and giggled through. It was important for him, essential to see things in some kind of clear, chronological tube. I knew my own history, the sewers through which I'd waded to be there. I didn't need to see the heatmap, I knew what the city looked like from the gutters.

Sensing Cooper had found a cul-de-sac in his reverie, knowing that something flanked us in the dark, I asked whether he had packed any booze, 'Something to warm us up, eh?'

'Course I have, Danny boy.' Cooper reached into his backpack, plucked out two thirds of a bottle of vodka. He twisted the cap, slugged it, sucked it deeply, suckled the rim until he winced from the burn, then passed it to me.

I took a deep sip too, felt the heat on my tongue, down the funnel of my throat, right into the shuddering gulag of my heart. Exhaling the fumes, feeling my face contort from the ugliness of the drink, I seemed to see the stars through the meanly knitted treetops, to see them clearer than I ever had before.

White arrows livid and furious on night's ebony, the burning planets winked and flared. An infinity of weightless bulbs beyond the roughly hewed canopies of leaves, the stars were pearls at the bottom of the endless sea, of space. They were downward tower blocks, meteoric high-rises plummeting through motorway ozone. They were a city above us. They were the first city, the chaos of galaxies, the workaday routine of a billion blistering moons. I saw it then, looking up, feeling the warmth in my chest. I saw an inkling of my dream, the echo of myriad cities. Seeing the one above, hearing the rustle of movement beyond our flame-lit clearing, I knew it was almost time to see those other cities, those cities below us.

Cooper finished the vodka in a few needy gulps. He needed it more than I did. He tossed the empty bottle into the night. We heard it land heavily against the trunk of a tree. He leaned back on his elbows, his face bloated with a yawn. He tugged at his pack, drew out a sleeping-bag. He didn't unzip it, unravel it, he just stuffed it behind his head, propping himself up against the fire, remaining there, pixilated by the heat.

I did the same, knowing there was nothing else to do but wait.

I knew something was coming, that the cities were busy below us. I knew the night wouldn't pass without a visit. I just didn't know that it would change my life forever.

I felt my eyes grow heavy, weighed down by tiredness and eagerness. I sensed I needed to meet them somewhere familiar to both of us, somewhere between dreams and waking. Cooper was snoring lightly as I went under. Everything ahead of me, from the fire to the splintered black of the night woods, faded into obscurity as I fell asleep.

⚬

I was awoken by the reek of wet soil, that now familiar perfume of their arrival.

As with the two earlier occasions, I could feel the muck in my throat, clagging there. Around my tongue and teeth also; a rank, earthy caramel.

I could breathe as normal, perhaps even clearer. I eased myself up, jacked on my elbows.

The fire was low, dying back. A few embers winked lustily from the gathering ash. Yet, despite the failing fire, everything was brighter, everything was more defined. I could see the fungi, those rheumy domes. They were as clear as my own hand. The trees too, the understory, it was all electric, all lit wildly, all buzzing and frothing with light. I felt confused, but only for a moment. Sleep-headed, I hadn't understood the source of the light at first, but that changed quickly as the movement increased around us.

They were here.

Faint figures frolicked. Barely visible, their dashing, their prancing, their hurry made them blurry and impossible to define. The thinnest, most meagre-fleshed ones I had seen so far, almost childlike in their playfulness. They were the ones who lit the clearing, their skin neon as they ran, as they danced and whirled.

I saw the hoods on them, that rolling meat which covered the mannequin nothingness of their slight faces. I stared over at Cooper, but his head hung slackly, his lips wet with dribble, his snore now exhaust-like, a deep rumble from his chest.

Despite their numbers, dozens, the figures were quiet, their steps on the slurry of leaves and roots only as audible as the breeze which meandered between the trees, stirring the fire slightly.

Then they were gone, the light with them.

I waited, gagging on the ethereal soil. I couldn't believe that was it, that was their only interaction with me, up there, in the northern woods, the place from which they seemed to come.

I couldn't see them, any of them, but I could still taste the mud and feel the pricks of sloppy dirt on my skin.

Then the woods grew lighter again, but from only one direction, from my right-hand side.

Through the barred willows and elms, the silver-black ash and leaning oaks, a single figure moved steadily towards us.

Larger, fatter, stooping slightly, the gossamer of the cobwebs it passed lit like crossing signs on the streets of the city. The figure moved easily, gently, confidently onwards, its features becoming clearer with every step.

It was the one from the first night, the creature with the tuxedo of a thousand fingers.

As it had done before, the creature lifted a pair of glasses to its face. It was closer this time, the rims of the goggles glistened from the light emitted by their owner. I watched the black eyes roll from side to side, almost camp in the theatrical movement. The head followed, mime-like, a second or so behind the eyes, catching up with them just as they changed course, as they returned towards the hacked nose and the sheer gob, over the stretched, labial skin of the face.

The fingers of the chest began to move, to fiddle. The tuxedo appeared to roll outwards, then inwards, changing, being reknitted as I watched.

This was another demonstration, something it needed me to understand. Not just the torso, but the thighs too, even the invisible feet, the stumps that seemed to literally meet the understory and intertwine. Everything seemed to be changing, revolving, sewing itself into a new outfit.

The creature finished its bizarre work, the fingers retreated into themselves, plaited, settled.

Where there had once been a tuxedo, there was now a shabby shirt, vaguely patterned. There were jeans, the yellow thread of the seams bright against the navy blue of the rest. There were tired walking boots, the leather dogeared, the laces untied.

It took a few moments for me to realise what I was looking at, what this being had done. I only noticed because one of my elbows slipped and I had to pull myself back to a seating position. When I did, I saw that the new clothing the creature wore was a copy of my own.

Some of the details were missing, but the creature was impersonating me, my clothing. It was trying to meet me in a way I would understand, in a way I could fathom. It had changed whatever it could of its appearance to make me understand that it wanted to communicate with me. I was sure of it.

I moved forward, onto my haunches. I squatted there, leaned towards the creature. It backed away slightly, but I lifted a hand, heard myself whisper *Wait, please*.

It seemed to hear me, to know what I said but, just as I began to stand, something thunderous began to move through the forest.

The creature scattered, leaving me drowned in the blackest night I had ever seen. Even the stars seemed to have sunk away to an inky hell.

I hadn't felt real terror before, but I felt it then.

An absence of even the slightest light, the stench of rotting vegetation strong enough to make me heave, I fell backwards, my left hand meeting some of the hot ashes. I tugged it away quickly, brought it to my side. Imbalanced, I rolled over, to where Cooper had been laying.

The clattering, hammering, pounding sound continued. It grew louder, heavier. I couldn't see Cooper through the glooms, couldn't even make out his shape but, as I lay there, waiting for the earth to shatter, I saw a distant light, a brilliant, haunted whiteness.

It came from behind Cooper, in the opposite direction to where the last creature had emerged. It came like a weightless boulder, like ball lightning. I couldn't make out the figure, but I could see that it smashed the smaller trees away as it came tumbling towards us. There was nothing I could do, nowhere I could run.

I waited there, every muscle locked in spasm, fear for blood, terror ripping my face into a soundless scream.

I couldn't look away, but I longed to.

As the nearest trees cracked, as those which had continued to bend into mockeries of plazas, arcades and beaten streets were torn away, I saw it...I saw the white stag, its enormous antlers scything through the silver night, their tips fast and monochrome against the darkness.

Expecting to be trampled, to be destroyed, I covered my face in some pathetic action, something people rehearsed on package holiday flights, some inane act of failure. I waited, one second, two. I waited for the wreckage, I waited to be crushed.

Silence.

The stomping, racing, battering hooves had stopped.

Through the fan of my shuddering fingers, I could see the brightest light yet. A spillage of pure whiteness, of a type of light impossible to comprehend.

I lowered my hands. I allowed myself to stare upwards, to look at up at where the creature had stopped, just off to the left of Cooper.

I have never seen anything as incredible, as unbelievable was what I saw then.

The white stag towered above us.

Brilliantly white, glowing with mercury skin, its antlers like cracks in the night itself, the creature huffed and snorted. Twice my own height standing, as wide as the van which had brought us there, the stag stood like a moon of fury, its intensity blinding, harrowing.

Too huge, too striking to comprehend at first, all I could do was gag with awe, stare unblinkingly upwards. A temple, a church, a god like no other, as alien as it was familiar, as frightening as it was peaceful, the stag seemed to inhale the universe around it, to own every reality possible.

I waited for the stag to stomp forward, toward me. I expected it to, but it didn't. It hung there, at the edge of our rough clearing, its eyes fixed so intently on my own that I hadn't been able to look away from them. Obsidian rocks, light glinting from their odd shapes, the stag's eyes looked lidless, looked void-like, endless in its immense skull.

I had to force myself to look away from them and, as I did, I wished I hadn't.

What I had taken for a thick, fur collar around the stag's neck as it hurtled towards us wasn't that at all. No, what the stag wore around its throat, what arched upwards to its shoulder was something awful, something able to bend the splintered comprehension I had left.

There, one after another, chainlike, matted by their torn flesh, a garland of human heads.

That alone churned my stomach. I felt my fingers dig so deeply into the dirt that my nails bent backwards and tore away from my fingertips. I was grabbing for earth, for something real, for ballast.

Worse than the existence of the heads, worse than that gory adornment, worse than anything I had yet seen, the faces were alive.

Gasping soundlessly, without bodies, swollen like buboes from the stag's own meat, the mouths opened and closed, gaped and snapped shut, gaped again. Their features tar and syrup, almost all of the faces were those of strangers, unfamiliar to me. They were suspended, moving with the stag's deep breaths, its breath rotten, mulchy, fetid.

Almost all of the faces were those of strangers.

Almost all of the faces.

Apart from one.

There, the final face on the stag's left side, looming out, pulsing from the muscle beneath it, a face I knew. A face I had seen so often in recent months. A face that I associated with being here, lost here, a face of a vanished love. Not my love, but Cooper's.

Shanice.

Her slender face, her child face, the face of Katie Pop, the face of a human fawn, of a lost soul, of a victim, Shanice's face.

Her dead eyes seemed to drill into me, more than even the stag's own eyes. They were round, they were shocked, they pleaded, they hated, they shone pitifully, consumed by forces neither she nor I could have understood.

Before I could issue another thought, another emotion, before I could raise myself from the muck, before anything, for the second time that day I was shaken by Cooper's screams.

Realities collided, smashed against each other. The marriage of clattering cities, falling, rising, collapsing, emerging.

Until then, until that very moment, the beings I'd seen, the visitors, I had seen them alone, unsure if they were anything other than my own imaginings, or the death psychedelia of Mom. Her mutterings about *the white stag* were no longer morphine fairy tales.

Everything I had seen belonged to me, until that second, until that appalling instant that I saw Cooper react to the white stag.

I had no idea whether he'd been conscious the whole time, whether he had watched as the other creatures lingered, as they wandered and visited. I couldn't tell. All I knew, all that became instantly apparent to me was that *then,* right there, as I lay muddied, crushed, Cooper not only saw the stag – *we see you Bone Stairwell* – but he saw Shanice's face too.

Guttural, broken, almost incomprehensible, all I could understand as Cooper reared up, staggered backwards past me, all I could hear was *Shanice, Shanice, Shanice.* A doomed shanty, a mantra of a man maddened by a single moment, Cooper not only vanished into the woods behind us, he teetered on the grinning teeth of the Undertundran spiral, falling quickly down into it, into that yattering maw, into oblivion.

Turning away, sprinting off into the dark, giggling forest, Cooper disappeared, his thudding steps and raking screams diminishing the further away he ran.

When I turned back to face the stag, it was already backing away.

Crushing sounds beneath its hooves, the wreath of doomed faces sinking into the glooms, the white leaving the bracken, just as maggots leave the bones. The stag retreated, leaving me there, alone once more.

20.

A garden of bones

I SNATCHED MY BAG AND ran after Cooper, bursting blindly into the blackness.

I didn't know what else to do, another way to react. All I knew, my head throbbing, winged, whirring away from my body, all I could think was that I had to catch up with Cooper, that I had to explain, that I had to tell him something, tell him *anything*. I had to save him.

I could hear the groans of the branches as they continued to change their shape around me. Pathways opened up, the understory reknitting itself into flattened pavement, as if it was showing me the way, guiding me with familiar routes, with the inherent blueprints of the estate, even of my old neighbourhoods, of every part of the city I knew so well.

I felt like I could close my eyes and be running from Cooper's place, through the moody arcade, past the Chinese takeaway, past the shuttered off-license, past the minimarket with its doomed staff and locked-up liquor. I could almost see The Gladiator, off between ethereal arches of bending elms, the dead tobacco faces of the punters glaring at me over their racing forms and tar-blackened teeth.

I ran as fast as I ever had. I ran without fear of the darkness, but with fear for Cooper.

The white stag wasn't following me, but I could see its face in my mind's eye, pulsing with every step, every thumping beat of my heart.

Beyond the others I had seen, the white stag felt like the most essential, the most important figment of this place. A gateway, a siren call, a god.

The branches seemed to lift away from me, duck from my face in order to hit my chest and shoulders instead. Where the pathway at the back of The Red House had blocked our leaving by road, now, just like the woodland had opened up to allow Cooper and me access a day earlier, it was spreading itself, morphing into my memory-streets, my bone arcades. It was carrying me along on a conveyer of hidden hands.

I couldn't see Cooper, but I could occasionally hear his cries, the bellowing of *Shanice, Shanice, Shanice.*

First in one direction, then another. Like a brutal birdsong, the sound was omnipotent.

My lungs burned. They felt like gunshots in my ribs. Mt throat too, it raked with every breath.

Where the white light of the others had lit the way at first, where it had bled through the bracken-land and the wood-world, now there was the emergence of another light, the universal light. Sunlight.

I hadn't thought of the time, because time means so little here, but day was breaking, the sun was coming up. Faintly, pinking the forest I crashed through, morning was coming to this part of the world.

Too early to see more than the spearheads of the trees around me, it was still a signal, a demand for me to stop, to wait.

I fell to me knees, gasping, puking. I had nothing in the tank, not a drop of energy left.

Once more, as I had done in the presence of the stag, I dug my fingers into the dirt, clawed at it in frustration. Cooper was nowhere to be seen. For all I knew, if I ever saw him again, he would be the next face on the garland of the stag, suspended on the flesh, reunited with Shanice in their laurel of death.

Overcome with fatigue, battered by it, I scrambled over to a tree, pressed my back against it, forced myself to take breaths as slowly, as deeply as I could. I closed my eyes, tried to ignore the gunshots of my heart, the roaring beats. In doing so, whether it was just exhaustion, or whether the woodland had the power to knock me out, I quickly fell asleep.

I wasn't out for long, less than an hour.

When I came around, the vague light was brighter, the higher leaves yellowed and silvered by the sun. The ground around me was less gloomy, the roots of trees visible and finlike. My legs were deadweight. I stretched them out, my arms too. I heard the clunk of my bones, the fanbelt recoil of my tendons. My heartbeat was slow again, gentle. It fluttered as I stood up, my head a little dizzy, a little lost.

I blinked myself awake, rubbed my face, searched the immediate woodland around me for a sign of Cooper, for a sign of anyone.

There were only trees, only brush, only the forest.

The reformation of the trees seemed to have ceased, for now. Behind me, in the direction I guessed I had come from, many of the trees were at right angles. Like the scaffolding of my mind, they were drawn in the outlines of places I had walked.

Maybe it should have frightened me, disconcerted me more but, given everything the place had shown me, from what I would know as Mr Milliman, to the stag called Bone Stairwell, to see only a woodland which wanted me to see it as familiar, as home...I was unable to fear it.

I had no idea which direction would lead me back to the house, back to Hickey. I had to assume it was behind me, opposite the direction which Cooper had taken, or at least the direction I thought he had. The only thing that told me this was the reshaped trees, the mimicry of the city.

Wherever I had walked within the northern woods, so the landscape appeared to have changed. In the direction I faced then, towards the sunlight, the trees seemed undisturbed.

I decided to head that way, just for a while, the hope I might find Cooper central in my thoughts.

Something strange hung on the air. A sweet smell, almost tangy. I couldn't place it, but I followed it, nonetheless. Woodland odours, the married scents of flowers. I had no idea. Without a sense of genuine direction, without knowing forests, all I could do then was pick a route and follow it.

The woodland had changed. The darkness and the dank void of the night was replaced by something brighter, fresher. I could feel a breeze on my face, a coolness. Unobscured by thick trees, by any buildings, the wind was able to splinter through the forest, to reknit itself again, like estuaries that meet in the sea.

I followed the unfurling carpet of light, noticing that small white and yellow flowers seemed to be more plentiful, almost abundant the further I went. In place of toadstools, their menacing red wax, the flowers seemed somehow purer, more vibrant, weightless, waltzing drunkenly against the wind.

I could see an end to the woodlands. They were thinning, the spaces becoming greater between them, the forest floor drier, more like a track.

I began to hurry, keen to see something, to snatch a view at the landscape around me.

The flowers grew in their intensity, the colours wilder, the thickness of them greater. They seemed to rise up in hillocks of burning brightness, the yellow flamelike, the whites as vivid and spotless as the bleached teeth of bad actors. They undulated, they leaned towards the sunlight.

I began to run again but, looking upwards, not watching the ground, I tripped and went sprawling ahead, only just managing to shield my face with my hands.

I landed heavily, but I landed in a pool of light, the sun unobscured by a canopy of deviant leaves.

As I rolled onto my side and began to stand, I saw the bones.

Something only the forest could show me, something only the beings who haunted the city beneath a city could create…a garden of bones, every perfect flower growing between them, enveloping them, dressing them.

I recognised the ribcages first of all. Unmistakably human, the yellowed bones fanned and fleshless, the chests were filled with flowers instead of meat, instead of hearts and lungs. I saw carnations, roses, gorse flowers, lilies, violets, buttercups and daisies, the few flowers I knew. They were the flowers of lapels at weddings and funerals, the flowers of verges between city roads, the flowers of cheap bouquets bought at the last minute for Mothers' Day. They were all I knew and they were there, *there* amongst the butchered bones, there in that mad garden, in that flowerbed of the dead and done for.

I stood and walked amongst them. I saw pelvises, tibias, fibulas, spines, even the carefully laid out bones of hands and fingers. Within them, as if held there, as if carried, the flowers grew upwards, hungrily, perfectly.

I didn't know what it meant then, I don't know now but, like the trees which changed their shapes to suit me, to welcome me, this too was something like that. It was a message but, as obscure as that message was, what I saw next was as clear as graffiti, as patently obvious as it could get.

I turned back to the light, to where the trees were no longer just thinned, but gone entirely. There was an edge, something sheer and definite. I moved towards it, slowly.

Beyond it, over a vast distance, a landscape unfolded.

Myriad woodlands, fields, lakes, lochs, alive with the silver skin caused by the sun as it eased over the wind-rolling waters. I could see for what felt like a thousand miles and yet, as I looked, I saw no signs of human life. No roads, no homes, no carefully drawn farmlands, nothing.

Moving towards that view, almost doped by it, I nearly fell from the lip of the ledge, the gnarled rock beneath my feet.

I caught myself just in time, staggered backwards and, looking down again, I saw a plume of smoke, a snaking funnel of black against the morning.

I quickly realised that I was stood at the quarry face, at its peak, to the west of the woodlands, above The Red House. The smoke came from its chimney.

What I saw then, how clear it suddenly was… what I saw told me everything I needed to know.

From that viewpoint, the property below me, the gift of topography mine to ingest, I saw that what I had taken as trenches, as deep, random ditches surrounding the house and outbuildings were no such thing. They weren't for sewerage, they weren't carved by the wheels of vehicles, they weren't dug by accident, they were a flag, a signal, a greenlight for the beings.

There, clearly drawn around the entire property, was a symbol I had seen far too often. A symbol I had seen carved into the skin of the targets who had fallen for the Katie Pop ruse. Enormous, compared to

198

those slashed with Hickey's knife, a huge version of the eye with two pupils, one looking upwards, one looking below. The ugly eye, the eye which saw all cities, all universes at once. What Hickey would call *The Undertundran Eye*.

Carved around the entire property, it looked upwards at me, unblinking from its face of dirt and brick, The Red House directly at its centre.

It seemed perfect, that image, that confirmation we were at the centre of everything that had happened, seemingly right from the start. The pieces weren't all assembled, but they lay nearby, partially jumbled, but all present, all at the reach of my thoughts.

To see the eye, to see the house almost as a third pupil within it, to know that those markings were there before Hickey began to carve them into the skin of his and Cooper's online monsters, to know that somehow the Katie Pop work was just another phase of a process which had begun long before it, to realise all this was, in some abstract way, a comfort to me.

Someone once told me that most human beings are implicitly desperate to surrender every ounce of autonomy they have, to simply relinquish each facet of control they possess, to unburden themselves of the responsibility of their own existence. They told me that they did it through governments, believing their votes would bring in some kindly necktie parent who would look out for their pensions, their salaries, their mortgages. They told me they did it through religion, through compelling themselves to believe in fantastic floating icons with lightning fingers and wizened commandments. They did it with fashion, with trends, with behaviours mimicked by the two-dimensional billboard heroes of their television minds. They did it however they could, *but they did it.*

I suppose, lingering in me like the root of a boot-shattered tooth, I had a shred of that same desire, the comfort of knowing that what had happened over these last few months, what was happening now, it was going to occur regardless, that I was flotsam on its waves, a mithering fly in the algebra of its web.

From the top of the quarry wall, looking over towards the northern woods, I could see a spattering of paths through the thick forest. They all lead down to the property, but all of them had seemed invisible to Cooper and me when we left there the previous day. I couldn't be sure if they had always been there, or whether the woodland had created them for me that morning, to allow the next phase to take place as it was supposed to.

Disconcertingly, the canopies of the trees gave no indication of the changes beneath them, the way so many of the trunks and arterial branches had reformed into snapshots of the city, of the estate. That mossy geography, the ultimate perversion of the landscape, was cloaked to any eyes above the woods. A dirty secret.

I edged along the quarry lip and pulled myself through some thorn-tipped bracken, towards the most immediate path I could see. Sheer, snaking down past right-angled ash and willow, it was a simple route, a clear, brightly-stoned escalator back to the house, back to Hickey.

Like a different land, a third universe of my thoughts, I seemed to be able to walk down through the trees with ease, hardly slipping as the ground below me sharpened into a steeper fall. The route was sensible, clear, defined and welcoming. I had the notion that I could have stopped walking completely, that I could have stood completely still and yet still have ended up back next to The Red House. I was on a conveyer belt, one geared to the earth beneath my feet, but more so to what I understood to be an inverted city, perhaps one of a rumbling infinity further below the crusts we knew. A two-way mirror world, a lake of static, a bottomless cascade of mimic cities.

I listened out for Cooper, but heard nothing. His shouts of *Shanice* still lingered in my thoughts, reverberating, rippling against the bone.

Perhaps I was numb with shock, but I could only picture him already dead and that seemed too remote from my heart to be anything other than a watercolour hanging in my skull, something I would wander past occasionally, notice, imbibe a little, but refuse to linger long enough ahead of it to be truly affected by the image.

I could smell the coal and wood of the fire within a few minutes. I began to see the plumes webbing the empty air.

Reborn from the softened bracken, I stumbled back onto the property, dazed by the sudden return to that place, to a place that seemed to exist a million years earlier.

Gathering my thoughts, wrestling with my disembodied clothing, I felt myself shake, probably from the exertion, the running, the lunacy. Who knew?

Crouched ahead of the outhouse, the large campfire burning ahead of him, Hickey looked over at me, nonchalantly, as if my reappearance was completely expected, perfectly punctual, an appointment adhered to.

I slung my bag down next to the fire.

Hickey blew the steam from the rim of his coffee cup, his eyes quicksilver, knowing. 'No Cooper,' he asked, glancing back at the bracken, then up at me.

I said he was up there somewhere; 'Maybe they got him,' I added, slumping down to the ground, suddenly desperate for the warmth of the fire, the sweat like a vest of ice on my skin.

'Here,' Hickey passed me his coffee. I sipped it greedily, scalding my lips and tongue.

I didn't need to prompt Hickey further.

He started at me intensely, nodded to himself, some recognition of a point reached. 'I best tell you everything I know. I owe you that, Daniel.'

21.

A congregation of ultimate truth

The Undertundra.

That's what he called it. The Undertundra.

'Different people have called it different things,' Hickey began. 'Often times it's been referred to as The Hallow, or Hallows. That's way back when, mind, back when people were living in hallows themselves. Fire-lit shitholes, huts, twiggy cottages, drinking piss water from the only well for miles around. It made sense then, made sense for them to see the other side of things as *a hallow*. It was familiar to them, something they could fathom. Tactile, just like home.

'Thing is, it's so much more.

'It's cities upon cities, Daniel. A universe unto itself. *The* universe. I could see how the woodlands changed for you, to show you, to reveal itself. This isn't a time for *hallows,* for beaten-up villages. That's what they showed *them.* For people now, for those who they want to bring in, those who *understand,* it's exactly what they need it to be. Towns, estates, cities, docklands, whatever we have, *they have.* Whatever we know, *they knew already.*

'Do you understand?'

I told Hickey I couldn't understand. I could only go on what I'd seen, on what I thought I had seen, at least.

'Which ones?'

'Eh?'

'Which of them have visited you, Daniel? Describe them.'

I did. From the tuxedo creature, to the flesh-hooded gang, finally to the white stag.

Hickey grinned as he listened, 'Mr Milliman,' he said casually. 'The stag is Bone Stairwell, at least that's the names I was given for them anyhow.'

I asked who gave him the names, who told him about The Undertundra. 'How the fuck could you have known about this?'

'I was brought in,' Hickey lifted a burning stick from the fire, twirled it in his hands, blew on the tip. 'Doors like this don't open by chance. You have to be invited, shown the way. I was instructed, you might say, guided by someone who already knew the deal, someone who had been working their way in for years, for decades. People called him an occultist, but he was just looking for the other side of the stars, the end of the end. He was burrowing beneath the meat of this bullshit planet, Daniel. He looked where others looked away. His name was Leopold Carr.'

That didn't mean a thing to me. The name, what Hickey was saying. I continued to listen.

'I was doing a three stretch. Three lousy years at the nick for ABH. It was just a fight, one more town centre with jug-eared chavs looking for a ruck. I shouldn't have bitten, but I'm a magnet like that. You can guess. I couldn't get away, so I roared and went to work. A few seconds later, I'm dribbling out two back teeth and two of those shitheads are out cold. One of them had his jaw halfway around the side of his face. They had it coming. I said as much in court. CCTV confirmed I wasn't the one who kicked off, but that doesn't matter when you've got previous, when you've got a past. Nothing matters then.

'No big deal. I took the years, swallowed the time. A Southern nick, outside the capitol, towards the coast. Makes no never-mind in some ways, but in others all you've got are the little things when you go down for a spell. Brine on the air when you're doing your hour outside, something different, something new.

'I was banged up on my jack for a while. Had a few weeks like that. Used to switch bunks, just for the hell of it, entertain myself. Nice to be able to use the bog without an audience too. Easy to forget what it's like, snatched up by pigs, sent down, everything taken, even the joy of a quiet shit and a smoke in the morning.

'A few weeks go by. Keep myself to myself. Best way to do your time. I worked out at the gym, passed the hours in the TV room after. Daytime telly, no sports allowed. Grinning idiots on their spotless sofas telling us doomed zombies about diets, fashions, the greatest getaways of the summer. Everything a prisoner could possibly want to hear.

'So one day, dinner done and dusted, I head back to the cell, dogeared paperback in my shirt pocket, some western shit. I turned in and there, stood by the beds, staring straight at me, this pale bloke, thin as a rake, hair so blonde it could've been white. He doesn't say a word, right. Doesn't introduce himself at first, nothing. He just looks me up and down, takes me in. I've never been looked at that way before, never had someone really stare at me that way. Only time anyone'd ever looked at me for that long, without blinking, without saying anything, well they wanted to fight, didn't they? Not this bloke though, nothing like that. He's just looking, but looking like he's thinking of buying me, like he's weighing it up, the value of the goods.

'I couldn't explain it, even to myself, but I just stood there, frozen, stock still. There was something about him, something that made my hairs stand up, you know? Ever had that feeling, like when you turn into a street at night and there's a few lads there, standing around, silent, looking your way. You have to make your way past, maybe they cross the road, walking slowly towards you, behind you. Everything's slow, everything goes so quiet that you can hear your blood and you're just waiting, *waiting* for them to pounce, waiting for the thuds to come.

'And then they don't.

'It all passes, time hurries on, catches up, all the noises of the street return. Cars start, ignitions growl, a kid screams in a terraced window, a dog barks from a cold yard. It's all normal, you're alive again.

'Well, that's how it was with Carr. His mouth eventually opened, arched in a thin smile. He introduced himself, held out a hand, like we were meeting for a business lunch. I shook it, said hello, all that jazz. I noticed that he limped. He walked with a cane, a polished wooden effort, all gnarled at the handle. First thing I thought was *Shit, I can't believe they let him have that in here.*

'After that, for a couple of days, it was fine, like he wasn't even there. He slept quietly, didn't snore, didn't scream out. He didn't gripe when I used the pan, but I noticed he didn't, at least not when I was in the cell.

'Carr didn't ask me much at first. He barely spoke. He read a lot, but not the cockeyed second-rate books from the nick's library, his own stuff. Large books, leatherbound. I figured they were worth a few quid, but I'm not a historian, so I left it alone. He was consumed by them, his thin face lit up, like the pages had bulbs in them.

'I had no idea of the clout Carr had until one afternoon.

'We're sat on the bunks. I had come across a TV and was fiddling with a coat-hanger arial, trying to get some kind of reception. The cell door opened and there was a screw, plate in his hands. The smell coming off it was wild, delicious. Restaurant stuff, Daniel, no kidding. "Mr Carr", he says, "I wondered whether you'd like this."

'Carr lowered his book, watched the guard for a second or two, then just nodded his head towards the table, next to the telly. He didn't thank that screw. Barely acknowledged him, in truth. He just went back to reading and this screw, this tubby guard, he backed out of the cell slowly, always facing Carr, scared to look away.

'Once the door was locked, I couldn't help but look up at him, look up at Carr, then back to the plate. Beef, rare as it comes, spuds, veg, the absolute works.

'Carr saw me looking and he lowered the book onto his knees. He asks me if I like the look of the grub. I tell him *Sure, what's not to like? The shite they serve in here, you see something like that and wow, it's paradise.*

'Carr smiled; he told me to have it.

'I couldn't believe it. After that simpering screw had brought it in, Carr didn't even want it.

'I asked if he was sure.

'*Of course,* he says, *I can have anything like that whenever I want it. If I don't ask Linton, or one of the other guards for something every day or so, they bring it anyway, just to keep our energies in place.*

'I didn't know what he meant, plus I wanted that chow more than anything right then, so I tucked in. I cleared the plate, licked it dry.

'There was no way back then. I had to know more about Carr.

'I asked why they treated him this way, whether he was a known face on the outside, someone people respected, a big-timer.

'He told me it wasn't quite like that. He said he represented a collective of alternate thinkers, of alternate believers. Carr said he was something of a figurehead for them, that they were everywhere. He called them a *Congregation of ultimate truth.*

'I assumed he meant a religion, Seventh Day Adventists, that kind of thing. He said it was something like that, but perhaps it was best to see it as *anti-religion*. It was a faith in the unfathomable, the forgotten order of things.

'I'm not an idiot, Daniel. I wasn't just some lunkheaded con, I knew a few things. I asked Carr if he meant a kind of paganism, a sort of worship of the land, not created gods. He was pleased I asked that, pleased I knew it. That was the first time he used its name, the first time he called it *The Undertundra.*

'What was I supposed to think? He spoke clearly, he spoke from experience. He told me he knew of four places, but there were countless others. These places weren't quite entrances to this universe, they were more like waystations, like shrines. They were places that a person could meet residents of The Undertundra, if they could demonstrate their fealty, their desire to be accepted to that world, if they could show their *value.*

'It would be easy for me to say I didn't believe him at first, that I thought he was a crackpot. There have been societies of these characters since ink met paper. I was never a religious man. It all seemed like bollocks to me. People are crazy for it though, you know that, Daniel. They lap it up, they live their lives by phony credos, by commandments they reckon were carved into rock by some holy beard. Wars are fought over opposing ideas of make-believe gods. Foreskins are lopped off babies, blessed water dunking, fasting in the name of one prophet, suicides in the name of another.

'Yet, even though I had always seen it that way, I *believed* Carr.

'What struck me most though, what sealed my belief in how legitimate he is, wasn't the lavish meals, the simpering screws, the way he carried himself, it was the discovery that he hadn't been sentenced to prison…he was there because he wanted to be.

206

'I couldn't understand it at first, the sheer idea of it. I thought it was a bridge too far, too much to believe. He insisted. He even summoned – and it *was a summoning* – another guard, another believer to confirm it for me. Sure as shit, Carr just walked in there, whenever he wanted, whenever he needed to be there.

'I had to ask *why*. I had to know why anyone would do that.

'*It's been there all along,* he said, *for everyone to see, from a dying liar on a cross of wood, to penance by blood. Churches, temples…they were never meant to be places of worship. They were meant to be places of torture.*

'Carr explained that access to The Undertundra, to the beings of the greatest, most ancient powers, access to their universe was obtained with *momentum*. Carr said it all related to sacrifice, to demonstration of belief, to an obvious lack of value in humanity. To ever stand a chance of being welcome in one of the four places, to ever be brought in and shown the cities beneath the cities, the way *you* see it, Daniel, to ever have a chance of snatching a glimpse of their world, a person needed to show their loyalty to the cause, to sacrifice their own kind, to hammer home that they are *beyond* their species.

'I began to understand then, Daniel. I began to see why Carr would be in prison by choice.

'The average person on the street is a zero sum when it comes to something like that. They would be more likely to run from violence than ever get involved. Not in prison. Just as a starting point, the average con, they've been part of it, they've done those things. Not everyone, but most of us. That's why we're there. People shower with killers, with rapists, with thugs who'd break every bone in your chest for a tenner. Carr knew that. He needed believers, disciples. He needed horsemen.'

I could feel warmth on my face as Hickey spoke. The sun was being winched higher, up into the heavens. Between that, the fire and the way Hickey talked, I felt dreamy, dazed. There was a scent on the air, something sweet, something rotting, something earthy, the Undertundran scent, our doomed perfume.

I wasn't surprised to hear how quickly Hickey agreed to be brought in by Carr. Maybe I would've been the same. It was too hard to say. For him though, bouncing from one dead town to the next, one failed scheme to another, to be promised knowledge, power beyond the millionaires and bosses he could never be, it was opium for Hickey, maybe for any of us.

As Hickey continued, I thought of Cooper, of what must've happened to him then. The pictures were fading to vapour, my feelings were gassed-out, knackered.

'Carr kept talking about *the momentum,*' Hickey tipped away his cold coffee as he spoke, 'he said it meant everything towards reaching the Undertundra, to being accepted there. I had an idea what we were getting to, where Carr was heading with his talk about proving adherence to them, to that other world.

'He showed me the Undertundran eye. He drew it for me, onto some scrap paper and, even then, when I saw it, the eye felt like it was looking into me, maybe even through me.'

'I saw the eye,' I told Hickey, 'from up there, above the quarry face. I saw it dug into the earth, around this place, around the quarry. Was that you?'

Hickey carried on, ignored my question completely. 'Carr told me that was a way for them to see. Wherever it was sketched, wherever it was carved, they could see through it, they would *know* why it had been put there. Carr told me that momentum was violence, that it was degradation, that people had to fucking *suffer* for that stamp, for that brand. It was about building a wave, Daniel, a red wave, a whole bleeding sea of sacrifice, something that would come tumbling over our fucking heads and crush everything. Eventually, Carr said, it would smash down the door between them and us, at least for those who believed and followed the course.

'I was stupid, an idiot, I asked whether it was riches, wealth, if that's what they had.

'Carr looked at me with absolute disgust then. His eyes went cold, rolled back into his head, like a shark. He was disappointed that I thought it those terms, that money was something to grasp onto, that it was the goal.

'I apologised. I told him it was just because of where I'm from…where *we're* from, Daniel. That's what we'd been striving for, the whole reason we ended up the bastard nick in the first place.

'Carr forgave me. I was elated, Daniel, blown away. Already, just from the moment that plate had arrived, already Carr had me on the line, my neck in a collar. He knew I was all in. What did I have to lose? The idea of leaving this universe behind, its pettiness, its ugliness, the cannibalistic, rapist mentality of the human race. The idea of leaving that beneath me, descending to greatness, to a city beneath the city, to a world that operates differently, to a wealth of knowledge, that kind of majesty, *fuck*, Daniel, I know you feel the same! *I know it.*'

It was my turn not to respond, but it didn't matter. Hickey could read my eyes.

'I just needed to be christened,' Hickey continued, 'I just needed to join the wave, to ascend in the waters.' Hickey stood up and unbuttoned his jeans. He lowered them, along with his boxers. Holding his prick to the side, cupped in his hands, I was able to see the deep, crosshatched scarring that covered his upper thighs, his groin, his buttocks. I thought it was random, just the fading worms of old wounds but, when I looked closer, I could see that it was more than that.

Between the slashes and deeply hacked cuts, there were dozens of Undertundran eyes cut into Hickey's meat and muscle. Oddly shaped, some gouged out of him, the Undertundran eyes were a bible, a testament to how much Hickey had allowed Carr to do to him.

He zipped up and sat back down, the fire moved with the gust from his movement. 'I submitted,' Hickey said, staring into the balletic flames, 'I let Carr abuse me for days, weeks. Whatever he wanted to do. I was a blank page and he went to work on me, wrote story after story of ruin and brutality. He could fuck me. He could cut me. He could bite me. Whatever it took. He drew an eye every time. One more nod to the world we wanted, one more wink.

'He disappeared from the prison as silently as he'd arrived. One morning, with me back from the showers, he had packed his things. He told me that he would be there to collect me on the day of my release. I believed him.

'I did the right thing. That morning, that sweet morning when the bars parted, Carr was there. Looking at me from the backseat of a limousine. His driver, Yando, opened the door, and I was there, sinking into plush upholstery, champagne in my hand.

'Carr brought me out here. He only spent a single night with me. It was long enough for me to see them, to see Bone Stairwell snorting in the trees, to see Mr Milliman, Floss the Teeth, Teardrop, the Unformed, for me to see dozens of them, waiting, watching, celebrating. They rode the wave, Daniel. They met us head on.

'Carr left me here for weeks. They came to me slowly, one at a time. They have only ever teased me. They have shown themselves to me behind curtains of bracken, only ever appearing briefly, always too far from my grasp, my true understanding. Once Carr had gone, they hung back, they seemed to find me…they didn't seem to think I'd done enough.'

I understood then. Hickey's involvement in the online vigilantism, in Cooper's idiotic steam-letting campaign of catfishing perverts, it was all so he could continue the momentum, continue to prove himself to The Undertundra. This Leopold Carr had shown him a way in, but had left him to it. All the while, in the background, growing stronger through disciples like Hickey; their efforts compounded, added to his own. I asked Hickey whether I was right, whether he had seen the Katie Pop game as his way in.

He nodded.

It all began to make sense, everything that had happened up until now, apart from a couple of things.

'They're drawn to you,' Hickey said bitterly, his lips curled into a sneer as he spoke to me, 'something about *you*, Daniel. They're keen.'

I told Hickey that made no sense. 'I've barely been involved in this whole bastard thing. I didn't want a part of it. I tried to get out of it every single way I could, but…'

At that moment the door to the outhouse creaked open. At that very second I knew just how manipulated I had been.

Skulking from the rank gloom of the shed, naked from the waist up, Watkins came walking into the sunlight, shielding his eyes with a hand as they adjusted to the glare.

Across his stomach, his chest, the ink fading away after years of being there, tattoos of the Undertundran Eye, of that otherworldly brand. Watkins wasn't a prisoner. He was a believer.

Hickey smiled as he looked over at Watkins, then back at me. I replayed the events in my mind, reeling, nauseated. The pitiful figure of the captured man, his mewling pleas for me to save his cat, the humming bushels of camera lenses. A set-up. I was nothing but a rube, an easy way to get us out here, for Hickey to continue his momentum, to bring it to a red crescendo.

I wanted to rush at Watkins, to smash his head to pieces with one of the nearby stones. I snatched around in the dirt for a rock, for something to kill him with. I was about to stand, to run towards him, but I caught his smile, the glittering eyes above that toothless mouth. I looked at the ink again, beneath the smears of dark blood, dried on his fatty torso. They *wanted* the violence from me. It would have been one more brick in the wall, one more win for the dead.

I let go of the rock, slumped in the dirt.

'Listen, Daniel,' Hickey leaned forward, onto his knees, his eyes wide, the smile not one that mocked me, not an evil grin, but a lightheaded, drunken, soul-doped smile of ecstasy, of fulfilment, 'it *had* to be you. It had to be. I tried to show you, to tell you. I tried to let you know, way before we came here. I could *see* that there was something in you, in the way you saw people, in the way you see me, Cooper, everyone. You're distant, Daniel, you're moving away. Human beings don't mean a thing to you, we're worthless, we're *shit*, Daniel. They know it, the Undertundrans, they can *smell* it on you, Daniel.'

I told Hickey it was insane, the idea they could want me, that I could be of interest to them. I'm nobody, I'm nothing, I'm zero. Yet, as he argued with me, I thought of Mom, of her dying, of her talking about the white stag she had seen in those bungled, morphine dreams. When she'd said it, laying there in hospice lamplight, I had seen a stag made of pills, some dope deer guiding the terminal to their furnace as painlessly as possible. But now...

'You've seen the forest!' Hickey screamed at me, 'You've seen it change shape, resembling the estate, the city. That's for *you*,' Hickey insisted, adamant. 'The trick, the shit with Watkins to get you here, it wasn't just for me, Daniel. It was for you!'

Before I could argue more, the sound of cracking branches shocked us into silence. I turned to the northern woods, to where a figure stumbled wildly into the morning light.

Naked, bloody, Cooper fell to his knees, his mouth wide, gasping, his eyes wild, shocked, maddened.

22.

The rain of porcelain figures

I LEAPT TO MY FEET, ran towards Cooper.

I caught sight of Watkins slithering back into the outhouse as I passed him. That snivelling bastard, it took all my willpower not to run after him.

Cooper fell forward as I reached him, his face crashed into the dirt, chapped lips pecking at the soil, jabbering in nonsense tongues.

I snatched him up by the shoulders. His skin burned hot, but he shuddered violently. Feverish, sickly, there was a weakness about him I had never seen before. Beyond the nakedness, it was as if the forest had atrophied his strength, sapped it up, drained him, crumbled the man I knew.

Still, I struggled to lift him to his feet. He had no petrol in the tank, nothing to give. His legs were like tripe as I hoisted him up.

I shouted to Hickey to help me, but he just watched us. 'Help me get him inside the house,' I pleaded, 'I can't lift him, Hickey.'

'You're wasting your time, Daniel,' Hickey yawned, 'he's theirs now. Whatever they want.'

I turned back to woods, saw the moistened space from which Cooper had been regurgitated by the Undertundra. There was no way he'd found his way back here, to the house. His pupils were like ink blots, he couldn't tell where he was.

They had slung him back down here, thrown him onto the fire, waiting to burn with the rest of us.

Still Hickey watched, still he ignored us.

'He trusted you!' I seethed at Hickey. 'He fucking *trusted you.*'

'He followed his own course.' Hickey stood up, but made no effort to walk over to us. 'He walked at my side, not on a collar behind me.'

I screamed at Hickey that he had used Cooper, that he'd used me too.

'Believe what you want,' he waved me away, 'you know better than that, Daniel. Forget the Watkins business, that was a cheap ploy, but so what? I see in you what Carr saw in me, a disconnection with the human race, with that ruined world. It's doomed, Daniel. You *know it.*'

I said that had nothing to do with Cooper. 'It isn't his fault. All he did was let you in.'

'Don't be so dull.' Hickey took a few steps in our direction, Watkins peered from a crack in the darkness of the outhouse behind him.

'Cooper couldn't be more of the problem,' Hickey continued, 'he couldn't be more human. Look at him, *look at him!* A glimpse of the Undertundra and his box's gone. He's blown-out, spaced out, broken up. He could never handle what we have seen. He could never understand it. Shit, look how quickly him and Shanice rearranged the cottage to look like the house on the estate as soon as we got here. A series of echoes, a desperation to cling to fish and chips on a Friday, soap operas at seven-thirty every night. What does that tell you, eh?'

I hated myself for having noticed the same thing, for having seen how they had rebuilt that living room, how they had turned it into their reeking familiarity. All of that whilst the Undertundrans tried to reshape their hallow into a city, into an estate, to change it completely, to bring me in...

Shanice. *Shanice.* Mention of her name caused Cooper to begin again. Whispers bloomed into screams, he called for her from his blind oblivion.

'Please,' I begged Hickey again, 'just help me get him into the house.'

This time he agreed. Hickey didn't say another word, he just meandered over to us, took hold of Cooper under his right arm, as I lifted his left and, sharing the burden, we dragged Cooper towards the cottage.

We laid him down on the sofa and, unsure why, both Hickey and I stared down at him, watched him. Whimpering, struggling, tangled in his own bloodied limbs, Cooper writhed on the cushions, his fever causing him to spasm.

'Better get him some water,' Hickey nodded back towards the kitchen, 'I'll cover him up.'

I wanted to believe he was helping at last, that he felt something for Cooper, for the friendship he had given him. I hurried off to the kitchen, ran the water until it was freezing, then filled up two of the plastic bottles, their bodies half crushed by thirsty clutches.

As I made my way back to the living room, I found Hickey hunched over Cooper, one of his knees on Cooper's back, holding him still as he went to work.

I dropped the bottles and pulled Hickey back by his throat, but it was too late. There, on the back of Cooper's thigh, joining the other wounds he had from the forest, the unmistakeable shape, the unblinking stare, the Undertundran eye.

I swung for Hickey, but he dodged my punch easily. The momentum carried me over onto Cooper, who barely reacted. He was too lost in shock to have even noticed Hickey branding him. 'You piece of shit,' I spat at Hickey, stood up, moved towards him, 'how could you?'

'Easy.' Hickey held the knife up ahead of him, facing me as he backed away to the door of the cottage. 'Best they know *I* brought him here, Daniel. Best they get it clear in their thoughts.'

There was nothing I could do. I just looked on as Hickey made his way out through the cottage door.

Stood there, featureless, silhouetted by the already fading light of the day, Hickey grinned a warning at me, at us, 'They'll be back tonight.' He drew a circle with the knife, 'More of them than ever. Get ready, Daniel. Pick a road out of the muck...or be swallowed by the night.'

◊

AS DARKNESS CAME IN PURPLE swells, I tended to Cooper as best I could.

I pushed a chair behind the front door, the table too. I was worried Hickey might come back, worried he and Watkins were intent on making Cooper the next sacrifice for Undertundran acceptance. Maybe they had already.

Even though Cooper had stopped shaking, he was still ruined, still babbling nonsense, still blinded by fright. I had never seen him afraid, never seen him shaken like that. I watched him shiver, watched as he clasped the blankets to his red chest, his knuckles white from the pressure of clutching them. The topless man at the gym, the face of the estate, strutting through the arcade, the immortal figure at the boozer, all of those sides of Cooper were gone, completely worn away, the details corroded by his night in the northern woodlands.

I went back and forth to the window, looked over towards the outhouse. The door was open, but I couldn't see Hickey, or Watkins. I stared up at the dense trees, leering over at the lip of the quarry face. As the darkness thickened, so the bracken brightened, so the trees shone, so it began, the rain of porcelain figures.

Crowds of them, a parade of them, a circus of the Undertundrans.

I cowered back from the window. I could taste the thrum of my heart, feel it rattling at the back of my throat.

Some stomped, some crawled, some scuttled, some slithered. Their shapes, their features, it was almost incomprehensible to me. Some of them were enormous. Tentacular limbs slashed around the trunks of aged oaks, gripped them, wove upwards to their leaves, anaconda-like. Swollen, gut-white creatures followed, their faces hacked into smiles that moved through the night like infinite crescent moons.

Others crashed through the trees, tipping them, wrenching them from the dirt. The cracks of the bark, the branches, they were like ten-gun-salutes out there, with no road sounds, no machine sounds to smother them.

Some were familiar... Mr Milliman paraded adroitly between uncouth brethren, as if he was scared to damage his tuxedo of fiddling limbs.

The unformed creatures in their skin-hoods had trebled in number. Dozens of them dashed past and over one another. They seemed like the younger creatures in every way. They were pushed by others, some who wore gnarled monocles, some who held up skirts of driftwood and animal flesh, their feet arched on heels of jagged slate.

At the centre of them all, heralding them, guiding them, agitating them, Bone Stairwell stepped slowly through the centre, parting the gossamer waves. The garland of faces around its throat, the black-eyed stare fixed down at us, down at The Red House, the white stag watched everything. Like the Undertundran eye, Bone Stairwell saw both worlds at once.

One and all, they seemed to be heading to the property, whooping, dancing as they came.

I ran back to Cooper. He lay there, on the sofa, his eyes wide. He stared at the ceiling, his expression lost in the damp, in the cracked plaster. I shook him, tried to speak to him, to snatch some kind of acknowledgment, some sign of awareness. There was nothing there. Cooper dreamed from a coma of fear and loss.

Back at the window, I finally saw Hickey and Watkins.

Both naked, their wounds and brands on display in the gilded night, they kneeled by the dying bonfire, bowing before the approaching Undertundrans.

I froze, my fingernails dug into the wood of the windowsill. I could feel the splinters. I expected them both to be killed, to be torn apart. I watched, but didn't want to see. I saw, but didn't want to watch.

They arrived, the Undertundrans. They weaved around the naked men, leapfrogged them, stepped over them, ignored them, denied them their touch.

They were looking at me. They were staring at the house.

I backed away from the window, the whiteness of their combined light like a meteor coming towards me.

I staggered back to Cooper, grabbed the poker from the fire. I held it out ahead of me, ahead of us. I didn't know what they were going to do. I felt as if I was stood on the very edge of sanity, the final moments of coherent thought.

In a flipbook montage that passed with the wings of a hummingbird, I saw Bone Stairwell, I saw my dead mother, I saw her face on his garland, her skin on his scarf. I saw the faces of everyone I had ever known, the few I had ever loved, they were all there, hanging from the white stag's neck, gasping wordlessly, severed from the universe, sewn into the night itself.

Cities above and below, eyes above and below, I clutched Cooper and waited.

The windows of the Red House shook. The door rattled. I heard scuttling on the roof. I heard the thump of enormous things against the outer walls. I heard the hiss of cracking plaster, the snap and scrape of tiles being slapped away from the roof.

I thought we were being swallowed, that the ground beneath us was splitting. I held Cooper and closed my eyes. I heard myself begin to scream, to shout Cooper's name, to shout for my Mom, to shout for anything. I just wanted to hear myself, to know I was still there.

Over and over, I listened to my own bellowing nothingness. My chest burned, I waved the poker at the air, heard it crash against lamps, against tables.

Breathless, the taste of cloying dirt clogging my mouth, my throat, I couldn't hold on any longer. Weightlessness, vacuumed into the black, I passed out.

23.

stnecsed gnillaripS

I CAME AROUND IN DAYLIGHT.

Splinters of it came through the wonky blinds of the cottage windows, from beneath the ill-fitting door.

My mouth was too dry to swallow. I was laid on the sofa, where Cooper had been. It took me a few minutes to realise that. Blanked, dumb, I just looked upwards at first, to where I eventually remembered Cooper had been staring as...

Cooper.

I swung my legs over, onto the floor. I adjusted my eyes. Blinked, rubbed them with flaking thumbs. The table was still against the cottage door. The windows weren't shattered, the ceiling hadn't collapsed, the walls still stood.

I found Cooper stood by the sink in the kitchen, his back to me.

He stood there silently, stained jogging bottoms hanging loosely from his arse. He was topless and the cuts on his back seemed to breathe independently of him. A hundred tiny laceration-mouths whispering their pain to the quiet room.

I walked over towards him. Cooper heard my steps and half turned to me. I could see his face was drawn, sapped. When he spoke his voice was deep, distant, cracked from his unending screams for Shanice.

'What's gone on here, Danny boy?'

I was pleased to hear those words, to know he was awake again.

I told him I didn't know. 'It's too hard to understand, Coop.'

'No,' he turned to face me completely, his eyes were trenches in his face, 'you saw what I saw…you know what I mean.'

'In the woods?'

Cooper nodded, 'Shanice, she…,' he stopped, took a purposeful breath, steadied himself, 'they took her, didn't they?'

I nodded. 'You couldn't have done anything.'

'Hickey knew, didn't he, Dan? Hickey set this up?'

I wanted to tell Cooper everything, the whole story Hickey had given me, everything I had learned about The Undertundra, but it wouldn't have mattered, not one bit.

'Hickey knew about this place,' I nodded, 'Watkins too.'

Cooper didn't seem surprised. I wasn't sure he could ever be surprised by anything human again, after everything he'd seen.

He asked where they were. 'Those cunts,' he showed his teeth as he grimaced, 'they out there?'

I thought of seeing them, the previous night, their genuflection in the face of tumbling Undertundrans, their kneeling in their antichurch. 'Last I saw of them…' I nodded towards the door, half unsure how to finish the sentence, half unsure why to bother.

Cooper came towards me, placed a hand on my shoulder. 'I know what you did for me, Danny boy.' He forced a smile, but it wasn't a real smile. It was a mask's smile, a toyshop expression. 'Get your things together, get yourself the fuck outta here, okay?'

I shook my head. 'Coop, *you're* the one who needs to make tracks, not me.'

'Not a chance.' He walked past me and began to fish around for something behind the sofa. 'I've gotta let her know I wouldn't have let it happen…if I'd known…' Cooper reappeared with the poker from the fire. He held it up, stared at it, then made for the front door.

I knew he was going for Hickey.

The way Cooper moved then, the way his legs jerked, his arms, reminded me of machinery puttering out, of engines sapped of fuel, running on vapours. He was there, but he wasn't. He was alive, but dead. Fundamental, arbitrary actions, the will of remaining nerves and tendons, Cooper was a puppet, his miserable strings fingered by forces none of us understood.

I thought about stopping him again, trying to convince him we were best leaving there together, but I already knew the outcome. I think I already knew how I felt about leaving, about staying there.

I saw Cooper struggle to move the furniture I'd piled behind the door. I staggered over, my movements awkward also. I tugged at the dining table, the chair.

As Cooper snatched at the door handle, missing it the first time around, I imagined we would find their bodies outside, Hickey's, Watkins'. The last time I had seen them, they were surrounded by the Undertundrans, kneeling amongst neon gallows, waiting for the ultimate moment.

When Cooper tugged the door open and we made it into the daylight, we saw nothing like that.

The trenches, the huge carved eye, it was there, as deep as ever. There were tracks, some lengthy, less like wheels, more like limbs. There were footprints, distorted, angular, infinite misshapes, but there was no blood, no flesh, no echoes of a violent night.

We stood there quietly, Cooper's breathing deep and raspy.

It was an unreal moment, maybe more unreal than anything else that had happened since our arrival. We waited in silence. The world seemed stunned and drunk.

Cooper rocked back and forth, unsure whether to march to the outhouse, or to stand there. He was lost in the warmth of his confusion. Before it all happened, there was already a sense of finality to everything in that scene, every last blackened molecule of the moment.

Before a decision could be made, the door to the outhouse opened and Hickey stalked out, towards us, one hand behind his back, the other held out in the air ahead of him, feathered for a handshake, his fingers trembling.

'You're up and about, eh, Coop?' he said, his face twisted, exhausted. His eyes had receded into the sockets. He looked like he'd lost half his bodyweight overnight. 'I'm glad you're feeling better, mate.'

Cooper groaned. He seemed to be struggling with his words, with how to express what he felt. They were there, the words, but they were jumbled up and locked in his throat.

'I know how you feel,' Hickey continued to move towards us, his eyes on Cooper the entire time, 'I know what you think, Coop. I can understand it, mate. It's been weird here, hasn't it? I know what you think happened to Shanice, but-'

The mention of her name rocked Cooper. It jogged him into action. He lifted the poker, held it out ahead of him, an arm's length from Hickey. 'You lousy bastard,' he spat, 'you two-timing fucker. *You* did this.'

Hickey licked his lips, flung a glance my way and then, from behind his back, brought out the knife he had shown me the previous evening. The blade was dirty, its edge blackened with old blood. 'That's how it is, eh?' His eyes shone, 'You want it to end like this, you wanna come at me?'

The moment arrived so quickly. Its power was kinetic and brutal.

Cooper leaned into the space between them. He brought the poker back across the face of Hickey. The sound was horrible. The metal rang deeply off the bone of Hickey's skull. The cut on his forehead seemed to open immediately. The wound laughed from bright red lips.

In the same motion, the whole thing seemingly crushed into one solitary second, Hickey reeled, then forced himself forward, bringing the blade in under Cooper's ribs. The knife vanished, buried up to the hilt in Cooper's torso.

Cooper made a sound, a kind of sigh. Guttural, exhausted.

Hickey withdrew the blade. His teeth bared, his eyes wild. He brought his arm back, as if he was going for another shot. I felt myself move towards him and maybe, maybe that distraction was enough for him to pause just long enough for Cooper to issue one final blow, all of his energy funnelled into it.

The poker held against his thigh, its tip facing Hickey's exposed stomach, Cooper grasped it with both hands and, screaming Shanice's name as he did so, drove the poker upwards, into Hickey's gut.

The poker lifted Hickey off his feet. For an instant, framed there, a lithograph of white on red, Cooper seemed to hold Hickey in the air long enough for him to kick his legs back and forth.

They both fell backwards, parting from that bloody marriage.

Neither man fell over, but both landed in a kind of crouch, their wounds making sudden sense to them.

Hickey stood again and looked down at his stomach. The poker jutted out at an angle. As he watched, it began to slide from him, dropping from the meat, hovering there, then falling into the dirt. He staggered backwards, the wound becoming more cavernous with each retreating step.

Cooper used his hands to steady himself. I skidded over in the dirt, next to him. I tried to lift him, to help him up. He made a desperate sound. The blood covered his entire left side, pouring out over his hip, reddening his leg, his foot.

He turned to me, away from Hickey.

Cooper's lips moved, but his eyes were vacant again.

Something moved behind him and, before I could see what, Cooper lurched forward towards me, falling onto me.

As I held him there, my arms around his chest, my chin on his shoulder, I was able to look past him. Stepping back from him, the spout of a broken bottle in his hand, its jagged edge wet from the wound it had carved into Cooper's back, Watkins looked on, his lips wet, his eyes lit, frenzied, bulbous.

Cooper shrugged me off, but didn't turn back towards Watkins and Hickey. Instead, his legs weary, knobbly with blood loss, he stumbled back towards The Red House.

I rushed towards Watkins, but he turned and ran, past the pallid Hickey, around the outhouse, towards the trees. They swallowed him quickly. They welcomed him into the happy bracken.

Hickey held his stomach. His face was flat with pain.

I stood there, in no-man's land, the trenches around me, Cooper lurching into the cottage behind me, Hickey pressed up against the outhouse ahead of me.

Hickey panted horribly, shook his head from side-to-side, 'They never wanted me,' he snorted, blood bubbled from his nostrils, 'not me…it was *you*,' he heaved. 'It was you, Daniel…you all along.'

With that, his legs faltering, Hickey fell backwards, into the shadow of the outhouse.

I turned and hurried back to the cottage, to Cooper.

As I stepped inside, I found him, sat in what had been his usual seat, the same position here as it was back there, on the estate. He faced the blank TV, his head back against the sofa, his eyes and mouth open, lifeless. I already knew he was dead, but I walked over and checked his throat.

That broad neck, those rolling shoulders, the heft of a man who was a god to himself. They didn't mean anything now. He was a cadaver. Yesterday's shank.

I don't know how I felt, seeing him there. I don't know what it meant. I ran a hand across his face, held it over the breathless mouth. I touched his eyes with my thumb, closed them.

Back outside, the pools of blood were already drying in the dirt. I searched the treeline for Watkins, but couldn't see him.

I walked over to the outhouse.

I expected Hickey to be dead too, but he wasn't.

Slumped, his back against the cold stone, Hickey wasn't far from death, but his eyes followed my movement, watched as I stood there, at the centre of the room.

I noticed the knife on the ground, near to Hickey's thigh. I leaned over and picked it up. I wondered if I was meant to finish Hickey off, to drive that blade through his chest, to end it all.

He must have thought the same thing. He looked at the knife in my hand, then up at me.

'Better get it done,' he wheezed.

I was finished with instructions. I was done listening to Hickey, to Cooper, to anyone in this world. Everything they had done, every manipulation, it had all come crashing down around us. The cities I knew, the universe of this level, it was kaput. It was choked out. The whole thing was starved to death.

I slid the knife into my beltline, then grabbed Hickey by the ankles. He couldn't fight back, he couldn't struggle.

I dragged him outside, into the daylight, next to the gnarled wood of last night's bonfire.

I turned Hickey over with my foot, so I had his back.

So familiar with it now that I could have carved it with my eyes closed, I kneeled down, turned the knife to Hickey's skin and branded him with the Undertundran Eye.

If that was what it took, if that was what they needed, then so be it.

24.

I See

I BURNED THE RED HOUSE with the remaining fuel from the generator.

I covered the furniture in that gurgling petrol, then the walls. I did the same with the outhouse before I stacked the remaining wood on the site of the blackened bonfire and covered that too.

Hickey died as I went to work. I heard his final breaths as I lit the tinder and watched the flames eat hungrily at the air.

I stood outside The Red House and watched the fire engulf Cooper's body.

Even then, even as he burned, Cooper remained there, in that recreation of his living room, all of it collapsing, all of it becoming ash together.

The outhouse went up quickly, toppling as its roof fell inwards.

As the afternoon wore on, as the sky greyed, then darkened, I heard Watkins scream.

It could have been terror, it could have been ecstasy. It didn't matter to me.

♦

THE FIRE IS DYING BACK now.

Only occasional flames lick from the shattered windows of The Red House.

The palls of dark smoke, only recently like enormous murmurations, have splintered and faded. Soon, all of the rage and violence seen here will be invisible.

Even the corpses will be nothing more than charred furniture.

Regardless, I am not even facing the stone cottage, I am facing the woodland. That perimeter of unblinking eyes. I am waiting for the Undertundrans to light the jagged bark and bracken.

I am waiting for the white stag, for the creature christened Bone Stairwell by Hickey. I have learned that when it appears, it heralds the arrival of the others, of the ethereal masses. When they arrive, that grinning parade, I will ask them to show me everything, to show me their world beneath the world, their city under dirt.

Hickey wanted that more than anything. He was content to kill, maim and maul to get even a glimpse of the inhuman universe and, well, he did. He was able to stare into that void. I have to wonder whether the image is now printed on his eternal eye, fixed there forever, the last frame on the cinema of the soul.

I couldn't care. He was everything I thought he was from the start. Every ounce of him, flesh, bone, marrow. If only Cooper had realised earlier on, if only he hadn't been hypnotised by his own anger, his own humanity.

Dusk is turning to night now. It shouldn't be long until Bone Stairwell appears between the ashes and oaks, its face stoic, hardened, on its throat a garland of human faces.

Until then, whether I want to or not, all I can do is look back.

I believe I know how this began, the very moment the door opened, the second the shadows began to face the figures who cast them. I can trace it, the way it unfolded. That blueprint is all I have now, all I will have until the Undertundra opens its maw to me.

I pull my coat tight as the temperature drops. I'm weak, I've barely eaten. It's hard to keep my eyes open now, but I must do the best I can.

❦

HERE THEY COME…

The forest is brightening again, the night-woods are whitening. High up, carving its slow path through the snapping bracken, Bone Stairwell is leading the parade.

The cities of that past are rubble, the cities above and below are mine to learn.

I am the eye now, the Undertundran eye.

I see everything all at once.

I see everything all at once.

I see.

End

Acknowledgements

Thanks to Stairwell Books, to Rose, Alan and Emily. You took a punt on me, and I'll be forever grateful for your faith. In particular, thanks to Rose for meeting with me on that December morning in Manchester. I knew as soon as we were face to face that Stairwell was the home I wanted for 'At Night, White Bracken.'

Long live independent publishers. They are the blood, bone and marrow of true literary art.

Thanks to the brilliantly talented Susie Williamson for turning her thoughts on my work into incredible cover art.

Thanks to CS Fuqua for his deep understanding of the novel and for providing a response that touched me to the core.

Thanks to the great Ramsey Campbell for his kindness, his words on novel and, above all, for creating the enormous, weird ocean on which my small ship can sail.

Other novels, novellas and short story collections available from
Stairwell Books

A Fistful of Ashes	Katy Turton
The Department of Certainty	S. C. Paterson
Widdershins	L.A.Robbins
100 Summers	Ali Sparkes
Skull Days	PJ Quinn
The Broke Hotel	Clayton Lister
Equinox	Ruth Aylett, Greg Michaelson
Not the Work of an Ordinary Boy	Victoria L. Humphreys
Black Harry	Mark P. Henderson
Eboracvm: Carved in Stone	Graham Clews
Down to Earth	Andrew Crowther
The Iron Brooch	Yvonne Hendrie
The Electric	Tim Murgatroyd
The Pirate Queen	Charlie Hill
Djoser and the Gods	Michael J. Lowis
Needleham	Terry Simpson
The Keepers	Pauline Kirk
Shadows of Fathers	Simon Cullerton
Blackbird's Song	Katy Turton
Eboracvm the Fortress	Graham Clews
The Warder	Susie Williamson
Life Lessons by Libby	Libby and Laura Engel-Sahr
Waters of Time	Pauline Kirk
The Water Bailiff's Daughter	Yvonne Hendrie
O Man of Clay	Eliza Mood
Eboracvm: the Village	Graham Clews
Sammy Blue Eyes	Frank Beill
Poetic Justice	PJ Quinn
The Go-To Guy	Neal Hardin
Abernathy	Claire Patel-Campbell
Tyrants Rex	Clint Wastling
How to be a Man	Alan Smith
Border 7	Pauline Kirk
The Geology of Desire	Clint Wastling
Close Disharmony	PJ Quinn
Wine Dark, Sea Blue	A.L. Michael
Foul Play	PJ Quinn

For further information please contact rose@stairwellbooks.com

www.stairwellbooks.co.uk
@stairwellbooks